W9-ALK-555

HELLO, GROIN

Learning Resources Center
Jordan High School
Jordan, Minnesota

HELLO, GROIN

BETH GOOBIE

ORCA BOOK PUBLISHERS

Copyright © 2006 Beth Goobie
All rights reserved. No part of this publication may be reproduced or transmitted in
any form or by any means, electronic or mechanical, including photocopying,
recording or by any information storage and retrieval system now known or to be
invented, without permission in writing from the publisher.

Library and Archives Canada Cataloguing in Publication

Goobie, Beth, 1959-
Hello, groin / Beth Goobie.

ISBN 1-55143-459-8

I. Title.

PS8563.O8326H44 2006   C813'.54   C2006-903098-7

First published in the United States, 2006
Library of Congress Control Number: 2006927980

Summary: Dylan discovers that friendship can get in the way of love.

Orca Book Publishers gratefully acknowledges the support for its publishing
programs provided by the following agencies: the Government of Canada through
the Book Publishing Industry Development Program and the Canada Council for
the Arts, and the Province of British Columbia through the BC Arts Council and the
Book Publishing Tax Credit.

The author gratefully acknowledges the Saskatchewan Arts Board grant that
partially funded the writing of this book.

Design and typesetting: Christine Toller
Cover artwork: James Kingsley

ORCA BOOK PUBLISHERS
PO Box 5626, STN. B
VICTORIA, BC CANADA
V8R 6S4

ORCA BOOK PUBLISHERS
PO Box 468
CUSTER, WA USA
98240-0468

www.orcabook.com
Printed and bound in Canada

08 07 06 • 6 5 4 3 2 1

for Sue

Chapter One

We were coming around a bend in the road just before the Dundurn Street bridge. I was double-riding my best friend, Jocelyn Hersch, on my bike, and we were running late, Diefenbaker Collegiate's last warning bell about to sound. So I was tearing along with my head down, pretty much oblivious to the local scenery, when Joc tightened her grip on my waist and let out a yelp that could have raised the dead. Of course, right away my head snapped up and the first thing I saw was the bridge straight ahead, a two-lane overpass that arced about twenty feet above the river. Then my eyes landed on a thick white haze that appeared to be rising out of the water. In the morning sunlight it glowed a brilliant white and was so tall it touched the underside of the bridge and over-rode the nearest bank by at least a hundred feet. Putting on the brakes, I stood, holding onto my bike and staring. The day was warm for mid-September and somewhat cloudy, but not foggy—whatever the haze was, it hadn't been caused by the weather.

"The city woke up, but the river's still dreaming," said Joc, her chin nudging the back of my shoulder. Then, sliding off the bike seat, she headed into the small park that ran this side of the river.

Laying down my bike, I took off after her, catching up just as she reached the edge of the massive glowing haze.

"What d'you think it is?" I asked, staring up at it. Now that I was closer, I could see the haze was made of a zillion bubbles, and the air was full of the soft sound of their popping. A gust of wind kicked up, scattering yellow poplar leaves across the surface.

"I told you, Dyllie," said Joc. "It's a dream. The river's dreaming."

Up on the bridge a car drove slowly past, the driver gawking maniacally through his window. Then the car was gone, the rumble of its engine sucked completely into the morning quiet. Another gust of wind kicked up, full of that sweet September smell, and twenty more leaves were scattered across the top of the haze. For a moment then, just a moment, I got a sense of the entire city spread out in all directions and settled peacefully into itself, the morning traffic rush over, kids safely in school. All that quiet made the haze in front of me even more mysterious, with its softly breaking bubbles, a world of undone hearts.

Putting out a hand, Joc scooped some into her palm.

"Careful," I said. "Could be toxic."

She gave it a sniff. "Smells like laundry soap," she said. "Dish soap or bubblebath."

Without another word, she stepped directly into the mysterious cloud. For a second I could still see her—the vague outline of a dark-haired, low-hipped, sixteen-year-old girl—and then she disappeared into the soft bubble-breaking haze.

"Joc," I called, but no sound came back to me. So I stepped in after her, leaving the city and its everyday sights and sounds behind, and was immediately surrounded by the faint sweet scent of soap, the constant whispering of breaking bubbles and an eerie all-around white. Then, somewhere up in the sky the sun must have come out, because the bubbles above my head suddenly lit up, glowing pink, yellow and blue. Off to my right, Joc cried out in delight, and I started toward her. The bubbles gave easily as I moved, and breathing wasn't a problem. The whole thing was a little like walking through a trance, thinking in soft colors, sweet scents and vague secret murmurings. Or like stepping into one of my five-year-old sister Keelie's drawings. Yesterday I'd caught her sitting in the living room with paper and crayons, staring straight ahead with an intense expression on her face. When I'd asked what she was doing, she'd said, "I am drawing silence. I am drawing the beautiful quiet in the air."

So that was what walking through the pink-yellow-blue haze reminded me of—*the beautiful quiet in the air*—and it took me deep into one of those inner watching places of the mind. As I moved toward Joc, she came gradually into view, a vague dark outline humming to itself and spinning lazy pirouettes. Because of the haze, I could only see her in bits and pieces, and it was a moment before I realized that she was naked. Stumbling to a halt, I stood staring, just *staring*, my heart pounding so hard it was about busting me open. Then, before I could stop her, Joc walked over and reached out toward me.

I don't know exactly what happened next, it went by so quick. Her hands reached toward me as if she was about to start unbuttoning my shirt, and instantly a hundred different thoughts slammed into me: *I can't, someone else might come walking into the haze, someone might see.* But mostly it was a giant panicky *No!* as my hands swung up to fend her off. Frozen, we stood staring at each other, and then Joc reached out again and grabbed my hands.

"C'mon, Dyl," she said and started spinning us in a slow uneven circle. At first my feet tripped a bit, but then we came into sync, leaned out from each other in perfect balance while everything we couldn't seem to say whirled white and sweet around us. Gradually we slowed, and Joc let go and staggered, giggling, toward her clothes.

"God," I heard her mutter. "Now I can't tell where I'm going. What if I can't find...Oh, here they are."

There was the quick sound of jeans being pulled on and a sweatshirt being zipped. "Dyl," Joc called, her voice muffled and low to the ground, and I walked over to find her, shoes still off and crawling around in the grass. "Y'know that ring Dikker gave me last week?" she said. "The one with the amber stone? I can't find it."

"What did you take it off for?" I demanded, dropping to my knees beside her and groping in the white-shrouded grass.

"Dunno," she mumbled. "It's just so beautiful in here. It made me want to take off everything extra—no interference, nothing but skin." Swearing softly, she pawed at the grass. "It was just a cheap ring, no big deal. He won it at the Ex at a target booth. It's not a family heirloom or anything, but—"

She paused, running her hand again over the same place, and my heart gave a painful kick, thinking she'd found it. "Nope," she muttered, just as my fingers passed over something small and hard in the grass. A swallow locked my throat, and I traced the object carefully. Circular, with a small hard knob set at one end—no question about it, I had Dikker's ring in my sweaty little hand.

Cheap, I reminded myself. *Not a family heirloom*. Holding my breath, I waited as Joc crawled farther into the haze. Then, getting to my knees, I hurled the ring in the direction of the river. A slight splash sounded, followed by more of the eerie white nothingness, me breathing and a zillion bubbles breaking all around.

"What was that?" asked Joc from my right, her voice oddly flattened by the haze.

"What was what?" I asked casually.

"That splash," she said.

"Dunno," I said. "A fish?"

A long thinking pause followed, and then a few more swear words, and finally I heard her making her way back toward me. "I guess I'll tell him I took it off in the bath and it fell down the drain," she muttered resignedly.

"Good thinking," I said, probably way too loud and enthusiastic. "He'll get lost in the bath fantasy and forget all about the ring."

"Here's hoping," she said, and we stepped free of the haze, blinking at the nine-thirty sunshine and the great blobs of bubbles riding our arms. Laughing, we piled scoops of it onto each other's heads, then got onto my bike and tore through the streets toward the Dief, trailing pink-and-blue bubbles behind us.

By the time school let out, we'd discovered that the mysterious haze had been caused by a factory soap spill upriver. Biking back to the Dundurn Street bridge, we found the haze considerably shrunken and police warning tapes strung along both banks. Two cruisers with flashing lights sat at the edge of the park, blocking entry.

"Just like the cops," Joc said disgustedly, her chin dug into my shoulder as we surveyed the scene from my bike. "Find a little harmless fun and they have to cut it off."

"Someone could fall in, I guess," I shrugged. "A little kid, or a drunk."

"We didn't," said Joc, and we took off down the street, headed for her house. Here and there huddles of green-gold poplars flashed by, murmuring their thoughts to the wind.

"I love this time of year," I said, tilting my head back to get a straight-on glimpse of the sky. "Everything's blue and gold, and the smell is so thick, it's like the earth is breathing."

"Yeah," Joc said quietly, her arms tightening around my waist. Braking to take the turn onto her street, I let out a whoop as I saw Joc's older brother Tim backing his car down their driveway. Well, *he* called it a car, but the thing was a '72 Chev, so ancient it was almost apocalyptic. Joc and I didn't even have to look at each other, just ditched the bike and took a mutual flying leap onto the car trunk. Arm stuck out the window, Tim gave us a casual wave, then putt-putted several blocks at golf-cart speed while we kicked back and watched the neighborhood roll by. At the first major intersection, he leaned on the horn until we got off, then revved the engine and squealed off around the corner.

"When was the last time he washed that junk heap?" I demanded, staring at the two very obvious bum prints now decorating the trunk of his car. Ruefully I checked the back of my jeans. "I bet I'm wearing the last three months of that car on my butt."

"Anyone asks," Joc drawled, "he'll say it was Marilyn Monroe and Jackie Kennedy returned from the dead to bless his trunk."

"Not far from the truth, I guess," I said.

Joc grinned and lit a cigarette. "I bought another Morissette CD," she said. "*Feast on Scraps*. It's just as jagged as her last one. You heard it yet?"

"Nope," I said.

"C'mon," she said. "It'll make you howl."

We headed back up the street, practicing our howling and taking the odd time-out on Joc's cigarette. When we reached her house, no one was home, so we grabbed two Cokes from the fridge and headed down the hall to her bedroom. Since it was the usual swamp zone, I kicked my way through the laundry and other debris camouflaging the floor, and settled onto the bed.

In the meantime Joc inserted *Feast on Scraps* into a small CD player that stood on her bookshelf, then flicked on her curling iron and started an intense stare fight with her dresser mirror. A base throb that sounded like a great reverb heartbeat poured out of the CD player, filling the room, followed by an upswell of music that was pushed and prodded along by Alanis Morissette's voice. I listened, bobbing a foot to the beat.

"Hey, that's good," I said. "What's this song called?"

"'Fear of Bliss'," said Joc.

"Huh," I grunted, bobbing my foot more energetically. There was always such tension in Morissette's music, a long fishing line of ache with a hook waiting to catch you—the hook of self-respect. She was different from most rock singers. Joc was right—this album was more jagged than her last.

"Come on," I said, taking a swig of Coke. "Leave it, okay? You're already gorgeous."

"Dikker doesn't think so," said Joc. Arcing her neck, she studied the long gleaming slide of her hair.

"He told you that?" I demanded. With a sigh, I propped Joc's pillow behind my head and settled in for yet another extended discourse on Barry Alan Preddy, more commonly known as "Dikker"—a guy who'd told Joc on their first date that he wanted to be dead before he turned thirty. Talk about being paranoid of commitment.

"He didn't have to," said Joc. Licking a fingertip, she tapped the curling iron to test it for heat. "It's all in a guy's eyes," she said. "Where they are when you're with him."

"So where are his?" I asked in a decided monotone. I mean, we'd been through every possible angle and permutation of this subject countless times. Too many of my conversations with Joc were beginning to feel like a repeat of a repeat of something that had been interesting three years ago.

"Everywhere but on me," she muttered, leaning toward the mirror and poking at a zit on her chin.

"Why doesn't he break up with you then?" I yawned.

"Because I'd kill him," Joc said casually, catching the edge of her bangs expertly with the curling iron. "And then I'd kill myself."

"Oh yeah," I muttered. I'd heard this comment before. Many times. "Romeo and Juliet," I added without thinking. "Front page news."

"Look, Dyl," snapped Joc. Releasing half her bangs into a perfect curl, she turned to glare at me. "It is, of course, obvious to you and everyone else that you're superior to the rest of the human race," she said acidly. "For some reason known only to His very divine self, God dumped us normal people with a shit-load of hormones and you just got a sprinkling, which you take care of with the occasional mastie."

Turning back to the mirror, she started up another stare fight with her reflection while I lay rigid on the bed, observing the ceiling. Here it was again, that conversational scorpion that leapt out of nowhere, poisoned the most innocently intentioned words and vanished as quickly as it had appeared. The last time Joc snapped at me like this, we'd ended up heaving large objects at each other. Tim had actually turned down his bedroom stereo and sauntered across the hall to find out what all the high-pitched squealing was about.

"Cat fight," he'd said, unimpressed, and left again.

It had taken a week to work our way back to speaking terms, and that had been only last month. Tension like this never used to happen between us. Sweet sixteen could really suck. Pressing my cheek against my can of Coke, I waited for the fire in my face to burn down.

"Okay," I said thickly. "Dumb thing to say, agreed. It's just..."

I never liked Dikker, you know that. He's always making you feel like crap. When's the last time he made you really happy?"

"Last Friday," said Joc, forgiving me with a smug grin. "Around 1:00 AM."

"Yeah," I muttered. "You were probably stoned."

"As a matter of fact, I was," she said complacently and set down the curling iron. Then, without the slightest warning she crossed the room, climbed onto the bed and straddled my hips. Leaning over me, she poked her intense narrow face into mine.

"C'mon Dyl," she said, her large purplish blue eyes trapping mine. "When are you going to let Cam get what he wants? You've been seeing him for eight months now. You're practically married. You should hear the poor guy moan when you're not around. Says he's almost forgotten how to use it."

The perfect curl of her bangs dangled from her forehead, and the rest of her hair dropped in a smooth, coconut-scented fall around my face. "Don't you like him?" she whispered, her lips inches from mine. I could smell tobacco on her breath. "He's decent enough," she added thoughtfully. "Doesn't two-time, has a great car."

At that moment she shifted, and the unexpected movement on my hips set off a wave of sweet singing heat that shot everywhere through me, suspending me in an edgy horrified bliss. Then the sensation passed and I came back to myself, eyes closed, fighting panic. *Shit*, how had that happened? It sure as hell hadn't been my fault—I wasn't the one who'd crossed the room and jumped all over someone else's body. Joc must have hit some goddamn hyper-alert nerve when she shifted, but I hadn't asked for it. I *hadn't*.

Well, the first thing to figure out now was whether or not Joc had noticed. Had I moaned, had my expression changed or given anything away?

"I dunno," I mumbled, keeping my eyes closed. "Sometimes I feel like it, but never when he wants to, y'know?"

Joc hesitated. I could hear the soft come-and-go of her breathing as she thought. "Is he rough?" she asked. "Pushy?"

"No," I said.

"What would it hurt to try it with him then?" she asked. "C'mon, you've got to give the guy some hope."

"Maybe," I whispered.

"Open your eyes, would you?" she said and tugged gently at my left eyelid. "I feel like I'm talking to a corpse here."

"Can't," I said, keeping them shut. "I'd go cross-eyed staring at you this close."

"Okay," she said. "I'll wallpaper myself to the other side of the room."

I waited, my eyes squeezed shut and counting heartbeats, but the only thing that moved was the tip of her hair teasing my neck. "What's the matter with you?" she asked finally. "You're all tense. If I didn't know you better, I'd think you didn't get it on for guys, you—"

Joc paused, her silence speaking for her, and then the tip of her coconut-scented hair buckled and she was right onto me. "But I know you better than that, don't I?" she whispered, her words puffing gently against my face. "No one knows you as well as I do, right Dyl?"

"No one," I said softly, and longing flared, slow and searing, in my gut. Turning my head to escape Joc's nearness, I felt her breathing angle up my neck.

"So, if I think it'd be good for you to get it on with Cam, it probably would be, right?" she said.

"Maybe," I hedged.

"Definitely," said Joc, and the coconut-scented hair wisped away from my neck. Returning to the dresser, she once again took up her battle stance in front of the mirror while I lay dishrag-limp on the bed, breathing in the empty air bit by bit, its hard lonely truth. Slowly I turned my head and watched Joc through slitted eyes.

"My hair sucks," she said bleakly, staring into the mirror. "My face looks like it's been pickled. I give it two weeks before Dikker dumps me."

Closing my eyes again, I shut her out.

Chapter Two

The problem wasn't that I was a virgin. I mean, I'd had sex—with a guy. As far as I could tell, my sexual experiences to date had been pretty much the usual—some lunch-hour kissing in junior high and the odd after-school groping session. Then, midway through grade nine, I started dating Paul Loye, and over the summer we had sex four times. It was always with a condom—the first time I was so nervous, I almost made him wear two! But even with protection, and even though I liked Paul, I could never relax and get off on it. I guess the whole thing just felt sweaty and grunty and bump-bump-bump. Plus I would always be in a funk, wondering if the condom was doing its job or if I was in the middle of getting pregnant. And then, to top it all off, afterward neither of us could look the other in the eye.

To be honest, sex with Paul was one big flat-out disappointment. Which was definitely confusing, because I'd always figured sex would be the most fantastic experience of my life. At least that was the way it looked on TV. I can't tell you how lonely I felt. And what made it even worse was that when Joc and I consulted, we seemed to be doing the same things, and she was, as she put it, "enjoying her karma." Or so she said, so of course that was what

I said too. But lying about it just made the situation worse, and the whole time I kept wondering when someone would finally see through the act I was trying to pull.

I think that was why I kept doing it with Paul. I was trying to *make* myself like it, prove to myself that I *could* like it. But all it seemed to prove was the opposite, and in the end I couldn't fight it off anymore—the certainty, the *knowing.* Because I did know what was going on, had begun to sense it way back in grade six when Joc and I had started growing breasts and pubic hair, and she'd wanted to compare. No big deal—lots of kids pull that kind of stuff when their bodies are changing and they can't get a straight answer from their parents. And our school sex ed class hadn't explained *everything* we wondered about, even with its extremely straight answers to questions we hadn't even known existed. Basically it was the little things we wanted to know about then, not the big ones. Like most eleven-year-old girls, Joc and I weren't interested in attaching our eggs to anyone's sperm yet. We just wanted to know if our boobs were growing too fast, or if there really was supposed to be that much hair you-know-where. And those weren't the kind of questions you could ask your health teacher.

So we did a few spot checks on each other, took off our shirts and checked to see whose breasts were bigger, that kind of thing. Once Joc reached out and touched one of my breasts, but I jerked back at the sudden soft explosion of sensation, and she never did it again. Still, she kept wanting to compare, so I kept telling myself that my reactions were normal—I was just feeling the way I was feeling because our shirts were off, and if she was a guy, then things would *really* get hot.

Then came a fateful grade seven sleepover at Joc's house, when she decided that we were going to strip head-to-toe and do a "scientific evaluation." Actually, it was a very helpful experience as far as science went—it's not all that easy to see between your own legs and I learned a lot about exact locations, especially with Joc's finger right on them. I kept a pillow over my face while she was examining me and refused to touch her, though when it came my turn to play doctor, I looked—I have to admit I looked for a very long time.

After that I knew. Even though I kept telling myself that Joc was just a substitute for a guy, I knew better. And the weird thing was that she was always hanging all over me. She's a naturally physical person, but guys took to calling the two of us lezzies. Just joking, of course—by grade eight Joc already had her rep, having officially done the deed with Larry Boissonneault, then dumped him for his best friend Terence Harty.

I think she knew too—about me, the way I was. Sometimes I would look up and catch her watching me, her eyes kind of glazed and her mouth pouty, the way it goes when you're dead center in your hottest sex fantasy. And every time I caught her watching me like that, she would look away. But first, just for a second, there would be this electric flash that leapt between us— something you couldn't see or hear but damn well felt—and then she would blink and turn her head. And it would be completely and utterly gone. Until the next time it happened.

The thing was, Joc hardly ever looked away. Sometimes we had stare fights that lasted five, ten minutes, and she never backed down. Never. After that sleepover in the seventh grade, we didn't compare again. At least, not that obviously. But the summer before grade ten, when she started dating Dikker and I was going with Paul, we double-dated a couple of times. Dikker was a year older than Joc and already had a car, so after the movie, they would take the front seat and we would take the back. And the whole time, even though she seemed to be *really* busy with Dikker, I could have sworn Joc was listening to me and Paul—so close, it ended up feeling like a competition, each of us trying to prove who was having the hottest time. Thinking about it afterward made me feel kind of sick, so I told Paul that I would rather do things with just the two of us. When I told Joc that I didn't want to double with her and Dikker anymore, we stopped talking for a while. No apparent reason—she didn't get mad or anything, it just happened. Then, at the end of the summer, I broke up with Paul, and Joc and I were best friends again.

Now I was going out with Cam Zeleny. And like Joc said, I couldn't expect him to hang around, *unfulfilled*, as she called it, forever. After all, Cam was prime dating material—smart, decent, good-looking and a member of the senior jock crowd. Dief girls lined up every day just to say hi to him. I mean, I was definitely not his only option for a Saturday night. And to add to the pressure, he'd put in his time with me. I was way overdue to start putting out, at least by most dating standards. What was I going to do when he finally lost patience and dumped me?

I could already feel it—that big lonely crater opening in my gut. Cam might not have been the one who secretly turned me on, but he was a worthwhile conversation and a damn good kisser. If I kept my eyes closed, he could get me pretty sweaty. The problem was that I couldn't take it any farther. It wasn't that I didn't want to. I would have given almost anything to have been able to respond to what Cam wanted to give me. But every time we tried, I turned off. I didn't think *no*, didn't protest or push him away. Some inner switch simply clicked off, and I turned into cold putty in his hands. He always stopped then—Cam wasn't the kind of guy who just wanted to get off. A few times he'd tried to get me to talk about it, but what was I supposed to say? I couldn't even *think* the truth inside my own head. How was I supposed to tell him?

And if I was going to be absolutely honest, I would have to admit that behind the fear of losing Cam was the complete and utter terror of what other kids would think if we split up. Ultimately there were only two reasons for a girl to reject Cam—she was religious, or deep inside herself she was skewed, she was wrong. Okay, maybe I'm being a little paranoid here. Couples break up for lots of reasons, but if Cam and I split, that would be why—I was skewed. And with all the talk about gays and lesbians these days, someone would eventually figure it out. Once they did, it would get around. Then everyone would know. Everyone would know that deep inside, in the deepest core place, Dylan Kowolski was *wrong*.

So there it was inside me, that wrongness, the way I felt about Joc. It lived, shoved down deep, a kind of spell or threat, like that song by Alanis Morissette—"Fear of Bliss." Though I knew they were there, I never let my mind open onto the deepest feelings I had for Joc. I could feel them sometimes, moving around my gut, but if they ever came into my mind—if I ever, even for a moment, daydreamed about kissing or touching her—I would shove those thoughts back down and slam the door on them. That kind of thinking was forbidden. If we were going to be friends—best friends, the *best* of best friends, I couldn't let myself even think about the secret flame she hadn't seen that night in grade seven, burning between my legs.

It was the week following the river soap spill, and I was halfway through my Tuesday lunch-hour shift at the Dief library checkout desk. Leaned against the other side of the counter and wrapped in each other's arms were Joc and Dikker, pretending to keep me company while they engaged in their favorite pastime. This meant, of course, that the last five minutes of the library's supposed domain of silence had been punctuated by some rather unusual sound effects, but what the hell—I was only a volunteer and not about to pull any authority trips.

It wasn't like me to volunteer for things, but the Dief library was different. To be specific, Ms. Fowler, the librarian, was different. The majority of teachers in my school were only interested in students with cubbyhole minds, the kind of kids who could take facts coming at them from any angle and shove them into the appropriate mental-storage unit. Ms. Fowler wasn't like that. She was more of a watcher than a coder. At first when I caught her looking at me, I would tense up, not sure what she was seeing. Because she really *observed*. Behind that mousy expression and erratic graying hair lurked more information about what went on at the Dief than in the front office computer database.

But no snaky forked-tongued comments ever came out of her—no criticisms, suggestions for improvement, or off-with-your-head statements. Maybe it was because I was a volunteer and she had to take what she could get. Or maybe it was because her career had been spent dealing with other people's thoughts. One day last year, while I was shelving books in the fiction section, I stopped for a moment and stood, just looking at the shelf in front of me. The weirdest sensation came over me then—almost as if each book had a voice and they were all calling to me. I mean, *extremely bizarro*, I know, but it happened. And as I was standing there, listening to that shelf of books call out to me, Ms. Fowler walked over and asked what I was doing.

"One shelf of books has so many completely different ideas sitting right next to each other," I said slowly. I wouldn't normally say something like that to a Dief teacher, but talking to Ms. Fowler was sort of like talking inside your own head. "It's like looking at a row of minds," I continued, just letting the thoughts come out. "A story from Moose Jaw could be sitting next to one from Johannesburg. Every shelf in this library is like that. It's fantastic."

Beside me, Ms. Fowler stood silently, her eyes roaming the shelves. "Yes," she said finally, a tiny smile crouching in one corner of her mouth. "It is fantastic." Then, without looking at me, she patted my arm and returned to her office. We hadn't mentioned it since, but from that point on, whenever she saw me come into the library her eyes would flick toward the shelves and she would get that tiny smile in the corner of her mouth. And it made me feel, I dunno—*located*—to think that there was an adult in this school who actually remembered something I'd said.

Yes, in this library, with its shelves of minds waiting to be opened and Ms. Fowler's tiny crouching smile, I felt *located*.

"Dikker!" said Joc, letting out a small shriek. Pressed against the check-out desk, she giggled breathlessly. All over the library, kids were turning to watch, some grinning, others glaring. From behind the desk, I gave them a shrug and went back to emptying the book return bin. Some days Joc's brain simply stopped functioning. As far as I could tell, it was usually connected to the presence of Dikker Preddy.

"Hey, Dyl," said a familiar voice. A wave of Brut washed over me, and I looked up to see Cam drop his gym bag and lean across the counter. Quirking an eyebrow at Joc and Dikker, who gave no hint of having noticed his arrival, he grinned and asked, "So, what's the major sign-out trend for today?"

Quirking an eyebrow in reply, I said, "Ancient architecture. No one looks too happy about it either."

"C'mon," he said, taking hold of one of my fingers. "One of these days you're going to tell me it's a bunch of guys fighting over *The Joy of Sex*."

"Not today," I quipped back, hiding a flicker of nervousness. "I've already got that one signed out."

"Ah," he said, his eyes zeroing in. They were blue, *very* blue—the color of soft faded denim. "And what class might that be for?" he asked.

"Ancient history," I grinned. "I decided not to do the assigned essay topic."

Cam grinned back. "That essay will be read aloud in the staff room," he predicted.

Next to him, Joc and Dikker's ecstatic make-out session was continuing nonstop. Then, in one especially ecstatic moment, Dikker pressed Joc against the check-out desk, and her shoulder toppled a stack of books I'd taken out of the return bin. I mean, the guy practically had her laid out across the counter. Suddenly all the frustration I'd been trying to hide reared up in me. Picking up a hardcover thesaurus, I swatted Dikker on the head with it.

Hardcover thesauruses are ideal for this sort of thing. Immediately Dikker's mouth detached itself from Joc's and he straightened, rubbing the top of his head. "Jeeeeeeezus, Dyl," he moaned. "What was that for?"

"There are people researching ancient architecture in this library," I said, giving him a melodramatic glare and hoping against hope that he and Joc would take it as a joke. "You are distracting them. Besides, my boss, Ms. Fowler—remember her?—is due back any minute."

"Oh, Ms. Fowler," sniffed Joc. Patting the top of Dikker's head, she slitted her eyes at me. "What's she going to do, revoke our library privileges?"

"Yeah," I said. "No more making out in the library."

"Big deal," said Dikker. "Thought we'd save you from another boring virgin library shift, but we can always use my car. C'mon, Joc."

Turning, he tried to walk through the turnstile, but the alarm went off.

"That book," I said, pointing to a paperback he was carrying. "Did you sign it out?"

"Nah," he grunted, tossing it onto the counter. "I was looking for pictures, but there aren't any."

I picked it up and looked at it. By Truman Capote, the book was called *In Cold Blood*.

"Figures," I muttered, as my extremely pissed-off best friend and her numbskull boyfriend headed out into the hall. Well, maybe not *extremely* pissed-off. Through the glass panes in the library doors, I could see Joc taking a tube of lipstick out of her purse and slathering it all over Dikker's mouth. Then she did her own. A second later they leaned in together and gave the upper pane in the left door a simultaneous hearty smooch.

Kiss off, I thought. Okay, the message could have been worse.

Snorting softly at their artwork, Cam picked up his gym bag. "Coming to the game tomorrow?" he asked. "It's our first one."

"You gonna win?" I demanded, jamming *In Cold Blood* onto a filing cart.

"If I know you're watching, beady little eyes fixed on my working butt," Cam grinned.

"Mmmm, yes," I said lightly. "It is a gorgeous butt. For your butt, I just might show."

Immediately Cam's face lit up, and I felt like the usual shit for keeping him in that ever-hoping, never-fulfilled position. "Okay, Dyllie," he said, slinging his gym bag over a shoulder. "I'll call you tonight."

With another grin he backed through the library doors, barely missing Ms. Fowler who was standing in the hall, observing the two lipsticked smooches. As usual she had on her watcher's expression, which was pretty much the same as no expression at all. Waiting until the doors had closed behind

Cam, she took out her own tube of lipstick and wrote something underneath the smooches. Then she came into the library
and headed for her office. After processing the end-of-lunch-hour
check-out rush, I stopped by her office to let her know that I was
leaving. As I entered, she looked up from her desk work, her head
framed by a large globe that sat on the counter behind her.

"That globe," I said, unsure as ever as to the best way to break
into her silence. "I've never seen one that large."

"That's why I bought it," she said quietly. "It's bigger than my
head. Isn't that symbolic?"

Tiny corner grins crept into both our mouths.

"Yeah," I said. "Yeah, it's symbolic, Ms. Fowler."

"Thanks for helping out today, Dylan," she said and went back
to her work.

Outside the library doors, a small crowd had gathered. Joining
them, I stood scanning the comments Ms. Fowler had written
in dull burgundy lipstick beneath Joc and Dikker's scarlet
smooches: READING CAN IMPROVE YOUR EXPERTISE
IN ALL SORTS OF SUBJECTS! GET LITERATE!

Chapter Three

Sometimes I secretly watched Mom and Dad and wondered which of them was to blame. I mean, sexual orientation is supposed to be genetic. So it was, of course, my parents' genes that were responsible for the body I ended up with—a skewed body, without normal hormones. Whatever was wrong with it had to have come from them. Only there didn't seem to be anything abnormal about their love life. It was definitely hetero, and even after three kids, it was hot and happening. Sure, they fought, but they also kissed a lot and "slept in" on Sunday mornings. Every now and then they bought each other flowers and went out on dates. There were even times when I caught Dad dreamy-eyed and staring at Mom as if he was still a virginal teenager trying to imagine her with her clothes off. I swear sometimes he was about to start drooling.

Maybe what I'd gotten was a throwback gene. Dad had an uncle who'd died a while back. I'd never met him, but I knew he'd never gotten married and was thought of as the black sheep in the family. There was some kind of shameful secret attached to him that no one would explain. And then there was Aunt Chrissy, a sister of Dad's, who was also unmarried. She hadn't been given the black sheep label, but she was considered odd. After graduating from high school, she'd taken off for Europe and now worked as a travel agent in Rome. I used to study her photographs for signs that she harbored skewed genes, but we didn't look anything alike. She was definitely a Kowolski, with blond wavy hair and broad bones, and I took after Mom, who was short and slight, with straight slate-black hair and dark brown eyes. Everyone on her side of the family was tight into marriage with numerous offspring, and any divorces were soon solved with a second marriage and another kid on the way.

So the problem gene had probably come from Dad's side of the family. And so far it looked as if I was the only one in my generation who'd gotten it. Most of my cousins were married, or heavy into dating someone from the opposite gender. My four-teen-year-old brother Danny was definitely hetero—his room was plastered with posters of Britney Spears, and by the time he'd reached grade seven, the phone was ringing off the wall with girls calling. Two weeks ago he'd started grade nine at the Dief, and I passed him in the halls at least once a day, surrounded by a bevy of girls clamoring for his attention. We looked alike—same straight black hair and dark eyes—and whenever he saw me, he would flash me a conspiratorial grin as if letting me know that he was following in my footsteps and keeping up the family tradi-tion. So the problem gene was obviously not part of his makeup. And Keelie, my five-year-old sister—well, she was too young to define one way or the other yet.

On the other hand, she was a genetic afterthought. Certainly unexpected. Mom and Dad had counted their diaper-washing days long over when she showed up in the womb. Mom was forty-two and a full-time accountant when Keelie was born, and Dad thirty-nine. The pregnancy really upended their lives—once I even overheard them discussing an abortion. But in the end they decided to go through with it, and the little hurricane was born seven months later. Just like Danny and me, she had Mom's dark eyes and straight black hair. Immediately the house filled with her shrieks and bellows, and when she got her "sea legs," as Dad put it, well, the universe became her backyard. Right now I could hear her on the other side of my bedroom door, dragging the kitchen broom between her legs as she tore up and down the hall, hollering, "Watch out, Harry! Draco's right behind you! He's got the snitch! No, I've got it. I've got it!"

Sprawled on my bed, I listened to her tear down the hall. About a year ago, Keelie and I started our own private tradition. Every morning at seven, she would ease open my door and poke her head into my room. She would wait there like that, her head stuck into the gap, checking to make sure I was still asleep, and then her short little figure would come tiptoeing toward me. I was always awake as soon as the door opened, but I knew my part of the deal and would continue to lie with my face burrowed into my pillow, faking sleep, while she grunted her way softly onto the foot of my bed and crawled up to my head. It was hard not to giggle as her small hand started brushing my hair back from my face, but that would have spoiled it. So I would lie with my eyes closed until she'd brushed all the hair from my face, then leaned down and whispered, "Wake up, Dylan. It is time to bring some happiness into this day."

That was my cue to erupt with a roar and grab her tight and squealing in my arms. We would roll around for a bit, giggling our heads off until Mom poked her head in the door and said it was time to get moving. Then Keelie would slide whooping off my bed and scamper out the door, and I would watch her go, wondering if I'd been like that at her age—barreling around in a body that felt like a promise or a wish come true, riding the wave crest of my own happiness.

Thursday after school, I lay sprawled on Rachel Gonzales' bed, bored out of my mind. I'd been invited here to play audience while Rachel put Julie Crozier through her idea of the perfect makeover—heavy on the eyeliner, massive on the mascara and absolutely brutal on the eye shadow and lip gloss. Both Julie and Rachel were core members of the Dief's jock crowd, and as such, considered themselves to be semi-divine. As far as they, and admittedly most of the Dief student population, were concerned, it was a privilege to be seen with them and an even greater privilege to worship everything they said and did.

As their invited audience, I was expected to remain in a near-comatose state, making single-syllable statements such as "ooh" and "ah." This wasn't because Julie and Rachel didn't understand two-syllable words. They regularly pulled *A*s and *B*s on class assignments, and Rachel was planning on studying engineering at McGill in two years. But they were both seriously protective of their semi-divine status, and no female outside their tiny inner circle was allowed to display anything beyond a basic Neanderthal intellect in their presence.

So there I was with my back to the wall, flipping through one of Rachel's *Sweet Valley High* books and trying to ignore the obvious fact that Julie's pale skin and blond hair were not meant for thick globs of olive eye shadow. In fact, Julie was beginning to look rather like an alien experiment gone terribly wrong, but no way was I saying anything. Rachel and Julie were not only two of the Dief's minor goddesses, they were also part of a group that Joc and I had dubbed "the phone patrol." Get on their bad side, and their phone network would be passing your name around like a helpless electron in a massive electrical current. The next morning you wouldn't begin to recognize yourself in the new rumors flying around school.

Generally speaking I wasn't into the worshiping thing, at least not unless it was absolutely necessary, and in this case it sort of was. As part of the jock crowd, Julie and Rachel were Cam's friends—not close friends, but they always sat together in the cafeteria and went to the same parties. For the past two years I'd played on the girls junior volleyball team with them, but neither Julie or Rachel had given me a second glance until Cam and I started dating. Then they'd stared in what can only be described as stunned astonishment. I mean, why would Cam Zeleny date a fringe jock with definite nerd overtones, when he could have been dating diaphanous nymphs like Julie and Rachel?

But when Cam's interest in me showed no sign of fading, the leaders of the phone patrol—Julie, Rachel and Deirdre Buffone—reluctantly began to include me in some of their activities. Which meant that today I got to lie here in an awed stupor, listening as Rachel and Julie attacked, mutilated and otherwise dragged through the absolute sludge the characters of various female students from the Dief. Survival of the fittest—that's the way it works, I guess. But y'know, it's so *boring*.

"Lindsay Horner's been carrying her ass pretty high these days," said Julie, eyeing herself dubiously in the mirror. Rachel had just finished layering the olive eye shadow on her right eyelid with a rusty red color, and the effect was indescribable.

"Lindsay!" sniffed Rachel. Shifting to Julie's other side, she let out a breathy laugh. "She knows all the guys are watching her like crazy because she's keeping Darryl Stronner so happy. She's been letting him do it to her without a safe."

"They're not using condoms?" asked Julie, turning toward Rachel in surprise.

"Watch it!" yelped Rachel, jerking back. "I almost stuck you in the eye." Carefully she erased a smudge of rust eye shadow from Julie's nose with her finger. "What was I saying? Oh yeah, Lindsay. Yeah, well, that's what she told me, anyway."

"But that's crazy," I said, ditching my stupor along with *Sweet Valley High*. "I mean, Darryl Stronner's definitely been around."

"I dunno," shrugged Rachel, working away at Julie's left eyelid. "Lindsay's on the pill."

My jaw dropped and I stared at her. I didn't know that much about sex—four times doesn't make you an expert—but I did know enough to always use a condom. No way would I have let Paul anywhere near me without one.

"Yeah, sure," I said slowly. "But there are a zillion STDs you can catch."

Even Julie was giving Rachel skeptical glances. "Yeah, Rach," she said. "Since when does the pill protect you from herpes?"

Rachel shrugged dismissively. "Lindsay says Darryl doesn't sleep around anymore," she said. "Not since he started seeing her. Besides…" She paused, slowing into her thoughts, then added, "Wouldn't you let Cam, Dylan, if you were on the pill?"

Neither Rachel or Julie looked at me directly, but I could feel them grow suddenly intent, waiting for my answer. And damn it all if I didn't feel my usual tidal wave of nervousness as they focused in on me. Later, when I thought back on this, I was going to be really pissed-off at myself. I mean, it wasn't as if Julie and Rachel were experts on the subject…or experience…of sex. Rachel had probably done it—last winter she'd gone out with a guy in grade twelve for a while—but my instincts told me that Julie was still virginal. Early last year she'd put out a story about how she'd done it with a guy at summer camp, but I figured it was a fib, concocted to impress the phone patrol. I mean, you don't have sex for the first time so you can *advertise* it.

Still, experts or not, both Julie and Rachel were frozen into position, barely breathing as they waited for my answer.

"I'm not on the pill," I muttered, trying to ignore the flush crawling up my neck.

"You don't neeeeed to be," Rachel singsonged deliberately, and Julie gave a quiet snort. My flush deepened, but I fought the urge to snap something back. It wasn't wise to rouse the ire of the semi-divine. In fact, it wasn't wise to even attract their attention. Last year in health class, the teacher, Ms. Harada, brought in a package of condoms for her annual talk on safe sex. It was an all-girl class, and the package was passed hand to hand with a lot of quiet giggling. No big deal for me—Joc and I used to snitch packages of Tim's safes from his dresser, then run around the house shooting them at each other. Childish, I know, but once we even snuck a large sausage out of the fridge and slid a condom onto it to see if it would fit. It did the job nicely. We were quite impressed with that condom's stretchability factor.

Anyway, there was a girl in my grade ten health class named Sharon Harder—a really shy, quiet Christian who was so religious, she carried a Bible everywhere she went. Unfortunately for her, Julie, Rachel and Deirdre were also in this class and keeping their eyes peeled as the package of condoms traveled around the room. The instant it was passed to Sharon, they simultaneously burst into shrieks of high-pitched laughter. For a moment it was just the three of them, cackling in absolute hysteria, while the rest of us scanned the group, trying to figure out the joke. Within seconds, the entire classroom had focused on Sharon Harder, who was still holding the package of condoms. The result was a wall of sound smashing into Sharon, and I have to admit I was part of it, roaring my head off with the others.

When the hysteria finally died down, Ms. Harada was speechless. "Well," she faltered, her eyes on Sharon, "that wasn't very nice." But she left it at that. I mean, what was she supposed to do—give the entire class a detention for laughing? Besides, she coached half of the girls' sports teams, and the phone patrol were her most valuable players. That was the secret of their power—it had to do with the way they operated as a group, pushing boundaries en masse, but never stepping over them as individuals. As Cam Zeleny's girlfriend, I was reasonably safe from their attacks—no girl, not even a member of the phone patrol, would risk her chances of dating Cam in the future by attacking his current girlfriend in an obvious manner. But they had their way of getting in small digs, and it was easiest just to go along with things, duck your head and keep your mouth shut when you disagreed.

"What d'you think of Michelle Allen?" asked Rachel, ignoring the angry burn that was festering on my face. She'd made her point. The phone patrol knew about my sex life, or lack thereof, and had filed the information in the appropriate mental-storage unit. They had probably heard about it from Gary Pankratz or Len Schroeder, two of Cam's friends—Julie and Len had been getting very friendly of late. But then, maybe they'd heard it straight from Cam. Like Joc said, he moaned and groaned about it enough when I wasn't around.

"The new girl?" asked Julie, also ignoring me.

"Yeah," said Rachel. "She's signed up for volleyball tryouts."

"She-male," Julie said significantly.

In spite of the flush that was eating up my face, I gave her a startled glance. This fall, Michelle Allen had transferred to the Dief from Confederation Collegiate, a high school across town, because she wanted to get in on the Dief's superior sports program. Though she was in grade twelve, I knew her somewhat because we'd played on the same summer-league baseball team two years ago. Nothing had seemed remotely off about her.

"She has a boyfriend," I said quickly. "At least she did last August."

"Can't see why," Julie said coolly. "Practically no boobs, and she's built like a horse. She should've been born a guy—it's written all over her."

"D'you think she's a dyke?" asked Rachel. Focusing on Julie's upper lip, she sketched a Smartie-sized beauty mark above it.

"It's as obvious as the nose on my face," said Julie, scowling at Rachel's latest brain wave in the mirror. "We'll have to keep an eye on her in the locker room. If she tries anything funny, she's toast."

With that, they ditched Michelle Allen and started in on someone else. Rigid on the bed, I lay silent, letting my thoughts race. Everything I knew about Michelle told me that Julie was wrong, but there was no point in saying anything. Nobody argued with Julie Crozier. She had just pronounced a death sentence on Michelle Allen, and there was nothing I or anyone else could do about it. The harassment Michelle would face if she made the team would never be obvious to Ms. Harada or the other coaches, simply an ongoing series of small shoves and pushes, personal belongings that constantly went missing and a wall of silence from the other players. I gave it three, maybe four weeks, before Michelle quit and headed back to Confed.

And all this was going to happen in spite of the fact that Michelle had a boyfriend. I'd always thought having a boyfriend meant you were high and dry, no one would assume anything.

"Hey," said Rachel, turning toward me. "You haven't signed up for volleyball tryouts yet. And you didn't try out for soccer. How come?"

I shrugged, avoiding her gaze. "Soccer practices are in the morning," I said guardedly. "Mornings are for beds. I'm still thinking about volleyball, though."

"What d'you mean, *thinking* about it?" demanded Julie, ducking another dose of olive eye shadow. "We need you on the volleyball team. If you're not there, Michelle will make it for sure, and who knows who else?"

My eyes slid across hers, then away. How inspiring to think that she wanted me on the team just to keep Michelle Allen, who was a ten times better player than me, off of it.

"Maybe," I said, picking up Rachel's *Sweet Valley High* book and pretending to be fascinated with it. "Like I said, I'm still thinking about it."

"Yeah, well you just think your butt down to the gym and get yourself signed up," snapped Julie, then waved a dismissive hand at Rachel, who was leaning in with more eye shadow. "Cut it out, Rach," she added irritably. "You have me looking like a corpse here."

"Not a corpse," Rachel protested quickly. "A killer sexy lady of the night, maybe."

"A corpse that *used* to be a killer sexy lady of the night," said Julie. "*Maybe*. Where'd you get the idea for this color combo, anyway? The last time your cat threw up?"

"Olive and rust look great on you," said Rachel. "It looks great on most girls. They just don't realize it."

"I bet they don't realize it," Julie said dryly. "I think you're the only one who does, Rach. But what about Dylan? How d'you think it'd look on her?"

Remorselessly they turned toward me, their eyes fixing on my face—the gaze of the semi-divine, considering the potential of the almost-human.

"Yeah," Rachel said thoughtfully. "That combo would look super with Dylan's dark hair and eyes."

"C'mon then," said Julie, standing up. "Your turn, Dylan."

I stared at the chair she'd just vacated as if it was electric. This bedroom was an execution chamber in disguise.

"C'mon," said Rachel, looking offended. "You look like I'm going to kill you or something."

Single syllable words, I thought. *The awe and worship thing.*

Setting down *Sweet Valley High*, I got to my feet. "Y'know," I said, trying to smile. "Olive is, like, my fave color. And rust is my second fave."

Watch it, I thought. *Second has two syllables.*

Slowly I walked toward the chair.

Chapter Four

It was the following Saturday evening, and Cam and I were driving down Main Street, looking for something to do after the early movie. Well, actually it was something to do for the next hour or so—we both knew what we would end up doing eventually, and as usual, I was trying to put it off for as long as possible. And also as usual, Cam wasn't getting on my case about it. Dates were never just grunt and jump with him—he liked to talk and do things first.

"You thirsty, Dyl?" he grinned. "Want to stop for a Coke?"

"Yeah, sure," I said. "And a large pack of Doritos. It's only nine and I don't have to be in until eleven."

"You bet," he winked, and pulled into a 7-Eleven that was located two blocks from the Dief. A typical high school hangout, the parking lot was crowded with cars and lounging kids. Everyone came here to show off their weekend dates or just hang around. The other major hangout for Dief kids was a pool hall three blocks west, but that place didn't start happening until the weather got colder.

"Cam, buddy!" shouted someone.

All over the lot, car horns started honking. Cam's car was an old blue Firebird that he'd painted with curling orangey red flames. While his artwork would never be confused with Michelangelo's, the car was immediately recognizable from several blocks away. Steering carefully into a parking space, Cam turned off the ignition, and I climbed over the gearbox and squeezed onto his seat in front of him. Then I leaned out the window and waved to Deirdre Buffone and some girls from the soccer team. They'd been giving me a rough time about not coming out for the team this fall, but when I reminded them of the warmth, softness and general all-around coziness of a 7:00 AM bed, they just groaned and gave up.

Cam was rumbling contentedly in his chest, so I leaned against him while Deirdre and I called a few comments back and forth. Just a few, though—it wasn't easy to concentrate on what she was saying with Cam nuzzling away at my hair.

"Hey," I said, turning around. "You looking for some attention?"

"Yeah," he said. "I'm lonely. Why don't we forget the Cokes and head off by ourselves?"

"For two hours?" I demanded. "You looking for a shotgun wedding?"

"I've got protection," he said quickly. "I know how to use it, Dyllie."

"I know you do," I said, and he grunted softly, a sign that he was pulling back, biding his time until things were right. That was how he'd fixed it in his head—with a girl like Dylan Kowolski, you had to find the right time and place. The issue wasn't whether it would happen, it was having the patience and observing the social niceties until the right time—the *absolutely* right time—created itself. Because that was what an absolutely right time did—it *created* itself, out of patience and conversations, and the kind of caring Cam handed out to the people who were important to him.

Opening the door, I got out, and Cam followed. The weight of eyes that descended upon us then was tangible, and it didn't take a massive intellect to figure out what everyone was thinking: *Are they doing it? How are they doing it? How often are they doing it? Have they done it yet tonight?* For the next few minutes, Cam and I had center stage in that secret sex video teenagers are constantly running inside their heads, and we played it up, holding hands as we walked through the crowd, then stopped to talk to Deirdre by the store door. Two girls from the soccer team came over and asked me about the movie we'd just seen. Still holding hands, Cam and I played with each other's fingers while we held separate conversations.

Suddenly an ear-splitting roar cut through the air. A whoop went up from a group of kids on the sidewalk, and everyone turned to watch as a rusty derelict Honda came tearing down the street and veered into the parking lot. Kids scattered in every direction as the car made an abrupt left turn and squealed out of the lot's other entrance. Halfway across the street, it braked, then backed into the parking lot, engine revving loudly. Swerving crosswise into a parking space, it revved a few more times and went quiet. The driver's door burst open, and a tall, lanky, dark-haired guy leapt out and began pounding on the car roof. Throwing back his head, he roared loudly.

Dikker, I thought in disgust. *What a way to kill the ambience.* My eyes narrowed to slits and I almost hissed. Beside me, Cam went stiff, and several of his friends snorted.

"Six pack," grunted someone.

"Twelve pack," someone else grunted back.

"Hey," Cam said easily, his hand tightening on mine. "Who would you rather feel like right now—him or you?"

An appreciative snort ran around the group, and I squeezed Cam's hand gratefully. Cam was like that, always defending other kids—not that Dikker happened to deserve it. Keeping my face blank, I watched Joc get out of her side of the car. The gods be praised, she wasn't swaying; in fact, she managed a rather athletic vault onto the car hood before climbing onto the roof. Still, I couldn't help the scowl that came stomping across my face. They were at it again—the two of them could never seem to stop putting on a public display. Okay, so maybe Cam and I were guilty of it too, but at least we didn't go around *begging* for an audience.

Scooting across the roof, Joc came to a halt with her legs dangling on either side of Dikker's shoulders. Even from the other side of the parking lot, I could see the calculating grins on their faces. Joc was wearing a mini-skirt. Everyone was watching, the air had a razor edge. If someone didn't intervene soon, things were going to get *obscene*.

"Hey, Joc!" I shouted, and as she glanced toward me the tension broke. Pulling my hand free of Cam's, I started across the parking lot. As I approached, Dikker laid his head in Joc's lap and gave me a slow grin. He was drunk and probably stoned. Joc looked about a two-beer happy. I wanted to slug them both.

"What happened to the car rally?" I asked. Joc's original plan for tonight had involved watching Dikker's older brother compete in a smash'm up car race.

"Car broke down," said Joc, playing with Dikker's hair.

"It sounds alive," I said and kicked the Honda's rusty front fender.

"Not *this* priceless piece of shit," said Dikker, giving me another dozy smile. He was definitely stoned. "My *brother's* goddamn wreck."

"Oh yeah," I said. If there was just...*something* I liked about this guy. But nothing—no matter how I wracked my brains, I couldn't come up with a single positive attribute.

"So," I said, glancing up at Joc. "You planning on descending to planet Earth for a Coke any time soon?"

"Not Joc," said Dikker, with a hiccuping snort. "She's flying."

This sent Joc into a flurry of giggles, but she stopped as Dikker abruptly doubled over and grabbed at his crotch.

"Shit," he groaned. "Do I have to piss."

"Mind your manners," Joc said sternly. Leaning down, she swatted the back of his head. "This is Queen Dylan you're talking to here, not street trash. Go do your stuff behind the store where she can't see you."

"Yes, boss," grunted Dikker. Pulling himself upright, he tiptoed an exaggerated arc around me, then meandered across the parking lot, waving amiably at the comments being tossed in his direction. Joc watched his progress without comment, an odd smile on her mouth.

"What was that all about?" I demanded as Dikker's worthless butt swaggered around the back of the store.

"What was what all about?" asked Joc, keeping her eyes on the place he'd disappeared.

"*Queen* Dylan," I snapped, fighting the hiss in my throat.

"Oh, you know how Dikker gets when he's drunk," said Joc, sliding her eyes lazily over me. "I was just reining him in a bit, so you wouldn't be shocked."

I don't know what it was—the way Joc was looking down at me, so cool and distant, almost as if we weren't friends...*best* friends... or the fact she was so obviously enjoying Dikker's company. I mean, couldn't she see what an absolute MORON he was?

"Oh really?" I said hotly. "Well, for your information, most of us normal people can't tell the difference between Dikker drunk and Dikker sober."

I was so mad, I was shaking—colossal, earth-shattering trembles. Without another word, I turned and headed across the parking lot. A mad chaos had erupted in my head, morphing the 7-Eleven into a confused blur of colors and voices. As I reached the store's right front corner, the lounging crowd of kids petered out and I was alone, storming down the side wall. From behind the store I could hear Dikker clearly, singing away at the top of his lungs—a completely tuneless version of "You Make Me Feel Like A Natural Woman." Needless to say, this did nothing to improve my state of mind. But then, I'm not sure you could call what I was in a state of "mind." It was definitely closer to a state of "no mind," as in rabid, crazed, insane. I mean, I wanted to do heinous things to Dikker Preddy, unmentionable *unbelievable* things.

Fortunately, before I reached the store's back corner, I got a basic grip. Collapsing against the wall, I closed my eyes and made a massive effort to calm down. What in the world did I think I was doing back here? What in the world had I been *about* to do? There were definitely better ways to communicate frustration, disagreement, even *fuck you*, weren't there? I mean, *legal* ways?

From the back of the store came a few more bellowed-out notes and the sound of a fly being zipped up. Abruptly it hit me—Dikker was about to walk around the corner and find me standing here, doing exactly...*what*? Frantically I turned and started back the way I'd come, just as Cam walked around the store's front corner.

"Dyllie?" he asked, looking concerned. "You all right?"

On his heels was Joc, but the expression on her face was not exactly what I would call concerned. At that moment a loud belch sounded behind the store, and we all turned to see Dikker swagger slowly into view. His eyes met mine, and for one brief terrifying moment all I could do was pray that he hadn't heard me around the corner, experiencing my hopefully temporary nervous breakdown.

"Yeah, Cam, I'm fine," I managed. "Just fine."

Giving Dikker my back, I grabbed Cam's hand and started hauling him toward the front of the store. "C'mon," I said. "Let's go get those Cokes."

"What's the matter, Dyllie?" asked Cam. "You mad at me or something? Tell me what I did and I'll make it up to you. I'll do anything you want, I swear."

He paused, his face in my neck, waiting for a response. Inside my shirt, his hand slowly stroked my bra. Parked behind an office building on the east side of town, we were in the Firebird's backseat, doing the usual Saturday night thing. Normally I got something off this—a soft gentle heat that let me at least pretend I was turning on. But tonight, no matter what Cam said or did, I felt nothing. I mean, I could have been made of rubber. An absolute funk had dropped on me after the thing with Dikker at the 7-Eleven—a cold rubbery nothingness that wouldn't go away.

All I could think about was the way I'd gone storming back there to find him. What in the world had gotten into me? A sudden inkling to stare at his privates? Uh-uh. Very little could have interested me less. Still, it didn't take a genius to figure out in advance what I would find back there, so I must have gone looking for it. But *why*? If Dikker Preddy was the way Joc wanted to spend her time, what did I care? It wasn't as if she and I were going to get together, not the way I wanted, anyway. We would never...

Halfway through this last thought, a massive wave of fear reared up inside me and I shoved the forbidden thought back down deep, where it belonged. *Cam*, I told myself furiously. I was here with *Cam*, parked behind Reiniger and Sons on a Saturday night, and we were making out and I liked it. I *liked* it.

Nuzzling his hair, I said, "I'm not mad at you. You're the last person I'd be mad at."

"Then what is it?" he asked quickly. "It's like you're on another planet tonight. I feel like I'm kissing a doorknob here."

I winced. Something had to change, and fast. "It was something Joc said, I guess," I admitted reluctantly. "She called me a queen, as if I was some kind of snot who thought I was above her and Dikker, y'know? It pissed me off."

"Is that why you went after him?" Cam asked slowly.

"I'm not sure," I admitted. "I think maybe I wanted to kill him, actually."

Cam laughed low in his throat. "You wouldn't be the first person," he said.

"No," I agreed, some of the coldness leaving my body. If Cam believed this, maybe it was true. Maybe then I could too. "My head went kind of crazy there for a bit," I said. "I wasn't thinking about what he was doing, I guess."

"So you found out how he got his nickname?" asked Cam, his voice going husky.

"Well," I said, "I stopped myself before I reached the back corner, so I didn't actually *see* anything. You got there right after that."

Cam sighed, then muttered, "The day he was born, the angels must've had a lot of extra stock lying around. That guy definitely got more than his share." Taking his hand out of my shirt, he lifted it to my mouth and traced my lips. Then he started kissing me softly, again and again. And this time it was working, I could feel a gentle heat start up all over me.

"You want to see mine?" he whispered. "It's not as big as Dikker's, but it's eager and it's all yours, Dyl. It's begging for you. Can you hear it calling your name? Dyllie," he singsonged into my ear. "Dyllie, Dyllie."

That made me laugh. "Shh," I said. "Don't talk. Just don't talk."

So we went at it for a while, kissing and kissing, and it was still working—I could feel the heat building, heartbeat by heartbeat.

"You are a queen," Cam whispered. "Joc was just telling the truth. You're way above her, Dyllie. I don't see why you hang out with her. You should join the volleyball team and get to know Deirdre better, or Julie and Rachel. They're more your type." Slowly his fingers traced my jeans zipper. "Dyllie," he whispered. "I'm calling to you. Dyllie, Dyllie."

And I went stone cold. It happened the second his fingers touched my zipper. No, just before that—when he'd made the comment about my being above Joc. Suddenly I'd felt distant, as if Cam and I really were on different planets. I mean, why would he criticize my being friends with Joc, as if there was something...*wrong* with it? There was nothing *wrong* with it. We'd been friends for years, we had tons in common.

Except Dikker Preddy, that is.

"Shit," sighed Cam. Taking his hand off my zipper, he burrowed his face in my neck and just sat there. I could feel the disappointment coming off him in waves. It was thick in me too, a sickness pulling at my gut.

"I'm sorry," I mumbled. "I guess I'm kind of weird tonight." Then we just sat there like that for a while—silent, him breathing, me staring out the window, blinking back tears.

"Just tell me what it is, Dyllie," Cam said finally, without lifting his head. "I want you to be happy, I want you to like it.

Just tell me what you want and I'll do it."

But that was the one thing I couldn't tell him, I couldn't even tell myself. So after a while I buttoned up my shirt, we climbed into the front of the car, and he drove me home.

Chapter Five

The main question here, I suppose, would be, What was the big deal? Most people didn't go into a major funk over sexual orientation anymore—a lot of lesbians and gays were out these days. TV sitcoms were full of gay characters, and the Internet had loads of chat sites for teenagers who wanted to talk about the issue. There were even five girls who were officially out at the Dief, and as far as I could see they weren't given a rough time—as long as they stayed away from the senior girls volleyball team, that is. If they had been guys, it would have been different, but most straight guys who got uptight about gays thought lesbianism was sexy. So as the Dief's five official lesbians, they got some stares and the odd dimwit comment, but they weren't harassed or shunned in any obvious way. They all had friends—homo and hetero, though admittedly none from the phone patrol.

No loss there, of course, but it was also true that I wasn't friends with any of them. It wasn't that I went into a massive panic attack whenever I saw one of them, though sometimes I wondered if they had a way of reading other girls, if they could tell about me. No, it was more that I just didn't click with them.

They were all really different than me—besides our hormones, we had nothing in common. I guess what it came down to was that their scene didn't feel real to me. *They* didn't feel real, I suppose, because they didn't feel like *me*. So they weren't *really* real, y'know?

The people who are *really* real in your life are the people you're close to. The rest are just a dream you wish you weren't having. And the people I was close to were my family, who reeked heterosexuality, and Cam, who reeked the same very straight vibes, and Joc, who was dating a guy whose vibes were so massively hetero, they were almost solid. That was what I was surrounded by, that was what was real to me. The rest, like I said, was just a virtual reality game I wished I wasn't playing.

It wasn't that I thought my family would reject me if I told them I was lesbian. I knew their love was deeper than that. But there were assumptions that ran through everything we said and did together, never spoken aloud but still there, part of every family gathering and the frequent jokes my parents made about the grandchildren they would someday have. These assumptions were like an invisible web of warmth and light that connected all of us, the understanding that some day the love we felt for each other would be carried on into the next generation. Coming out as a lesbian meant that wouldn't happen.

Well okay, I suppose there was the option of a reproduction clinic, sperm donors and all that. But it was kind of impersonal compared to the husband-and-wife thing. And besides, how would you know for sure what you were getting? I mean, *really*? I mean, NOT!

And NOT meant, of course, no next generation coming out of Dylan Kowolski's womb. No next-generation Dylans would mean massive disappointment for my family—not just my parents, but my grandparents, aunts and uncles, brother and sister and cousins, *everyone*. More importantly, it would mean massive disappointment for me. Because I *wanted* to fit into that web of warmth and light. I *wanted* to have children, a husband and a happy home. If I was hetero, I figured it was pretty much guaranteed. If I was hetero, I would be happy.

And, of course, there was also my friendship with Joc, my best-friend friendship that had been a core part of my life since grade three. She was part of the way I laughed and breathed. So if I walked up to her one day and said, "Joc, I'm in love with you, and I have a mad passionate urge to kiss you," and it freaked her into a total funk and I lost her, well, it would be like losing part of my body. Like I said, we'd been friends for a long time, she was the way I breathed. I didn't know how to lose that.

So I couldn't just up and tell her how I felt about her, unless I was absolutely sure of the reaction I would get. If only there was some way to figure out in advance what it would be. Because sometimes, in spite of the fact that she was dating Dikker, I could have sworn Joc was really attracted to me. Like I said, she was always hanging all over me. And there was that electric flash that occasionally leapt between us, as well as that moment in the soap spill haze when she'd almost started unbuttoning my shirt.

But there was also, of course, Dikker.

Monday morning, following the 7-Eleven catastrophe with Dikker, I got onto my bike and headed to Joc's house the way I usually did. The weather had cooled somewhat since the weekend, but snow was still a ways off, so the neighborhood was dotted with adults clearing leaves off their cars and kids in windbreakers, walking to school. Normally everything I passed went by in a bright blur, simply an extension of my thoughts, part of the early morning buzz I felt biking toward Joc's place.

But this morning there was an odd feeling to the ride, as if things were out of sync. Joc hadn't phoned last night the way she usually did, and I hadn't called her. It was like a tradition between us, we always called each other Sunday night to plan the coming week.

So when neither of us called, it was a sign that something was definitely off. My guess was that Joc had asked Dikker what had happened behind the store and he'd told her "Nothing," but she was brooding over it anyway, working her way toward nuclear detonation. And of course I was still in a major funk, trying to figure out what exactly had made me storm back there the way I had. So when I got to Joc's house, I coasted up to the curb and just stood with my head down for a bit, trying to figure out how to handle the next few minutes. Because if Joc was mad, the all-important moment with her was the first one. If you managed to pull the right grin or say the right thing, you had a chance of heading off a major explosion. If not, you were busy picking up the pieces for the next few days.

Unfortunately she didn't give me much time to mull things over. Almost the second I pulled up, the front door swung open, and there she was, leaning against the doorframe and watching me. And as soon as I saw her, it happened to me the way it always did—an electric shimmer that lit every nerve in my body so I was suddenly riding hyperspace.

She was eating toast from one hand and drinking coffee from a Tweetie Bird mug in the other. Her hair wasn't brushed and she still had to put on her makeup, but she was gorgeous, her large purplish blue eyes flat on me, watching and speculative. For a long moment neither of us spoke, just stood and stared at each other. Then Tim came barreling through the doorway, bumping Joc out of the way with his hip.

"Hey, Dyl," he called, coming down the porch stairs. "Want

a lift downtown? That's where I'm headed."

Tall and dark-haired like Joc, Tim had graduated from the Dief three years ago and now worked at an auto-body shop in the city's west end. The rest of his time he spent tinkering with his friends' cars. That, and pouring beer down his throat.

"Can't," I called back. "The school thing, y'know?"

"Prison!" he bellowed, punching his fist into the air. "Break free!"

Getting into his car, he revved backward out of the driveway and took off down the street. Eyes fixed on his taillights, I watched for as long as possible, until the absolute tip of his muffler had vanished around the corner. Then slowly, very slowly, I turned back to Joc. As expected, I found her gaze still on me, heavy and loaded with meaning. Too loaded. Nervously my eyes flicked past hers and glued themselves to the wall beside her head. Guilt—I was crawling with it, the evidence all over my face. "Power blush" was what Cam called it.

But then, all of a sudden, I just thought, *Screw it!* And I dumped the whole guilt thing. Because even if I didn't know why I'd gone storming after Dikker at the 7-Eleven, it hadn't been to hurt Joc. Besides, she'd started it. She called me a queen.

"You coming or what?" I called, too loud, but definitely not ass-kissing eager.

At that Joc's eyes narrowed, and without responding she backed into the house, letting the door slam behind her. For a moment I just stood there, wondering if I was supposed to follow her in, or wait at the curb like a dog with its tail between its legs.

Screw that too! I thought and dropped my bike onto the lawn with a melodramatic crash. Then I stomped into the house after Joc, letting the door slam behind me too.

Immediately I was hit with the dense odor of cigarette smoke.

Ms. Hersch, Joc's mom, was a heavy smoker, and so were both
her offspring. Officially, Ms. Hersch didn't know Joc smoked, or
that her frequent evening shifts at the local library branch gave her
daughter unrestricted access to the household ashtrays. This was,
of course, a very different situation from my undercover nicotine
habit, since my mom happens to be the Clean Lungs Patrol.

"Hey—go easy on the door, would ya?" called Ms. Hersch from
the kitchen. "It works just as good if you close it gently."

"Sorry," I called back and headed down the hall toward Joc's
room. The Hersches' house was a bungalow, everything on one
floor, with Joc's and Tim's rooms facing each other across a hall
on the east side. When I got to Joc's room, she was standing in
front of her mirror, curling iron in hand.

"You're talkative today," I said, flopping down onto the bed.

Keeping her eyes fixed on her reflection, Joc shrugged. Slowly
the silence ticked by, a grenade waiting for victims.

"So," I said finally, trying to kick-start a conversation, "what
fascinating things did life bring you yesterday?"

"What did it bring you?" countered Joc, rolling her bangs into
the curling iron.

"Took Keelie to the park," I said. "Raked the lawn. Met
Danny's new girlfriend. Flavor of the week, y'know. They're lining
up for him."

"He's gorgeous," shrugged Joc. "No surprise, he's your brother."

The compliment was so unexpected, coming at a time like this,
that it sent me into an immediate funk, the heat crawling up my
neck. Power blush. I *hated* doing the red thing.

"We look a bit alike," I said carefully, trying to put the brakes
on my manic blood rush. "But I'm nothing—"

"Guys are crazy for you, Dyl," Joc said quietly, setting down
the curling iron and picking up her mascara bottle. "Cam's lucky
to have you and he knows it."

"Oh yeah," I mumbled, trying to ignore the heat stampeding across my face. Fixing my eyes on the ceiling, I thought about icicles up my butt, freezing cold showers, life in the Arctic—anything that would take me down ten or twenty degrees Celsius.

"Even Tim's gaga over you," Joc continued as she cleaned her mascara brush with a Kleenex. "And Dikker's friends are always asking about you. God, even the teachers watch you."

"Oh, come off it," I snapped, sitting up. "Teachers watch everyone."

"Not like you," said Joc. Leaning toward the mirror, she began applying mascara. "Not *Queen* Dyl—"

A tsunami-sized wave of frustration slammed through me, yanking me to my feet. "Don't call me that!" I yelled, the words pouring unchecked from my mouth. "Just because I'm going out with Cam. Just because *he's* popular and Dikker's—"

"Cam!" Joc said incredulously. Mouth open, she stared at me. "This doesn't have anything to do with Cam, Dyl."

"Then what?" I bellowed, the anger huge and hot in me. No, not anger. *Fear.* Fear like a trapped bird, its wings flapping desperately inside my chest.

"It's just you," said Joc, her eyes hard on me. "The way you are. As if everyone around you is your subject. We're all here to please you."

"I am *not...*," I spluttered helplessly, then just stood there, staring at her. I mean, I was speechless, a complete void.

"If you think you can wait *one* minute," Joc said airily, turning toward the door, "I've got to brush my teeth. Then I'll be ready."

With that, she stalked out of the room. As she left, absolute chaos erupted in my head. Flopping back onto the bed, I listened to the sound of running water coming from the bathroom. Was it possible Joc was telling the truth? Did I really come across like that kind of snot? But how could I? I mean, I was hardly a candidate for sainthood. Anyone who *half*-knew me knew that. And lots of girls at the Dief were prettier than me, way prettier. I was lucky Cam wanted to go out with me. Joc made it sound as if it was the other way around.

The thing was, Cam and I weren't having sex. And the times I'd done it with Paul in the summer before grade ten were ancient history now. So it was probably my twelve-month stint of abstinence that was behind all this queen stuff Joc had been throwing at me lately. It made her suspicious, but she didn't know what to be suspicious about, or maybe didn't *want* to know. "Queen" was the only word she could come up with to define the situation. As usual, everything came down to the same old problem. Hormones, I didn't have the proper hormones. I was out of sync, skewed, *wrong*.

At the other end of the hall the bathroom tap shut off, and Joc's sullen footsteps started toward the bedroom. Brushing her teeth obviously hadn't cheered her up, and the situation called for emergency measures. I was going to have to cut deep, bleed a little. Maybe a lot. Taking a long breath, I waited until she reached the doorway, then said, "Okay, so I was pissed-off Saturday. Because you called me a queen, and I *hated* it. And..."

I paused, racking my brains as I tried to come up with something she would believe. Something *reasonable*. "And I guess I wanted to prove I wasn't—a queen, I mean," I added grudgingly.

I kept my eyes glued to the ceiling. No way was I chancing a direct look. "So," I said, taking another long breath, "that's why I went storming after Dikker. To..."

I paused again, trying to figure out the best way to put it. I mean, it just wasn't the kind of thing I had to explain every day.

"To...*well*...look at him peeing, I guess," I said in a rush, my eyes still on the ceiling. "But I stopped myself before I reached the end of the side wall. And he was around the back. So I didn't see him, I didn't see *it*, I didn't see anything. Nothing happened, okay? I just went crazy for a bit, and then I got over it."

Silence leaned down ominously onto the room, so close I could almost hear it breathing. Finally Joc said carefully, "You're telling me you went back there to look at Dikker's dick?"

"*Well*," I said, keeping my eyes on the ceiling, "not *really*. It was more to prove I wasn't a queen, I think. But like I said, I got a grip and stopped halfway down the side of the store. So I didn't see anything, anything at all."

She took a few hesitant steps into the room. "That's what he said," she said slowly. "But I wasn't sure…"

"Well, now you can be sure," I said. Chancing a quick glance at her, I felt relief hit me flat out. Joc looked confused, a little on the astonished side, but nuclear detonation definitely wasn't in the picture.

"I mean, really, Joc," I added dryly, "can you see Dikker and me, in a *million* years…?"

A grin flashed across her face and she giggled. "No," she said. "Not in a million billion *centuries*."

Darting across the room, she jumped onto the bed and began bouncing gleefully. "And he's mine, he's mine, he's mine!" she crowed, knocking my head against the headboard with each bounce.

"Great," I said slowly. Problem solved, she was no longer pissed-off. Swallowing the very lumpy lump in my throat, I got to my feet and said, "We'd better get moving or we'll be late."

"Yeah, all right," said Joc. Quickly she stood and followed me to the door. But instead of walking directly into the hall, she stopped and said, "Hey, Dyl?"

Hearing the wobble in her voice, I turned to find her watching me, an uncertain expression on her face. She blinked, her eyes flitting nervously, then said, "You're sure...nothing happened?"

"Nothing!" I said, my astonishment so obvious that she relaxed.

"Okay," she breathed, hugging herself. "What was I thinking? You're my best friend, right? Besides, you've got Cam. C'mon, let's get going."

A dazzling grin took over her face, she leaned into me and started force-walking me backward toward the front door.

Two days later we were sprawled on the floor at the rear of the Dief's auditorium, Joc curled into a semi-coma while I sat with my back to the wall and a book propped on my knees. Around us kids were scattered in various groups, their eyes focused on the stage. Classes had let out for the day, and we had all gathered to watch the first rehearsal for this year's fall drama production, *Hamlet*. The curious crowd contained some distinctly non-drama types, here to support a distinctly non-drama-type member of the cast. Because to the absolute astonishment of everyone at the Dief, including Joc, Dikker Preddy had landed a part. It was just Marcellus, a soldier of the king's guard, and a very minor part who did nothing more than walk on and off stage a few times, but still it was serious theater, real Shakespeare—Dikker in tights, quoting jokes that people had stopped laughing at several hundred years ago.

Joc hadn't made up her mind whether to be proud or pissed-off at Dikker's success. After all, he hadn't told her that he was auditioning for a part. She'd been abruptly introduced to the fact yesterday afternoon, when someone had called her over in the hall and pointed out his name on the cast list posted beside the drama room. An hour later, Dikker had been wearing cat scratches on his left arm, but the tiff had since been resolved and here we were, his loyal fans, sprawled at the back of the auditorium behind a scattering of Shakespeare groupies, several future recruits for the Hell's Angels, and various cast members who were waiting to be called up for their scenes.

"Hey, Joc," said Gary Wainbee, another minor part sitting directly in front of us. Vicious acne had pockmarked the poor guy for life. He coped by hiding out behind long droopy bangs and shooting everyone shy sideways glances. "Wakey wakey," he whispered, his gaze tiptoeing delicately around Joc's dozed-out face. "They're doing Dikker's first scene."

"Wha—?" mumbled Joc, half-opening one eye.

"Dikker," I said, poking her with my foot. "The Shakespearean nutcase in your life."

Instantly she was on her knees, babbling, "Is he on, is he on?" Leaning heavily on Gary's eager shoulder, she peered toward the stage just as Dikker swaggered out from the wings. Immediate ear-splitting whistles rose from the future Hell's Angels, then subsided under the annoyed glance of Mr. Tyrrell, the drama teacher. Rolling my eyes, I glanced at Joc, who was still kneeling with her back to me and giggling with Gary. In the auditorium's dim backlighting, her hair was a long dark river that ended an inch above a line of smooth skin that could be seen between the bottom of her T-shirt and the top of her jeans. For a second, then, in the room's back shadows, while everyone else's gaze was focused on the stage, I let it happen in me the way I never did—just let the feelings rise up through my body in a long liquid ache.

Abruptly a girl sitting close by shifted, as if about to turn around, and I slammed the feelings back down. Closing my eyes, I leaned my head against the wall, ground my teeth and fought back everything that was begging to be released. When I opened my eyes again, Joc had scooted back to her position beside me on the floor, once again in a semi-coma. Dikker's brief moment of fame was obviously over.

"Call me the next time he's up, Gary," she mumbled, and he nodded enthusiastically, ducking another shy glance at her from under his droopy bangs.

"Sure thing, queen of Dikker's dreams," he mumbled back.

"You've got that right," said Joc, a pleased smile curving her lips.

Queen. The word hit me just as she opened one eye and fixed it on me. For a fleeting second, I could have sworn she was gloating.

"Why are you reading, Dyl?" she asked. "Can't you tell we're in the presence of great art?"

"Yeah yeah, go back to sleep," I replied, faking an enormous yawn.

But she didn't. Instead she kicked me lightly and asked, "What are you reading?"

"*The Egyptian Book of the Dead*," I replied, flashing her the cover of the book I was holding. "It's for my history class."

"Cheery," she mumbled, then closed her eye and started to slip back into her coma.

"Yeah," I said. "Especially 'The Negative Confessions'."

"The negative what?" she asked without opening her eyes.

"'The Negative Confessions,'" I enunciated precisely. "It's a list of things the ancient Egyptians were supposed to say before they died—a list of the sins they didn't do while they were alive."

"Oh," said Joc. "Short list."

"Uh-uh," I said. "Very long."

"Short life then," said Joc.

"Boring life," I said, "if this list is true. Let's see, the first confession is about sin in general, as in 'I have not committed sin.' Then it gets more specific—robbery with violence, stealing, murder. Then stealing again, only this time it's grain."

"I've never stolen grain," Joc said lazily. "Does that mean I get to go to heaven?"

"If you can recite it properly," I said. "You have to include the god's name, and each sin goes with a different god. Repeat after me, Jocelyn Hersch: 'Hail, Neha-her, who comest forth from Rasta, I have not stolen grain.'"

"Forget it," Joc grunted sleepily.

"No heaven for you then," I said. "Let's see, the next sin listed is purloining offerings."

"Does that have something to do with loins?" asked Joc, waking up slightly.

"Uh-uh," I said. "It's stealing. They're really big on stealing in this list."

"Oh," mumbled Joc. For a moment she lay quietly, her eyes still closed, then said, "So far I have three negative confessions I can make—no murder, no stealing grain, and no purloining loins. Oops, I mean offerings." She smiled contentedly.

"Ah, but you have to say it correctly," I said. "'Hail, Ruruti, who comest forth from—'"

"Shut up," Joc said.

I did shut up, just to bug her, and pretended to read silently. After a bit her toe nudged my foot and she asked, "What's the next sin?"

"More stealing," I said. "This time it's the property of God."

"Haven't done that either," she murmured.

"Ah," I said, "but you're screwed on the next few."

"Oh yeah?" she asked, opening one eye. "What are they?"

"Lying," I said, "carrying away food and cursing."

"Cursing's not a sin," said Joc. "It's a natural instinct. Lying's just a different way of looking at something. That can be very good for your mind. And everyone's carried food. How else do you get something out of the fridge?"

"Okey-dokey," I said. "Next sin: adultery."

"Nope, no adultery," said Joc.

"Ah, but it goes on," I said. "It says here: 'I have not lain with men.'"

"Oops," said Joc. "No heaven for me. No *Egyptian* heaven." She sniggered.

"Except," I said, my mouth leaping ahead of my mind, "I think this list is for a man, so if this sin was written for a woman, it would say, 'I have not lain with women.'"

As I said this, Joc's one open eye widened, and an excruciating jolt of electricity leapt between us. Then her eye closed and she lay motionless, without speaking. In the sudden silence I felt raw, charred to the bone, as if someone had zapped me with a flamethrower.

"The next sin," I stammered, dragging words, *any* words, into the jagged air, "is 'I have made none to weep.' And the next—"

Stunned, I halted, reading and rereading the phrase.

"What?" asked Joc, her eyes still closed, her lips barely moving.

"'Hail Basti,'" I said softly, "'who comest forth from Bast, I have not eaten the heart.'"

Joc lay absolutely still, as if absorbing the words through her skin. "I have not eaten my heart?" she repeated.

"Pretty much," I whispered.

Her eye came open and she nailed me with it. "No heaven for you then, eh Dyllie?" she said quietly, and closed it again.

Chapter Six

So that was the way it was between us—known but indirectly, a kind of hidden story always going on beneath the surface. For the most part, I did my best to ignore it. But the problem was that it wouldn't stay ignored. I mean, I'm talking about a basic body function here. No matter how much you try to ignore something like that, no matter how much you tell yourself that your body is just a subplot in your life, it isn't. It's the main plot. Which is kind of weird, considering that the average teenager is surrounded by people telling her it's her mind that's most important, her school grades, and her future. I'm not saying these aren't important—they are. But the body is the main plot. That's where you live the story of your life, that's where you *are*.

And if you try to ignore all of this—I mean your body and what it's trying to tell you, well, things get twisted. Because the main plot never likes to be shoved down under a bunch of subplots. So while you're up in your head, pretending your body has everything wrong, it's looking for a way to prove to you that it's got it all right. And believe me, the body is devious. It'll take any opportunity that comes along, *anything*—even something as mundane as a class discussion about an assigned reading—to make its point.

The mundane class discussion that I'm referring to took place two days after Dikker's first drama rehearsal. For the past week, my English class had been reading the novel *Foxfire: Confessions of a Girl Gang* by Joyce Carol Oates. In a nutshell, the book is about five high school girls in the 1950s who formed a gang called Foxfire. Though Foxfire was exclusively made up of girls, it was tough, taking on the guy gangs in the area, even stealing a car at one point. But most of their activities were more along the lines of Robin Hood, stealing from the rich to help the poor. Even so, their leader, Legs Sadovsky, landed in jail for a while, but when she got out, the gang rented a house in the country and continued their Robin Hood activities, hanging around hotel lobbies and bus stations, pretending to be sweet and naive, then taking the married men who hit on them for everything they were worth. A twisted sense of justice maybe, and in the end they went too far, kidnapping a guy and holding him for ransom. Then a new girl, who had just joined Foxfire, shot the hostage, and the gang had to split up to escape the police.

In an attempt to kick-start a discussion about the novel, our teacher, Mr. Cronk, asked the class whether we thought justice was a universal or personal principle, and what the difference between the two was. As on most days when he tried to get us talking, the majority of kids continued to sit sprawled in their desks, eyes dull and heavy-lidded as they worked on their non-response skills. Like the others I was in shut-down mode, slouched in my usual position in the back row beside Joc, who was slouched in the next desk. Just looking at me, no one would have guessed I was actually listening as the front-row keeners gave the expected responses: one—justice by definition is universal, and two—everything is subjective, even God, so how can justice be universal?

We were supposed to have read to part four of the novel, but the lack of response made it obvious most of the class hadn't cracked the cover. Still Mr. Cronk kept at us, his eyes skipping the front row and focusing in on us back-row slackers. And damn it all if it didn't feel as if he had his eyes specifically peeled for me, as if he'd somehow tuned to the fact that for once Dylan Kowolski, back-row dreamer extraordinaire, had managed to complete an assignment ahead of schedule. Because it just so happened that I'd finished *Foxfire* last night, had actually read the entire novel in one sitting, tearing through it with my heart in my mouth and feeling each scene as if it was happening inside my body—the gang's initiation of bloody tattoos and bared breasts, the attack as they'd come crashing through the office window onto Uncle Wimpy, their crazed flight in Acey Holman's Buick DeLuxe, and Legs Sadovsky trapped in the Red Bank State Correctional Facility for Girls, watching eleven sparrow hawks through the small high window in The Room. Even now as I sat slouched at the back of English 11, watching the rest of the class slouched in their desks ahead of me, I could feel Legs standing in the schoolyard, knife in hand as she faced down a gang of boys and shouted, *Fuck off!*

And in that moment, as Mr. Cronk tried once again, prodding the class for a response, any response, a simple goddamn sign of intelligence in the universe, it connected with me—the *meaning* of the apathy Legs had been fighting, the enormity of it, the absolute weight.

Without warning a voice started coming out of my mouth— an unfamiliar, raw, gravelly sounding voice. And to my astonishment it said, "Justice is like sex, really. There are rules for when and how and what you can do, categories you fit into depending on how far you'll go, and how often and with who. And it's only when you buck the system and break the rules that you find out what it's all about, isn't it?"

All across the room, dull slouched bodies were coming awake. Straightening in their seats, kids turned to give me dubious looks.

"Find out about what?" asked a guy in the far right corner. "Justice or sex?"

"Um," said one of the front-row keeners, "I don't really think this book is about *that*."

"About what?" asked Mr. Cronk quickly.

"Well," hesitated the girl in the front row, "*sex*. I mean, you asked us about justice…"

"Of course, it's about sex," said the gravelly voice coming out of my mouth. Once again it had managed to bypass the thinking, reasoning, *sane* part of my brain, and cut loose with my secret thoughts. "Everything we do in life is sex, isn't it?" the voice continued, while I sat there hardly able to believe what it was saying. "I mean, it all comes from the same place inside you, doesn't it? And that place is either a place of following rules and doing what you're told, or figuring things out for yourself. Besides, Foxfire was an all-girl gang. Their justice was completely about sex. It *was* sex for them. Or maybe a replacement for it."

"You mean if they were getting laid properly, they wouldn't have been doing the gang thing?" asked the guy in the far right corner.

"Properly?" I shot back, too quickly to think about what I was saying first. "You mean with a guy, don't you?"

"Of course," shrugged the guy.

"Dyke city," muttered the girl sitting in the desk ahead of me.

Bye bye, sane reasoning brain. Suddenly I was leaning forward in my seat, my blood pounding furiously. Like I said, the body is devious.

"That means you're thinking universal, doesn't it?" I blurted to the guy in the far right corner. "As in mainstream, what everyone else around you is doing? But I don't think that just because Foxfire was a girls' gang, they had to be dykes. I mean, maybe they were and maybe they weren't, but what matters is that they were a group of girls who decided to think for themselves. Because isn't that the way you really learn—about sex, love, justice, reality, anything? I mean, how can you figure out the universal meaning of something if you don't work out the personal meaning for yourself first?"

"But you can't have people running around kidnaping and shooting each other," objected a girl near the front of the room. "You need universal things like rules and laws. And you should obey them. They're there to protect you."

"Sure they are," interrupted a guy halfway down the window aisle. "But Dylan's right too. If you don't work things out for yourself, you're a robot."

"Yeah," I said, nodding emphatically. I mean, I was so pumped, I was almost levitating. "I'm not saying you should break every rule," I added, trying to backtrack a bit. I didn't want Mr. Cronk thinking I was about to start a terrorist cell or something. "But if you live inside a rule, or a law, or *whatever*, all the time, without ever thinking about it, then you *are* that rule. Nothing but."

"Hey Dyl, what're you doing Friday night?" asked the guy in the far right corner, and a wave of laughter engulfed the class. For a second I stiffened, feeling it all being swept away—the raw, half-baked things I'd been saying and the pure uncoiled sensation of strength that had come with them. But then I relaxed and laughed along with everyone else. So what if we were back to mainstream universal thinking? I'd been able to say what I really thought, something weird and out of sync, and the class hadn't written me off as a freak. Mr. Cronk was even giving me one of his specialty piercing looks, as if he'd just discovered the next Margaret Atwood. Sure, the only reason I was getting away

with it was because I was Cam's girlfriend, and nobody would
suspect, but—

Mid-thought I glanced at Joc, and my brain ground to an
abrupt halt. Because out of the entire class, she was probably
the only person not laughing. In fact there wasn't even the hint
of a grin on her face. Leaned against the wall with both eyes
closed, she was frozen into such a careful hyper-alert slouch
that she looked as if she hadn't breathed since my first comment.

"Hey," I hissed. "We're talking about sex here. I can't believe
you haven't said anything."

She swallowed, the naked line of her throat rippling, then
settling. "Dikker's been over a lot lately," she mumbled, without
looking at me. "I haven't started the book yet."

Then the bell rang and she opened her eyes as if coming out
of a long uninterrupted dream. Gathering her lean sprawled
body, she unleashed it from the desk, got to her feet and sauntered out of the room without a backward glance.

That evening I lay in bed, thinking back to the class discussion and going over it word by word. The experience had been
a rush, almost like a drug, but better. Sure, uncertainty had
come crashing down on me as soon as I'd walked out of the
classroom, but that was to be expected. I mean, there was the
question of what Cam was going to think when he heard about
it. Then there were his guy friends and the phone patrol. Even
now, hours later, when I tried to imagine their responses, a vivid
electric worm started crawling around my gut.

But then I remembered that voice coming out of me, so
raw and determined. *Of course, it's about sex*, I heard it saying
again. *Everything we do in life is sex, really. I mean, it all comes
from the same place inside you, doesn't it? And that place is either*

a place of following rules and doing what you're told, or figuring things out for yourself.

I still couldn't believe I'd actually said those things. How had I gotten away with it? I mean, no one had called me a dyke in the hall afterward, even as a joke. But then probably no one had wanted to take a chance on facing Cam's wrath. He was my insurance, my disguise. And what would he have thought of the strange gravelly voice that had come out of me? Not much, was my guess. It wouldn't have fit the queen image he had of me, sitting quiet and pretty on a throne somewhere inside his head. But that wasn't me, it *wasn't.* I just hadn't figured out the best way to let him in on the secret yet.

Rolling onto my back, I loosened the tie on my pajama bottoms and slid my hand between my legs. As usual, the first thought that hit me as I started to do this was, *Yuck!* I mean, when you think about it, the groin is a really grotty area of the body. The smell is enough to put anyone off, there is rank stuff coming out of it on a regular basis, and if you're female, you also get to do the bleeding thing once a month. I don't know who was in charge of designing the original female body, but if it had been me, I would not have put the major pleasure center right next to the waste ejection sites. I mean, NOT!

Waves of sweetness started spreading slowly through my body, and I thought, *If only Cam could see me now, feel what I'm feeling.* This was what he wanted after all, dreamed about—me feeling this with him. A grin crossed my face as I realized that he was probably lying in his own bed right now, doing pretty much the same thing. But then my grin faded. Because I knew what he would be thinking about—me. And the truth was that I couldn't say I was thinking about him. Not if I was honest.

Usually when I did this kind of thing, I made myself think about Cam for as long as possible. Closing my eyes, I would imagine us sitting in his car and kissing, but the truth was that the hotter my body got, the quicker Cam faded from my thoughts. Not once had I made myself come while thinking about him, and the images that kept flashing through my head tonight were straight out of *Foxfire*, specifically the gang's initiation scene, where the girls take off their shirts and crowd in against each other. Though I pushed it out of my mind, the scene kept coming back to me—all that skin, heat and fierce nervous laughter...the *forbiddenness* of it. Because, of course, girls aren't supposed to think about breasts, at least not another girl's breasts.

With a groan, I once again pushed the scene out of my mind and made myself think about Cam. And just like that I lost it—the body sensation, heat and sweetness. It all vanished and the whole thing became mechanical, as if I'd lost the *me* of it, the soul.

Suddenly I thought, *Why am I stopping myself? I mean, it's just pictures in my head. It's not like I'm actually two-timing.*

And so for the first time I actually let myself do it—let go of the rule, the *law* of Cam. With another groan, I stopped fighting the pictures in my head and let them happen any way they wanted. Immediately I felt myself flat up against it, the raw pleading need of myself. I'd never felt it this way before—brilliant, as if I'd been skinned alive, some rubbery surface peeled off me so I'd become complete sensation. And then, without warning, Joc was there with me in my mind, leaning over me, her hair in a long coconut-scented fall about my face. And we were kissing, kissing again, the soft drift of our lips sending an incredible sweetness everywhere through me. I cried out then, almost shouted at the fierce wave of longing that swept through me—I hadn't known it could be like this, so intense, such a deep *opening* within myself. Lying on my bed with the imaginary Joc leaned over me, I came again and again, the sweetness like an ocean crashing over me, like a scream, a crime.

Finally, *finally*, it faded, leaving me soaked with sweat, my bed sheets stuck to my skin. But my body was at peace, floating on a vast calm, without the usual lines of edginess that ran through it. Soaked and smelly in the dark, I lay quietly with a goofy grin plastered across my face. No wonder Cam wanted to give this to me, I thought. No wonder he kept after me, begging and pleading with me to try it. And the real wonder of it all was that he was actually holding himself back and waiting for me. I mean, I knew he wasn't doing it with another girl on the sly—he really was *waiting* for me.

So what was I supposed to do now? Because if I'd needed final proof that this kind of sensation, this way of being together, would never happen between us, I'd just gotten it. For the first time I'd asked my body to tell me what it knew, to show me completely and absolutely who I was in that deep raw core where everything comes from—*that place without rules*. And it had. Sweetly. Explosively. Conclusively.

Should I phone Cam and tell him the truth? Break up with him without explaining? Or just let things continue as they were, while I explored this newness inside me and tried to figure out what it meant?

Nothing had to be done immediately, I decided finally. No one seemed to have figured out what was really going on with me, so why not let things continue as they were for a while longer? After all, it wasn't as if anyone was *begging* me to change.

Kicking the stiffness out of my legs, I got up, stripped the sheets, and headed to the bathroom for a shower.

Chapter Seven

As I biked to Joc's place the next morning, everything glowed, the houses wet and glimmering from last night's rain, the trees a brilliant yellow gold. Everywhere the earth was giving out that sweet scent you get only in the fall, and the sky ached with a forever-going-on kind of blue. And I was pumped, my mind still full of what had happened to me the previous night, that new way of knowing and the feelings that had come with it. As I zoomed along, the entire world seemed to be in on the secret, trees nodding at me, houses smiling. Then I was pulling up in front of Joc's place and the screen door bursting open as she came jogging across the lawn, jean jacket flapping over one of Tim's old Metallica sweatshirts.

"Hey, Dyl," she said. "I saved the last bite of my toast for you. Here, it's loaded with strawberry jam."

With a grin she held up the gooey bit of bread and the world lit up like a wish, my whole self living in my lips as she slipped the toast into my mouth. But if Joc noticed, she didn't say anything, just slid onto the bike seat behind me. Then we were off, headed down the street, me trying to ignore the warm circle of her arms around my waist, then deciding not to ignore it at all. And that just made the streets sing by faster, the earth smell sweeter and the sky go a sheerer, more forever kind of blue.

Part of me shouted that I was a fool, best girlfriends didn't fall in love, and I was setting myself up for kick-ass pain, but the rest of me kept pumping away at the bike pedals, knowing I would probably spend the rest of the day just thinking about the soft secret of Joc's head resting against my back. Secret, because I couldn't let on to her what it meant, couldn't even let on that I'd noticed it, but still I *could* notice, and for the first time let myself feel it in the deep private parts of my soul.

"Finish your French assignment?" I asked, knowing it was a dumb question, a boring one, but if I didn't focus on something mundane, I might suddenly start belting out "You Make Me Feel Like A Natural Woman"—something obvious like that.

"Un petit peu," murmured Joc, bumping her head slightly against my back, and I left it at that. I mean, Joc is très bien at French, a real conversationalist, and when she gets going, all I can say is, "Je suis stupide. Lentement, lentement, s'il vous plaît."

So I concentrated on trying to pedal without moving my upper body so Joc's head wouldn't get bumped around, and then all too soon the Dief was coming into view and I was coasting slowly up to the bike racks. As I came to a halt, Joc slid off the seat and just stood for a bit, leaned against my shoulder. And in that little bit of time I felt the entire world come to a standstill, as if all of it, every last single part was focusing in on that small warm place where our shoulders touched.

"Coming to the game after school?" asked Joc, glancing at me with a dreamy expression on her face. Then she took a quick breath and glanced away again, her eyes scanning the crowd. "Dikker said he'd give us both a ride and put your bike in the trunk. If you want, that is," she added, still scanning the crowd.

Dikker. When I heard her say that name, my heart gave an ugly thud and basically died for five seconds. Then it came miserably back to life, a life that sucked big-time.

"Sure," I said, ducking down to lock my bike to the nearest rack. "No prob, that sounds great."

"Okay," said Joc. "Meet you in the student parking lot at three."

Sliding my lock closed, I straightened to reply, but she was already gone, probably headed in a beeline for Dikker's locker. And because I'd been such a fool, not shutting things down like I usually did but letting it all rise to the surface, the disappointment that hit me then was nuclear—an agony bomb, exploding in my gut. There was nothing to do though but let it happen, so I just stood by my bike, waiting as bits and pieces of me flew off in every direction. Then it was over and I was back in gear, one more body in a stream of kids headed for the nearest school door.

"Hey, Dyl," said Dikker.

As he leaned against his car, he sent me a loaded grin. It was 3:00 PM, the student parking lot swarming with kids getting into cars and heading out to the football game. Hundreds of kids surrounded us, all of them hooting, hollering and revving their engines, but the second Dikker sent me that grin, the entire scene disappeared into the angry churn of my gut. I'll admit it, my reaction was pretty much automatic. The moment I set eyes on Dikker, I morphed into one hundred percent bitch.

"In case you're wondering," I said, keeping a tight grip on my bike so I didn't give in to the massive urge to chuck it at him. "Don't take this personally or anything, but no, I don't want to see it."

It was the first time we'd talked since Saturday, and the incident was written all over his face. Believe me, it wasn't easy to look him in the eye. I mean, I knew Joc had told him what I'd told her about my storming off after him. And of course Dikker had chosen to believe what came natural to Dikker Preddy to believe. But my protesting or explaining would only make things worse.

"Pity," he singsonged, faking a British accent. "Only in Canada you know." Reaching for my bike, he heaved it into the trunk of his car. "There," he said, tying it to the back fender. "I used all my Boy Scout knots, so it should stay put if I keep it to five, ten kays."

"Will this help?" I asked, pulling a wad of Double Bubble out of my mouth. "Use it to stick the bike into place, and then maybe you can take it up to twenty."

Giving me another loaded grin, Dikker took the wad of gum and popped into his mouth. "The closest I'll probably ever come," he sighed and blew a large pink bubble.

"You've got that right," I said emphatically. I mean, Dikker wasn't giving me much of a compliment—for him, come-on mode was automatic around anyone who looked remotely female, even his girlfriend's best friend. So, giving him my disgusted back, I scanned the parking lot for Joc. As I did, a passing car braked, and Julie Crozier leaned out the passenger window.

"Coming to the game?" she asked. Beside her, Rachel honked the car horn and waved.

"Yup," I said, trying not to stare at the olive eye shadow plastered on Julie's eyelids.

"Want a ride?" called Rachel.

"I've already got one," I said. "I'm going with Joc and Dikker."

Julie's eyes flicked to Dikker and she grimaced slightly. "Okay, see you there," she said, then pulled back inside, and the car moved on.

Great, I thought. *Just scored another point with the phone patrol.* Dikker seemed to be on everyone's dog list but Joc's. Keeping my back to him, I scanned the parking lot again. Still no sign of Joc. How long was she going to leave me here, stuck in a one-on-one with the planet's most neglected brain?

Still, neglected brain or not, I was being a royal bitch, standing there with my back to him like that. "Hey," I said, turning to face him, and found him leaning against his car, still watching me with that loaded grin. "There's something I want to ask you," I added, crossing my arms and staring at him so hard, he absolutely *had* to look me in the face. The guy's eyes had no morals. I mean, absolutely none.

"Holla, Barnardo," grinned Dikker. Hiking himself onto the car hood, he dangled his legs and looked at me expectantly.

"What?" I demanded.

"Holla, Barnardo," he repeated agreeably. "It's one of my lines from *Hamlet*."

I rolled my eyes. Of all the lines to quote from Shakespeare, he would pick something completely insignificant. "Very good, Dikker," I said. "You've got that one down pat. Okay, here's my question: Why do you want to be dead by thirty? You don't get Alzheimer's until you're sixty, you know."

A look of surprise crossed his face and he shrugged. "I don't want to get *old*," he said. "Gray hair, limp dick, Viagra. Just knock me off at twenty-nine, and I'll reincarnate and come back in full glory."

"Yeah," I said, "as a flea. Or someone growing up in Afghanistan."

He shrugged again. "Tell you what—I'll give you a phone call when you're seventy-five and living with your lawyer husband in a five-hundred-thousand dollar house on a zillion RSPs, and I'm fifteen and on my third time around, and we'll compare notes. I bet you I'll be having more fun."

I rolled my eyes again. The problem with one-on-one conversations with Dikker was that he was so insane that every now and then he actually made sense. "You're just looking for an easy way out of all the child support payments you're going to get landed with," I said. "You'll have an easy dozen by the time you're twenty-five."

Dikker just gave me another shrug, then said calmly, "Ah, there has been much throwing about of brains."

"Huh?" I asked, staring at him.

"Another line from *Hamlet*," he said. "Only I don't get to say it, Hamlet does. Anyway, for your information, since you seem to be *so* interested, I always use a safe. If I didn't, Joc would pull one over my head." He shrugged again. "Hey, I may not be able to think and piss at the same time, but I do know enough not to get my sixteen-year-old girlfriend pregnant."

"Think and piss?" I said. I was really staring at him now.

"Haven't you ever noticed?" he grinned. "Your bladder gets going and your brain shuts down. Must be something about the nervous system—can't handle two jobs at the same time, I guess. Try it the next time you're on the can."

"Yeah. All right. Fine," I snorted. Then I turned and scanned the crowd again. As much as I was working very hard not to, I was starting to like the guy. It happened to me in brief spurts every now and then when Joc wasn't around, and we were forced to actually engage in conversation. I mean, Dikker could be on the verge of interesting sometimes. You had to have some kind of smarts to be as deliberately stupid as he seemed to be.

To my relief, I spotted Joc on the far side of the parking lot, talking to someone. "There she is," I said, waving madly at her. Lifting a hand, she waved back.

"What's taking her so long?" asked Dikker. Jumping off the hood of his car, he peered over my shoulder. "Who's that guy she's talking to?" he asked, his voice suddenly irritable.

"Brian Cardinal," I said, fighting a smirk. "They're doing a presentation together in Geography. Didn't she tell you?"

"Not yet," scowled Dikker. Crossing his arms, he slouched against the car and sent a steady glower in Joc's direction. As if on cue she laughed, slapped Brian's shoulder, then turned and headed toward us. Several feet from Dikker, she launched herself at him, and they congealed into a tangle of arms, legs and smooching lips.

"What were you talking to Brian about?" grunted Dikker, his mood obviously improved.

"How much he'll have to pay his sister to research a Geography presentation for us," grinned Joc. "C'mon, let's get going so Dyl can get a good seat at the game to watch her man."

Opening the passenger door, she got in and plastered herself against the gearbox to make room for me. Dikker turned the ignition. The Honda's engine kicked over with a mind-shattering roar, and he pumped it even louder, watching kids scatter in every direction.

"Respect," he said. "You know when you've got it." Blowing a huge bubble with my Double Bubble wad, he peered around it as he backed out of his parking space. This, of course, was Joc's cue to pop it with her finger, then pull the wad out of his mouth and put it into her own.

"Mmm," she said. "Dikker germs. Love bugs. My mother warned me about these."

"You've got that right," said Dikker. Giving her a wide grin, he winked at me. "Better watch out," he said, glancing back at Joc. "They might make you pregnant."

With a groan, I slouched down until I was nose level with

the glove compartment. This afternoon's football game was at Confederation Collegiate, which meant I was going to have to endure fifteen minutes, trapped in close contact with these two while we drove across town. Why hadn't I just said I would bike to the game? On the other hand, because Joc and I were sharing the front passenger seat, her right leg was pressed flat against my left. If I just sort of relaxed and didn't pull away, the sensation was kind of pleasantly distracting. It also made me remember the new policy I'd come up with last night, of letting my mind do whatever it wanted, instead of always putting on the brakes.

So instead of learning my lesson from what had happened that morning at the bike racks, I closed my eyes, shut out the idiotic banter going on to my left, and let my thoughts roam. Almost immediately I was hit with the same image that I'd gotten last night—Joc leaning over me, our lips touching, touching again. But this time the fantasy was so vivid, so just *everything* in my head, that I could have sworn it was actually happening between us, hot and heavy, right there in the car.

"Dyl," said a voice in my ear, interrupting another long imaginary kiss, and a shoulder bumped against mine. "C'mon, we're here," the voice said impatiently. "What's with you? You on something?"

My eyes flew open and I sat up, blinking stupidly in the afternoon sunlight. *What's going on?* I thought, bewildered. *Where am I? Wasn't I just ki—*

Remorselessly, Dikker's car took shape around me—fuzzy yellow dice hanging from the rear view mirror, filthy dashboard and bug-encrusted windshield with a smeared view of Confederation Collegiate in the distance. Then, to add to the ambience, I was blasted by the scent of my Double Bubble wad, coming from Joc's mouth as she stared at me.

"C'mon," she said, bumping me again with her shoulder. "You moving any time this century?"

Without looking at her, I pushed open the door and half-stumbled, half-ran from the car. As I put some distance between me and the Honda, the heat pounding through my body faded and my mind began to clear. Still disoriented, I wiped a hand across my mouth, and to my surprise it came away sweaty. Abruptly a sharp wind kicked up, cutting through my jacket, and I realized that my clothes were slightly damp. If this wind kept up, it was going to be a cold game.

"Hey, Dyl," Joc called after me. "Where are you going so fast?"

A huge gulping breath came out of me, then another. As I stood staring at Confederation Collegiate, I realized that letting my mind go like that had been a mistake. The fantasy had been too vivid, too strong. It was one thing to play with it in my head when alone in bed, then give myself a full night's sleep to get over it. But here, next to Confed's football field and a milling crowd of kids, there was no way to release the feelings that had built up inside me. It was like being stuck inside another agony bomb, but one that was going off continually, over and over.

"Dyl," Joc called again, nearer, this time. Joc—my best friend, Dikker's queen, and I was her lady-in-waiting.

So I turned toward her, a forced smile on my lips and my eyes slitted so she was just a blur headed toward me, something I could see and not see, halfway between reality and dream while the wind sent another cold blast between us.

Chapter Eight

Cam and I usually had one date per weekend, though sometimes we saw each other twice if there was a sports event or something family-related going on. That Saturday I managed to wheedle two dates out of my parents, or rather two dates packed into one with an extended curfew, because the latest Disney movie had hit town and we were taking Keelie to the early show. Cam was great with Keelie and never seemed to mind spending time with her, and she adored him. When the doorbell rang at 6:15, she immediately dropped her spoon and squirmed down from her chair. Then she grabbed her Quidditch broom, which was propped against the nearest wall, and tore out of the kitchen screaming, "Cam's here! Cam's here! Watch out, Cam, Valdemort is going to get you!"

Cam must have heard her coming, because he didn't wait for her to open the door. Right behind Keelie, I reached the front hall in time to see the door burst open and him swoop in on her short squealing figure. For the next few seconds, everything was my boyfriend roaring into my little sister's hair while she screamed with delight, and then the universe settled down again.

"Look, Cam, look!" shouted Keelie. Pushing her broom at him, she stood watching expectantly as he examined it.

"Ah, this is a great-looking broom, Keelie," said Cam, shooting me a you've-got-to-help-me-here look. "Must be great for swee—"

With a massive scowl, Keelie yanked it out of his hands. "Not for sweeping!" she said sternly. "It's a *Quidditch* broom." Then she swung one leg over it and stood looking up at him. When he didn't move, she said, "Aren't you coming to play Quidditch with me?"

"Keelie, we don't have ti—" I began, but Cam had already gotten onto the broom behind her and they were off, trotting into the living room. Except that with Cam being so much taller than Keelie, and Dad having sawed the broom to half-size so Keelie could manage it, Cam was hunched down and almost tripping over his feet in his efforts not to mash Keelie into the floor.

Abruptly she stopped, frowned up at him and said, "Get off, Cam. You don't ride this broom too good. Your bum's too big."

"I'm crushed," said Cam. Stepping off the back end, he watched her carry the broom to a corner and prop it carefully against the wall.

"Don't feel bad," I said. "She hasn't even *asked* me to ride on it."

"Me neither," said a voice behind me, and I turned to see my father standing in the kitchen doorway, smiling broadly at Cam. "She must think of you as a second Harry Potter to let you on that thing," Dad continued, stretching out his hand. He and Cam shook, and then Mom came out of the kitchen and gave Cam a hug.

"Good to see you, Cam," she said. "Did you have dessert? We have ice cream."

"Thanks, Ms. Kowolski. I already ate a ton," Cam grinned.

Keelie wasn't the only person in my family who adored Cam. Both my parents did too. More than that, they respected him. When we first started dating, they gave him the third degree, asking him about his interests, inviting him along on family outings and watching every breath he took, that sort of thing. But once they'd figured out what kind of guy he was, they relaxed. It wasn't that they expected him to treat me like a virgin—after our fourth date, I'd gotten a carefully explicit condoms-and-safe-sex talk, along with a very decided sex-is-better-if-you-wait-until-you're-older reminder. Still, it was obvious from the beginning that both my parents really liked Cam, so much so, that their entire bodies lit up in a smile when they saw him. Even Danny thought Cam was cool, and lived for the moments he was called over to sit with the senior jock crowd in the Dief cafeteria. Right now he was hovering behind Mom, watching intently as Cam gently worked Keelie's squirming arms into her jacket, then knelt to do up her shoes. In the week to come, I knew I would see Danny go through the exact same routine with Keelie each morning, helping her into her jacket and shoes before she left for school.

"She can do that for herself, Cam," Mom said with a smile.

"No prob, Ms. Kowolski. I'm a sucker for little kids," said Cam, and I watched Mom melt.

"Yeah," said Keelie, crossing her arms and frowning at Mom. "He's a sucker for little kids LIKE ME." With immense satisfaction she watched Cam finish her second shoe, then took his hand. Looking up at Mom, she said importantly, "We'll probably be late, so make sure you brush your teeth and go to the bathroom *before* you go to bed."

"Okay, Keelie," grinned Dad. "We'll make sure we brush every tooth."

"Don't let her eat too much candy, Cam," Mom called as Keelie dragged him to the door.

"No prob, Ms. Kowolski," Cam called back. "I'll probably eat it all myself."

"Don't listen to her, she's too bossy," ordered Keelie, her voice floating back through the open door. Halfway down the front walk, she dropped his hand and took off for the Firebird, which was parked at the curb. "I'm driving, I'm driving," she chanted, jumping up and down as Cam unlocked the passenger door. Then she scooted into the front seat and placed her left hand firmly on the wheel. This was what she and Cam called "driving"—he steered and kept up a constant description of various monsters, labyrinths and UFOs that supposedly surrounded us, while Keelie hung onto the wheel and imagined herself getting us victoriously through the melee.

"Watch out, Keelie," hissed Cam as we started off down the street. "There's a drooling, snotty-nosed, one-eyed boogeldy-bear coming at you from behind."

Immediately Keelie whirled around in her seat, her eager eyes honing in on me.

"Not me, not me," I protested from the backseat, raising both hands.

"Ah," said Cam, sending me a grin in the rear view mirror. "My mistake. It's the queen of the Sirius galaxy *disguised* as a drooling, snotty-nosed, one-eyed boogeldy-bear. Legend has it that years ago she was kidnapped by an off-planet tribe of drooling, snotty-nosed, one-eyed boogeldy-bears. How shall we rescue her, brave Princess Keelie?"

Reaching around the back of her seat, Keelie grabbed my hand. "Don't worry, Captain Cam. I rescued her," she said. For a moment she looked at me intently, a thoughtful, almost sad expression creeping across her face. Then she said slowly, "But the queen isn't happy, Captain Cam. She doesn't have enough happiness in her life."

Cam's and my eyes met, startled, in the mirror, and the inside of the car was suddenly very quiet. "What d'you mean, Keelie?" I asked, forcing my voice past an odd graveliness. "I'm happy. Of course, I'm happy."

In the dusky evening light, Keelie continued to gaze at me, then shook her head. "You're lying," she said. "The queen of the Sirius galaxy is lying, Captain Cam."

"Well," said Cam, quirking an eyebrow at me in the mirror, "the queen and I will talk about that later. But right now, Keelie, you and I have to watch out for that giant suction pocket over there, between those two stores. Can you see it?"

He pointed and Keelie nodded fiercely, her eyes beady with anticipation. They were both back into their game full force, Keelie's comments about my happiness sucked into the imaginary suction pocket Cam was pointing out. And if I was lucky, I thought, leaning into the backseat shadows, Cam's memory of those comments had just been sucked away too.

The movie was the usual—an animation feature with a lost princess heroine who had to be rescued by a brave hero. Seated between Cam and I, Keelie leaned against his arm and devoured popcorn nonstop, giving him the odd poke when she wanted a slurp from the large container of pop he was balancing on one knee. When Keelie was with us, she got all of Cam's attention, which meant it was pretty much time off for me. So I just sat there in the dark, pretending to watch the movie while I thought about Cam, the way he would be fifteen years from now with his own kids, helping them into their jackets and shoes and making up stories for them to star in. And *that* made me think about how massively the future sucked. Because I loved Cam; he was the exact kind of person that I wanted to spend my life with, but I knew I didn't fit into that picture with him. It sucked, it really sucked. Big-time.

Leaning over Keelie, I rattled the ice in my pop container and told Cam, "Gotta visit the can."

He nodded, and I headed down the aisle toward the washrooms. The theater's front lobby was pretty much empty—just a couple of adults buying candy—and so was the women's washroom. As I sat there on a toilet, doing my thing, sounds from the movie oozed through the wall behind me—muffled shouts and screams, swells of scary music. An image of Keelie came floating through my mind, bug-eyed and openmouthed, staring at the screen. *The queen isn't happy, Cam*, I heard her say again. *She doesn't have enough happiness in her life.*

So, someone besides Joc had finally noticed. It didn't really surprise me that it was Keelie. She had a way of watching you so intensely that you felt as if her eyes were stuck to your soul. And like most little kids, she could spot a lie a long way off. When it comes to lying, little kids are different than adults. I mean, they haven't lived long enough to learn the art of lying continually the way adults have. Sure, they come up with incredible whoppers sometimes, but only in a crisis, to save themselves from a time-out or an early bedtime. They don't live a lie all the time like some grown-ups, plodding through each day resigned and defeated, all the while smiling tiredly and saying, "Oh, I'm good, great, fine. Everything's okay." Happiness, there's no happiness in them anywhere.

What if that happened to me? I mean, what if, in spite of what I knew about myself, Cam and I someday got married, and because of my skewed wrong body, we weren't happy? Because how could we be, how could I make him happy when I didn't... well, feel *normal*, the way girls are supposed to feel about guys? How long would it be before that resigned defeated look settled onto him? Five or ten years? Two or three weeks? It wasn't fair what I was doing to him now. I didn't have the right to go out with him under false pretenses like this. Not when he liked me so much, not—

Mid-thought, I heard the washroom door open, and then someone entered the cubicle beside me. A minute later the outer door opened again and someone else entered, so I waited until I heard both women leave before coming out of my cubicle. I'd been crying a bit—not too bad, but I wanted to check my mascara in the mirror before heading back to my seat. To my surprise, when I opened my cubicle door I saw a girl standing at the sinks. She looked to be about my age—sixteen or seventeen—with shoulder-length, wavy, brown hair and brown eyes. Not the kind to wear makeup, and maybe a little plump and not really pretty, but there was something about her that made you look at her twice—just the way she held her head, chin up, demanding your eyes. She didn't attend the Dief, but I'd seen her around, at the library and in cafés. Always alone, though—she didn't seem to hang out with anyone.

Without saying anything, I went up to a sink and started washing my hands. A quick glance at the mirror told me that my mascara was fine, but my eyes seemed a bit red. So I glanced at them again, more carefully this time, and as I did, my gaze met that of the loner girl in the mirror. And in that moment an electric vibe passed between us—heated, singing, shimmering—the way I'd so often felt it with Joc. Astonished, I ducked my head and rode out a warm flush of heat. This was impossible. It couldn't be happening here, in a public washroom, with someone I didn't even *know*.

"Hey," said the girl, turning toward me. "What's your name? Don't you go to Diefen—"

Massive panic slammed into me. Why was this girl talking to me? Had she felt the vibe that had just passed between us? Could she tell about me, the way I was?

Without replying, I grabbed a paper towel from the dispenser and walked out the door. In the lobby I didn't look around, just kept going, headed for the safety of the theater and its dark shadowy aisles. If the loner girl followed me out, I didn't hear her and I didn't look back. All the way to my seat I kept my head down, telling myself that what had happened wasn't important. There was no way the loner girl could have known what I was feeling and if she'd guessed, she was nobody, anyway. Even so, when I slid into place beside Keelie, my blood was pounding. I mean, it was *pounding*.

What's going on? I thought frantically. *Is this going to start happening with every girl?*

Quickly I stood up, edged past Keelie and sat down on Cam's other side. Then I leaned against him and laid my head on his shoulder.

"Hey," he said softly into my hair. "What's with the paper towel? You keeping it as a souvenir?"

Startled, I looked down at my lap. Clutched in my hand was the paper towel I'd grabbed as I was leaving the washroom.

"Oh," I said and dropped it to the floor.

Fortunately there was so much going on at Deirdre Buffone's place, the house party Cam and I went to after we dropped off Keelie, that we didn't have much time to talk. Since Deirdre was part of the jock crowd, as well as a senior member of the phone patrol, only popular kids were invited to her parties. That meant the energy was pumped, but so were her parents. Mr. and Ms. Buffone liked to get *involved* in their kids' lives—down to the very last detail. They always sat down with Deirdre ahead of time and organized her parties so every breath you took was fun, but also *supervised*. There was no wandering off to bedrooms or dark deserted corners at the Buffone house, and if a couple took off early in a car, Mr. Buffone would call their parents to let them know their dearly beloved offspring were headed *straight* home.

Tonight they'd organized a hay ride, with hot chocolate and charades afterward. The party was officially over at 11:30, but a few of us got talking with Deirdre and her parents at the door. Suddenly Cam looked at his watch, swore softly and said, "We'd better get moving, Dyl. It's five to twelve."

He kept it to the speed limit all the way to my house, but just, and when we got there the living room light was on. As usual, Guardian Angel Buffone had called ahead. So there was just time for some quick kissing before Cam's watch alarm went off, signaling 12:15—my extended curfew. Or, as Cam put it, "execution time," though when he was with his guy friends, he called it "the castration hour."

"Uh, Dyl," he said hesitantly as I opened the passenger door. "Y'know what Keelie said earlier, about you not being happy?"

"That's Keelie for you," I said quickly. "She's little. She gets ideas in her head and makes herself believe they're real."

Cam's eyes hovered on my face, uncertain. "You're sure?" he asked awkwardly. "Because if—"

"Of course, I'm sure," I said, forcing a smile. "Why wouldn't I be sure? Call me tomorrow, okay?"

Relief crossed Cam's face, and I could feel him ditching his doubt. Just like that, it was gone. "I'm going out with the guys," he said, flashing me a grin, "but I'll work it in. Y'know, I can't believe we wasted the entire evening at Deirdre's. Not even a half-hour pleasure cruise."

"Dream about me," I said, getting out. "And I'll dream about you. We'll dream the same thing, okay?"

"You bet we will," he called after me, waiting as I unlocked the front door, then waiting again as I closed it and drew the dead bolt. Even then he didn't drive off, and I stood inside the locked door, listening to the Firebird rumble contentedly in the driveway. Cam was thinking about me, I knew that, and it wasn't Keelie's comment about my happiness either. No, he was imagining all the ways he wanted me and was probably lost in the fantasy, staring off through the windshield and humming low under his breath the way I caught him sometimes when I snuck up on him from behind. He wanted me bad and it was a good bad, the way you were supposed to want someone. Pressing my palms against the door, I stood listening to the quiet rumble of the Firebird and guilt rose in me—something ugly, I was disgusted with myself, filled with self-loathing because of what I couldn't seem to do, the healthy natural things I couldn't make myself feel.

After Cam finally drove away, I turned out the living room light and headed upstairs to my room, stopping en route to knock on my parents' door and let them know I was home. They were both in bed, Mom watching a video and Dad reading a book, probably about astronomy or time travel, his two favorite subjects.

"Did you have a good time, sweetie?" asked Mom, putting her video on pause.

"Yeah," I said. "The Buffones had a hay ride for us."

"Keelie talked nonstop about driving Cam's car when she got home," said Dad. "We could hardly get her to go to sleep."

"It's a game they play," I said quickly. "He doesn't really let her drive it, she just imagines she does."

"I figured," grinned Dad, and I leaned down to give them each a goodnight hug, everything warm and affectionate, both of them smiling as I left, pleased with the way their eldest daughter was turning out, the choices she was making. There were some pretty mixed-up user guys out there, but she'd chosen a decent caring one—that Dylan really had her head on straight.

When I got to my room I didn't bother to undress, just crawled into bed and curled into a ball. Mom had left my desk lamp on, and the room was a glow of colors at low ebb—salmon walls, amber quilt, a scarlet throw rug on the floor. Cam had never been in here, but he'd asked me to describe it in minute detail, and twice he'd given Danny a box of chocolates to leave on my bed. *Sweets for the sweet*, the notes had said. Okay, maybe not original, but the meaning had been his, a thought coming from him to me. And here I was, lying to him, leading him on toward...what? It wasn't ever going to happen between us, the relationship was a charade, a dead-end—something I seemed to have to go through to prove to myself it couldn't work. Why couldn't I just face reality and give Cam up? I mean, I'd felt more tonight for a girl I didn't even know than I had for him.

As I lay there, staring at nothing, it came to me that my life was like a negative confession, that list of statements the ancient Egyptians used to say before they died. That was it—my relationship with Cam was one long negative confession:

Hail, Basti, who comest forth from Bast, I have not told the truth.

Hail, Ruruti, who comest forth from heaven, I have not let my heart beat.

Hail, Unem-Snef, who comest forth from the execution chamber, I have not sought my own happiness.

Hail, Neba, who comest and goest, I have not let myself feel pleasure and love.

Hail, Set-qesu, who comest forth from Hensu, I have not broken out of my fear.

Hail, Her-f-ha-f, who comest forth from thy cavern, I have not crawled out of the grave.

Hail, Qerrti, who comest forth from Amentet, I have not lain with women.

Turning off my desk lamp, I lay in the dark, listening to an inner voice repeat endlessly, *I have eaten my heart, I have eaten my heart, I have eaten...*

Chapter Nine

The following Tuesday I was back in the library, doing my volunteer shift at the check-out desk and sorting books that had been returned for reshelving. Beside me, Joc leaned against the counter, looking utterly morose as she unwrapped a piece of Double Bubble. Yesterday, to her dismay, she had discovered that drama rehearsals had been scheduled every lunch hour this week. This obviously put serious brakes on her love life—today was probably only the second school lunch hour in over a year that she hadn't spent with Dikker. Withdrawal symptoms were setting in.

"Y'know," she said, staring moodily at the comic that had been enclosed with the gum. "I must've read hundreds of these things in my life, and they've all been boring. Every single one of them."

"Yeah," I said, sliding a book onto the fiction filing cart. "Double Bubble must hold the Guinness world record for lousy jokes."

"Not a single funny one," muttered Joc, still staring at the comic. "Mom told me that when she was little, you could buy two Double Bubbles for a penny. Now they're five cents each.

That's nine hundred percent inflation in forty years. You'd think for nine hundred percent inflation, they could come up with one funny joke."

"At least print them in color," I agreed.

"Boycott," said Joc, looking grim. "We'll start a petition. No more Double Bubbles unless they're funny bubbles."

"Mmm," I said. "Does that mean you're going to start observing the library's no gum-chewing rule?"

"Uh-huh," Joc said carelessly. "As soon as I finish this one."

"Ah," I said and went back to alphabetizing the fiction cart for shelving. A small group of kids pushed through the turnstile, headed for the exit, but didn't sign anything out. Several others came in and wandered over to the study carrels. Today, blessed by Dikker's absence, the library was decently quiet, with only Joc's gum chomping and the whirring of the wall clock for sound effects.

"What d'you think of Shakespeare?" she asked, gloomily surveying the library.

"Shakespeare?" I repeated, glancing at her. "Dunno, really. Did he write jokes for Double Bubble?"

"If he did, they wouldn't be funny," grumbled Joc. "And no one would be able to understand them. Why does everyone in his plays talk so weird?"

"That's the way they talked back then, I guess," I shrugged.

"In rhyme?" she demanded, staring at me. "I don't think so. Anyway, I don't see why we have to study one of his plays *every* year. At least someone could translate them into normal English, so you can understand it. I have to look up every other word in a dictionary, and even when I know what all the words mean, the characters still sound weird. And Dikker is starting to talk just like them."

"Dikker," I said emphatically, "always talked weird."

"Maybe," said Joc, "but this is *Shakespeare*-weird. Like, he doesn't say hello anymore, it's 'holla.' And if he wants my opinion on something, he says, 'Stand and unfold yourself.' Then if he's giving *his* opinion, he says, 'In the gros and scope of my opinion.' I mean, really, Dyl—'in the gros and scope'?" She sighed heavily. "Last night when we were saying goodbye on the phone, he told me, 'Get thee to a nunnery!' He was just joking, but...I dunno, d'you think maybe he's losing his mind?"

What could I say? I had no gros or scope of an opinion on that whatsoever. At least nothing I could say out loud. With another emphatic sigh, Joc wandered off to the main study area, looking for someone else to gripe with about Shakespeare, and I got back to the fiction filing cart. I had just finished alphabetizing all of the authors up to the letter *J*, when I heard a shuffling sound behind me and turned to see a short skinny minor niner standing at the check-out desk. Eyes glued to the book she'd just placed on the counter, she looked distinctly nervous. A lot of kids got nervous when they saw me at the check-out desk, even kids from the upper grades. I guess they expected to see an academic type, or someone from the library club. Not a member of the jock set, even a fringe member, and certainly not Cam Zeleny's girlfriend.

Sometimes this nervousness got to me and I would play with it, to see how a kid reacted. Because it bugged me, I guess, when someone morphed into an uptight state around me. I mean, why would anyone do that? Because I was Cam's girlfriend? Because it looked like I was in tight with the phone patrol?

Picking up the girl's book, I read the title and said, "*The Small Words In My Body*. Cool title. What's it about?"

"It's poetry," the minor niner mumbled, so quietly I could barely hear her. Ducking her head farther, she stared intently at her hands.

"Oh yeah," I said. "Poetry about what?"

And then I stood there, just looking at her—not demagnetizing the book and not scanning her student card to complete the sign-out. Instead I waited for her answer, half because I did think the title was interesting and half because I knew it would send her deeper into her funk. Which it did immediately: a beet-colored flush crawling up her neck, then shooting up to her forehead. The kid was in utter misery, staring at her hands so hard she was almost bug-eyed. I mean, we're practically talking a near-death experience here.

"I don't know," she mumbled, rubbing a finger along the top of the check-out counter. "I haven't read it yet. That's why I'm signing it out."

And still I stood there just looking at her, even though I knew what a power blush felt like and what it could do to you. It was something about myself that I hadn't figured out yet, why I got like this sometimes—I mean, *mean*. Not as in bitchy, the way I was with Dikker; I mean pure snake head, hissing its venomous little tongue.

"Poetry," I said coolly, keeping my eyes fixed on the minor niner's beet-red face. "*Why* do you read poetry? Do you like everything to *rhyme*?"

The poor kid didn't respond, just stood there, staring down at her hands.

"Double Bubble," I said, kind of singsongy. "Juicy Fruicy. Shy fly. Me oh my."

The girl's hand made an agonized jerk, as if she wanted to grab her student card and take off but didn't have the guts. And instead of showing sympathy, my venomous little snake-head self opened its mouth again, ready to hiss out a few more rhymes. But at that moment a loud "Oof!" came from the library's main study area, followed by the sound of a chair being pushed back.

Turning to check out what was going on, I saw Geoff Simone, one of the Dief's grade-ten low levels, half-sprawled over Diane du Bois, a grade twelve student who was seated at the closest work table. Right behind Geoff were two of his friends, more low levels. From what I could see, it looked as if one of them had shoved Geoff from behind as he was passing Diane, and he'd ended up in her lap.

Normally this wouldn't have been a big deal. It was just the way these guys' minds worked—kind of dumb, yuk yuk, guffaws from the gutter. But Diane happened to be one of the Dief's five official lesbians, and her lap was, technically speaking, not the kind of turf Geoff dreamed of diving into. With an agonized yelp, he leapt to his feet and danced melodramatically backward.

"Dyke germs!" he shrieked, waving his hands frantically in the air. "I've been contaminated. I'm going to turn into a queer!"

Raucous guffaws erupted from his buddies. Turning, Geoff gave one of them a shove, and his buddy shoved back. Lewd comments started pouring out of them—I mean dumb, stupid, *absolute* gutter. While they yukked it up, Diane sat leaned back in her chair, silently watching, her face in neutral. Neither of her friends, who were seated across from her, said anything either. Generally speaking, no one said much to Geoff Simone. He'd been suspended twice last year for coming to school drunk and had also managed to score several trips to Youth Court.

All across the library kids had gone quiet and were watching, like I was. I mean, it was difficult to figure out the best thing to do. No one liked what was happening to Diane, but at the same time Geoff wasn't the kind of guy you normally took on, even when he was in a quasi-civilized mood. And even if you were crazy enough to speak up, how did you go about communicating the obvious to him—*Like, you're being a moron here.* He probably already heard that ten times a day.

"Dyke warts!" howled Geoff, shoving both his friends. "That's what you just made me catch. Or dyke gonorrhea. Eeeeeeeuw!"

My jaw dropped. I mean, I'd heard some nasty things in my day, but nothing quite like this, broadcast at full volume in the *library*. Some of the watching kids gasped, and an angry-looking Diane started to stand up. But as she did, Joc suddenly appeared out of the study carrel area at the back of the library and made a beeline toward the work tables.

"Excuse me," she said, cutting in front of Geoff, her voice so loud it carried to every corner of the room. "Mind if I join you, Diane?"

Without waiting for a response, she pushed Diane gently back into her chair, then plunked her butt onto Diane's lap and put an arm around her shoulder. "What're you studying?" she grinned at her. "If it isn't Shakespeare, I'll give you a big fat kiss."

For a moment Diane just stared at her, then let out a short angry laugh. "You're on," she said, "it's algebra," and without hesitating, Joc smacked her on the cheek.

A relieved snicker ran through the watching kids, and Geoff stepped back with a high-pitched shriek. Then, waving his hands as if warding off the Black Plague, he and his friends beat a hasty retreat to the study carrels. Ignoring them, Joc remained sitting on Diane's lap, probably bitching about Shakespeare as the surrounding kids went back to their interrupted conversations.

All I could do was stand there and stare. I mean, as far as I knew, Joc didn't know Diane. She'd never even talked to her. It was brilliant, what she'd just done. How had she *ever* gotten the guts?

Turning back to the check-out counter, I saw the minor niner still standing across from me and staring down at her hands. And it hit me then, what I'd been doing—little snake-head me, bitchy little *queen* snake.

"Uh, sorry about bugging you about your poetry," I said, glancing at the name on her student card. Tracey Stillman—even in her ID photo, she was looking down. "I'm in kind of a weird mood today," I added, completing the sign-out and handing back her book and student card. "Nominate me for the Geoff Simone Award, eh?"

Another flush hit Tracey. Grabbing her book and card, she mumbled, "I'm not a dyke," and took off for the exit.

Stunned, I watched her go. How in the world had she gotten the idea that I thought she was lesbian? For a long moment I stood there trying to work *that* one out, then gave up and went back to organizing the fiction filing cart. My volunteer shift was almost over. A few more kids passed through the turnstile, checking out books. I'd just demagnetized a copy of *Dune*, one of my all-time faves, and was handing it back to another skinny minor niner, when Ms. Fowler entered the library, returning from her lunch break. But instead of heading into her office the way she normally did, she stopped in front of a large display case that was mounted on the wall directly across from the check-out desk, and stood staring at it bleakly.

"Hello, Ms. Fowler," I said. "Planning October's display?"

"I'm afraid I'm rather behind schedule," she replied, her eyes still fixed on last month's display—a picture of a school entranceway that was being swarmed by a crowd of students. A banner over the doorway proclaimed: WALK INTO A GOOD BOOK. Definitely dullsville, something to fill up space. Grimacing slightly, Ms. Fowler glanced at her watch. "It's already October third," she sighed, "and I haven't come up with an idea for this month. October's only the second month of the year. I've got eight more to go."

Leaving the check-out desk, I went over to stand beside her. "What about that globe in your office?" I asked. "You could make a large planet Earth with different books for the countries. Or just do Canada, with a different book for each province and territory."

A smile snuck into a corner of Ms. Fowler's mouth. "That's interesting," she said quietly.

"Or…," I said, then paused, my heart skipping slightly as I thought of Tracey Stillman and her book of poetry. "What about a girl and a guy," I said, my words stumbling eagerly over each other, "and their bodies are made up of a bunch of books? The parts of their bodies could each have a different book title."

Ms. Fowler blinked rapidly several times and her shoulders straightened. "Now that is really an excellent idea," she said, still not looking at me. "Yes, I like that one very much."

A brilliant cosmic kind of grin hit me, and I almost gave one of Keelie's enthusiastic little skips. Already I could see Ms. Fowler perched on a stepladder in front of the display case, staple-gunning various book titles into the silhouettes of a girl and a guy. Over the next month, hundreds of students would read the titles in those silhouettes, and they would be looking at an idea that had come out of my head. Wonders never ceased. The next time I saw Tracey Stillman in the hall, I was going to have to tell her what she'd inspired. It would probably send her into another near-death experience, but what the hell.

Still grinning, I started back to the check-out desk, but was stopped by Ms. Fowler's voice. "How would you like to do the display, Dylan?" she asked.

"Me?" I demanded. Stunned, I turned to look at her. "But I'm not an art student," I stammered. "I'm not even good at English."

"That's not what Mr. Cronk tells me," said Ms. Fowler, smiling slightly. "Besides, it is your idea. I'd like to see what you can do with it. How about it? Would you like to do the display?"

For a long moment I just stood there, gaping at the display case. Me, organize something that would be seen by every student and teacher in the school for an entire month? It was sure to be a flop, an utter failure. I mean, I was half-decent at kicking a ball around a soccer field, but artistic I was not.

On the other hand, what could be worse than what was up there now?

"Okay," I stammered as book titles began swarming my mind. *Foxfire, In Cold Blood, The Small Words In My Body.* "Yeah okay, I'll do it. Thanks."

"Thank *you*," said Ms. Fowler, turning toward her office with a look of relief. "You have no idea how much I hate doing display cases. Just let me know what supplies you'll need, and I'll get them from the Arts Room."

Chapter Ten

Immediately I started scavenging everyone's mind for their favorite book. From my afternoon classes, I got a long list that included *Beloved*, *The God of Small Things*, *Hate You*, *Confessions of a Remorseless Teenager* and *Hamlet* (I bumped into Dikker in the hall between classes). Then, after school I waylaid Cam and his buddies outside the guys locker room on their way into football practice, and got another barrage: *Superman*, *Batman*, *The Hardy Boys*, *The Cat in the Hat* and *Playboy*. Reading was obviously not these guys' favorite activity.

"Hey, put me down for *War and Peace*," added Len Schroeder, puffing out his chest and giving it a dramatic thump. "I read it for a book review I had to do in grade seven."

Dubious groans erupted from the group.

"Yeah right," said Gary Pankratz, punching his shoulder. "The *Coles Notes* version, maybe. That kind of stuff is for fags, anyway." Dangling a wrist, he lisped, "*Ulysses*. That's what I read before I go to sleep. A page a night for the past ten years."

A guffaw rocked the group, and in spite of what had happened earlier that day with Diane and Geoff, I have to admit I laughed along with them. Not at the fag joke, but the idea of Gary Pankratz actually reading an entire page every night.

"What d'you want this for, Dyl?" asked Cam when the laughter had died down. As I explained about the library display, a broad grin took over Len's face.

"Ditch *War and Peace*," he said, "and change it to *Treasure Island*. And make sure you put it right across the guy's dick in your display."

Once again the group dissolved into laughter, taking me with them. These guys could occasionally be funny, even if they were illiterate. "Maybe I'll use it for the girl," I said, writing *Treasure Island* on my list.

"Uh-uh," Len said quickly. "The girl's would be *Sweet Valley High*."

My mouth just dropped. I mean, I'd heard drug jokes about the series' title, but never any sexual ones. "Okay," I said, after everyone had calmed down. "What's your favorite book, Cam?"

The other guys glanced at him, waiting for his reply, but Cam just stood there, staring at the floor.

"C'mon, Cam," I said, elbowing him gently. "What's the big secret?"

Reluctantly he glanced at me, his eyes kind of startled, almost frightened. For a second he reminded me of Tracey Stillman.

"I'll think about it," he said tersely, then turned to the group and said, "C'mon, we've got to get moving or Coach Gonie'll be on our asses. See you later, Dyl."

Then he was gone, the locker room door swinging shut behind him, while I stood staring at it. That hadn't been like Cam. I'd never seen him freeze on an answer before—he was always ready with a quick reply. Something had to be bugging him. I'd get it out of him later on the phone.

Filing the incident at the back of my mind, I headed to the auditorium where I found Joc sprawled against the back wall behind a crowd of Shakespeare groupies while Mr. Tyrrell gave some feedback to several actors standing on the stage. An expression of infinite boredom on her face, she was reading a copy of *Hamlet*.

Dropping down beside her, I said, "Hey, I'm taking a survey of everyone's favorite book. Shall I write you down for *Hamlet*?"

"Uh-*uh*," she said emphatically. "Diane du Bois said she liked it, so I decided to try reading it. But so far the story sucks. It's about some loser who spends all his time wandering around telling everyone else off. His dad is the king, and Hamlet thinks he's the greatest. But then his dad gets murdered and comes back as a ghost, and tells Hamlet to kill his murderer. What kind of dad tells his son to go kill someone? Hamlet's so screwed up, he can't even get it on with his girlfriend. No wonder he couldn't decide whether to be or not to be. I don't get what Dikker sees in this stuff."

"Maybe he's decided to improve his mind," I said, sucking back a grin.

"Yeah, well I think it's screwing up his mind," Joc grumbled. "He's even started quoting entire speeches from other characters. Why should I have to listen to gobbledygook that isn't even from *his* character?"

I gave up and let loose with a big grin. "C'mon, it is a step up from *In Cold Blood*," I said. "You've got to admit that."

"At least then I could tell what he was talking about," Joc snorted. She darted me a suspicious glance. "Do you like *Hamlet*?"

"I'm with you," I assured her. "I think he needed a good kick in the butt."

"A definite kick in the butt," agreed Joc, tossing the book to the floor in disgust. "Y'know, Dikker hardly even wants to make out anymore. He just sits there reciting lines and making me read

along to make sure he's got them right. He's obsessed. I think
he's decided to memorize the entire play. This afternoon he told
me he wants to become an actor." She looked at me in horror.
"He could be like this for the rest of his life."

I tried very hard not to bust a gut laughing but was not
what you would call successful. "You mean ten years from now
I'm going to see him on TV doing used car commercials?" I
wheezed.

"Oh, don't," moaned Joc. Collapsing against me, she buried
her face in my shoulder. "Just don't, okay?"

"Okay," I said, feeling a flutter pass through my heart. A quiet
thud-thud, thud-thud started up in my body—warm, soft and
everywhere.

"Hey, Joc," said a girl from the groupie crowd in front of us.
"Dikker's on."

"Oh yeah," Joc said disinterestedly, her face still buried in my
shoulder.

Another girl turned around. "But it's his big scene," she said.

"He doesn't have a big scene," Joc said glumly. "He comes on,
farts, and goes off again."

The groupies observed her in shock for a moment, then
shrugged and turned back to the stage.

"Dikker's going to hear about this," I hissed at Joc. "The
Shakespeare grapevine will be sure to get it to him."

"I'll tell him I have my period," she mumbled.

"Hmmm," I said, not wanting to get into *that.* "Hey, I'm still
waiting for you to tell me your favorite book so I can add it to
my list."

"*People Magazine,*" Joc said dozily and yawned. I glanced
down at her. Here my body was going thud-thud, thud-thud,
and she was about to lose grasp on consciousness and slide
into dreamland.

"Not a mag," I said, "a book. Y'know, with lots of words and *no* pictures."

"I don't like those," said Joc. "They remind me of *Hamlet*."

"There are lots of books that aren't *Hamlet*," I said. "Pick one, any one."

"*Gone With the Wind*," Joc said finally. With a sigh, she snuggled deeper into my shoulder. "I liked that one. It had lots of words and no pictures, except on the cover."

"The cover doesn't count as a picture," I said, writing it down. "And as far as I remember, Hamlet doesn't show up in the plot anywhere."

"Uh-uh," said Joc. "Scarlet never even heard of him. He was just gone with the wind, and he should've stayed gone." Pursing her lips, she puffed fiercely and said, "Go away, Hamlet. Go *away*."

"He's a goner," I said, patting her head. "No sign of Hamlet anywhere. Except on that stage over there."

"Keep him on that stage," mumbled Joc, "and far away from me. If I have to listen to any more of that gobbledygook, I'm gonna barf, I swear."

With that, she drifted off to sleep.

It was later that evening. Keelie had been put to bed, Danny was in his room playing video games and Mom and Dad were watching the late news. The house had settled into the quiet that comes with that time of day, all corner shadows and coffee-table lamp light, and I was where I usually was on a school night, doing you-know-what in my bed. As I got deeper into it, image after image started free-floating through my head—since I'd decided to let my mind go wherever it wanted, it definitely went there, straight to Joc, bringing sensations so vivid that I was left shuddery and gasping. But there's no rest for the wicked. Just as

I was hit with the sweetest, most vivid lightning bolt of sensation yet, my bedroom phone started ringing. Groaning loudly, I lay for a moment, letting my breathing slow as I returned to solid reality: bed under my back, amber quilt over my knees, one very grotty hand and a goddamn phone. With another groan, I rolled over and reached for it. Whoever this was, it had better be worth it.

"Hello?" I grunted.

"Dyl?" asked a voice. "You weren't asleep, were you?"

It was Cam, his voice low and husky, so I knew he was probably lying in his bed and calling from his cell phone. What I would have given for one of those things, but Mom and Dad insisted on my having a regular phone—something about electromagnetic waves and brain tumors.

"No," I said, taking a long slow breath. The images of Joc that had been invading my brain were fading now, almost gone. "How was practice?"

"The usual," said Cam. "Grunt, slam, bash. It was great. What'd you do tonight? How's Keelie?"

"Asleep, thank god," I said. "She spent all evening zooming around the house on that broom. I swear she really thinks she can fly."

Even on the phone, I could see the grin creeping across Cam's face. "Maybe she can," he said. "Maybe you just can't see her doing it."

Not sure what he meant, I said "Huh" and waited for him to explain.

"I've been reading about the wave particle theory for Physics," Cam said hastily, as if embarrassed by the oddness of his statement. "Did you know that particles are also waves, and they only take particle form when you look at them? That means everything you see as solid is actually only solid when you're looking at it. The rest of the time it's in waves." He paused, his voice wobbly with excitement. "And here's the really weird thing—a particle doesn't just exist in *our* universe, it slips back and forth between parallel universes."

"Huh," I said again, trying to keep up with what he was saying.

"So you see," continued Cam, "it's just possible that Keelie's particles actually are flying when you're not looking at her. She could be slipping into another universe where she really is playing Quidditch on a magic broom with good ol' Harry."

As Cam said this, I was hit full force with the memory of what I'd been doing before he called. What if...what if the particles in my body had been switching into waves and slipping into another universe where I actually was making it with Joc? Was that why it had felt so real? I mean, was it *possible*?

"Huh," I said again, and Cam laughed low in his throat.

"I know," he said. "Crazy Cam and his way-out ideas. But just think of it, Dyl—what if the present, the future and the past are all parallel universes, existing next to each other? And we can turn into waves and slip between them?"

"How would we do that?" I asked.

"With our thoughts," he said. "We could think ourselves into the future and find out what's there, maybe even change it. I read somewhere that there might actually be loads of parallel future universes, and by slipping into them with our minds, we can pick which one we want and make it real in this one."

Again I thought about what I'd been doing before he called. "Huh," I said.

"Bored?" Cam asked quickly.

"Uh-uh," I said. "Trying to work it out in my head."

"Yeah," he said. "That's what I've been doing all evening— trying to figure it out. It means anything is possible, y'know. You can create your own future just by thinking it."

A burst of phone static erupted as he rolled over on his bed and reached for something crinkly. Doritos, probably. Yup—a second later I heard him chomping away. Barbecue flavor, I could almost taste it.

"Hey," I said, as the Doritos bag crinkled again. "Now that we're here and focused in *this* universe…"

"Yup," he said, chomping away. "Here and focused, Dyllie."

"What's your favorite book?" I asked. "And why wouldn't you tell me what it was this afternoon?"

There was a pause as Cam swallowed, the glugging sound traveling down his throat. "The guys," he said finally. "They would've called me a fag. It just didn't fit into the mood of the moment, y'know?"

Fag, I thought and winced. "Well," I said, "the mood is now very moody. So tell me, I'm all ears."

"I read it in grade nine," Cam said slowly. "In the summer, up at the cabin. It's a really great book."

"Out with it," I said. "The actual title."

"*The Once and Future King*," he said quietly. "By T. H. Whyte. Ever read it?"

"Uh-uh," I said.

"It's about King Arthur," said Cam, "and his life as a kid with Merlin. His nickname was Wart, and then he became king and married Guinevere and got to know Lancelot. Lancelot's the best part, really. No, Arthur is. No, maybe them both."

On the word "both," Cam's voice quavered slightly, and my eyes widened. It sounded as if he was on the verge of tears. Giving a bit of a sigh, he said, "Anyway, I think that's the title you should put on the guy's dick. Not *Treasure Island*."

"*The Once and Future King*?" I said, my eyes widening further. "Isn't that kind of like calling yourself Dikker?"

"You have to read it, Dyllie," Cam said earnestly. "It's not like that at all. Arthur's humble, almost like a servant. Yeah," he said, his voice quickening, "a servant-king. And there's this scene where Lancelot has to do a miracle to prove he's pure, only he knows he isn't because he's been doing it with Guinevere behind Arthur's back, and God won't let him perform the miracle because of that. Only God does let him, and Lancelot heals a man. And then Lancelot bawls his head off, because he knows he's been forgiven for everything wrong inside him."

I lay silently, staring at the low glow of my walls in the lamp light. I'd never heard Cam talk like this, so raw, open from the inside out.

"We're all like that, don't you think?" he said, rushing on. "Like Lancelot—stuff wrong inside us but still wanting to do miracles. That's why I think you should put *The Once and Future King* over the guy's dick. Because that's where a guy lives, in his dick. It's his kingdom. If he's right or wrong in his heart and head, that's where it'll show up—in his dick. He'll be a bad king or a servant-king there. Or a Lancelot, performing miracles."

"Huh," I said again, listening to Cam breathe.

"Dyllie," he asked after a bit. "You still there?"

"Yeah," I said. "Just thinking about what you said."

He sighed again, a warm gush of sound. "I'm a bit of a kook, aren't I?" he muttered.

"You're the best damn guy on the planet," I said fiercely. "Len and Gary and the other guys should've heard you say this."

"Maybe," he said softly. "Sometime when the mood gets moody enough. Read the book though, okay?"

"Yeah, I will," I said. "I'll sign it out of the library tomorrow."

"Great," he said, and I could hear him smile. "So, what are you going to put over the girl's...uh, you-know-where? *Sweet Valley High*?"

"And get Ms. Fowler fired?" I said. "No, I was thinking of…"

I paused, my heart thudding slow and deep in my chest.

"Of what?" Cam prodded.

"*Foxfire*," I said and waited. A long pause followed on the other end of the phone.

"That's about a gang of dykes, isn't it?" Cam asked finally.

"Not all of them," I said. "The book never says any of them are for sure. And some of them got married. One of them even had kids."

Another long pause followed. "Someone told me what you said about it in class," Cam said slowly. "Justice and sex and categories, something like that."

"Yeah, something like that," I said. My heart was really thudding now. "Don't you ever feel the walls closing in on you?" I went on quickly. "It's as if everyone has a personal box inside them labeled 'This Is What I Am,' and all they want to do is squish themselves inside it and live there forever. Don't you ever want to bust out of yourself, and this place and everything around you?"

"Sometimes," he said quietly. "I guess. It just…didn't really sound like you."

"A very moody moment," I said. "Y'know how it is."

"Yeah," he said. "Yeah, okay. Well, I'm kissing you goodbye now, Dyl. You know what I'll be thinking about when I hang up."

"Me too," I said, giving the phone a big smooch. Hanging up, I turned out the light and lay staring at the darkness. That had been close, telling him about *Foxfire*. I'd thought I was about to have a near-death experience, I really did. But now it was over, and it didn't sound as if Cam had guessed. So it would probably be all right to use *Foxfire* in the display—sort of like saying it and not saying it. I could look at it as I passed the display case and get used to it being out in the open, without actually having to tell anyone directly.

Closing my eyes, I let the particles of my brain slide into the long dark waves of sleep.

Chapter Eleven

Over the next few days I collected about a hundred book titles from kids at school, and on Thursday evening I divided the most interesting ones into two lists. Next I laid out two extra-large pieces of bristol board that Ms. Fowler had gotten from the Arts Room, and drew the outlines of a pony-tailed girl and a short-haired boy, standing so they were facing the viewer head-on. After some constructive criticism from Keelie, as in, "That don't look good, his head's too big," I shrank the boy's head from alien to human size, and cut out the silhouettes. Then I used them to trace a second pair of silhouettes onto newsprint, each of which I cut into thirty outlines of books, both open and closed.

Friday after supper Joc came over to help with the next stage. Hunkered down at the dining room table, we traced the outline of each newsprint-book silhouette onto a colored piece of construction paper and cut it out. As each construction-paper book was finished, I fit it into the original bristol-board silhouette of the girl or boy. It was important they fit exactly, so there wasn't any bristol board showing.

Mom and Dad were out, burning up the town on one of their "dates," and Danny was upstairs with Keelie, teaching her a video game on his computer. So other than the fact that Joc had

Alanis Morissette's *Feast on Scraps* CD blasting from the living room stereo, things were pretty sedate.

"Last one," she said, as she finished cutting out a green book silhouette. "Good thing, too. I'm getting a blister from these scissors." With a satisfied grin, she fit the book into the single remaining space in the boy silhouette.

"Give me a sec," I said. "I've got a couple more to do for the girl."

She waited, fidgeting while I fit the last two books into the girl silhouette, then said, "C'mon, I need a smoke. Your parents aren't home—let's go out back."

"Can't," I said quickly. "Keelie'll see. Her bedroom's back there."

"The front, then," said Joc.

"We've got neighbors," I reminded her. "They get along *very* well with my parents."

Leaning forward, Joc banged her forehead gently on the table. "Nic fit," she grumbled. "I'm getting the jitters. It's been over an hour since my last drag."

"Near-death experience, I know," I said. "Okay, let's go out front, and I'll sit with you while you smoke."

"Bless you, sweet one," said Joc, and we headed out to the front porch where I made sure I was in full view of the neighbors—full *non*-smoking view, that is.

"Oh yeah," said Joc, lighting up and dragging deeply. "That's better. Now my brain's working again."

She shifted, and the side of her foot bumped mine. Just that little bump, and right away I was swamped by a wave of heat. Then images started popping into my head, but this time I was smart enough to get a grip.

Uh-uh, I thought. *No way I'm doing the lust thing now. Not with the neighbors watching.*

Carefully I edged my foot away. Joc didn't seem to notice.

"Mmmm," I said, taking a dramatic sniff of the smoke coiling off the tip of her cigarette. "Problem is, now *I'm* getting a nic fit. I was fine until you lit up."

"Near-death experience, I know," Joc grinned unsympathetically. Holding out her cigarette, she cooed, "Live a little, Dyllie. Have a drag on me."

"Uh-uh," I said, frantically waving the cigarette away in case the neighbors had their eyes peeled. "Mom would absolutely kill me if she found out."

"You worry too much about what your parents think," said Joc, taking another blissful drag. "They're not going to disown you if you smoke one cigarette."

"I know," I said. "They'd get mad, though. *Really* mad. But it's more than that. They'd be…I dunno…disappointed. I mean, they want me to be healthy, right? I figure—I like smoking, so I'll keep it to a minor hobby. Y'know, every now and then, when I get desperate. Like Mom says, it's really just sucking in toxic waste. And she also told me that in ten years none of the major companies will be hiring smokers because it hikes up their employee benefits costs."

"Oh yeah," said Joc, tapping off some ash. "Yeah, I guess, if you want to think that way—twenty years down the line." She paused, considering. "Yeah, I can see it—twenty years from now, you and Cam, both working for major corporations and set up in a ritzy split-level with three or four kids."

"Supreme bliss," I said casually, trying to ignore the kick of unease in my gut. "And what about you? What do you see yourself doing in twenty years? Besides spending half your time getting chemo treatments, that is?"

Joc sat silently for a moment, studying the curl of smoke coming off her cigarette. "Probably working at a race track somewhere," she said finally. "Or doing environmental stuff like Greenpeace. Or…" Turning to me, she grinned. "Maybe I'll be a two pack-a-day librarian like my mom."

"Yeah right," I grinned. "Exactly like your mom."

"That wouldn't be so bad," said Joc. "She's done some pretty interesting things. She told me about some protest stuff she did in the eighties, down in the States. Even got arrested for climbing onto a nuclear silo once with a nun."

"A nun?" I demanded, staring at her.

"Yup," said Joc. "Some of those nuns are pretty lively." She grinned slyly. "I bet some of them even smoke. That's what I'll be—a nun who sneaks onto American military bases and climbs onto nuclear silos. And I promise I'll send you and Cam and your four kids postcards—"

"Hey, maybe not *four* kids," I said abruptly, cutting her off. "And, anyway, how do you know I'll end up with Cam?"

"Oh, you will," Joc said immediately. "You're that kind of person, Dyl—the marrying kind. It's weird, in a way, that we've been friends for so long, seeing how we're so different."

Again, I felt an uneasy kick in my gut. "How are we different?" I demanded.

Joc shrugged. "You're smarter than me, for starters," she said. "And moodier, deeper inside yourself. Cam likes that about you—you two belong together, and he knows it. And me…well, you know me. Crazy." Staring across the street, she snorted softly. "My entire goal in life is to become a stable citizen."

The uneasy kick in my gut was quickly morphing into an uneasy sinkhole. I mean, I'd never thought about it before, really—how different we were and what that might mean for our friendship after high school.

"What about Dikker?" I asked, my voice suddenly hoarse.

Again, Joc shrugged. "He wants to be an actor," she said in

disgust. "Actors spend their lives *faking* things. How much time would you want to spend with a professional faker?"

Leaning forward, she butted out her cigarette on the front walk, then slid the unsmoked part into her purse. "C'mon," she said. "Dikker's picking me up when he gets off work, and we've still got to write titles on all those book outlines we cut out."

We went inside and got back to work, Joc following a master plan I'd drawn up for the boy silhouette while I wrote out titles for the girl. *Feast on Scraps* had finished while we were outside so the room was quiet, with just the squeak of magic markers as we wrote. Abruptly, three-quarters of the way through the job it hit me—Joc hadn't said anything for over five minutes. That was not like her. In fact, it was very much not like her.

Suspicion slammed into me. Reaching for her stack of completed book silhouettes, I sifted through them.

"Joc!" I yelped, horrified. "What the hell are you doing?"

"Don't take a hairy," she said, grinning at me. "I got bored writing down the titles you gave me, so I made up some of my own."

"*Hamlet Is A Turd*?" I bellowed. "*Holla Bolla, Moron*? *Get Thee to a Monastery*?"

"Well, I couldn't say what I really thought," Joc said reasonably. "It had to be something Ms. Fowler would let you put up in the display case."

"It took us ages to cut out all those books," I wailed, glaring at her. "Now I'm going to have to do these all over again. How many did you wreck?"

"Cool your toots, Dyl," said Joc. "Just five or ten, for a joke. Hail, Basti, who comest forth from the morgue, I promise never to have any fun."

"Easy for you to say—it's not your display," I mumbled, counting the altered titles. Fortunately, I'd caught her after seven. Twenty minute's work would replace them.

"Watch it," warned Joc, slitting her eyes at me. "You just rhymed. You're starting to sound like Shakespeare."

"A rhyme is a crime," I shot back, just as a car horn honked loudly outside.

"A rhyme is a *slime*," Joc corrected sternly. "And it sounds as if my darling foot soldier has finally arrived. Can I have the books I screwed up? I'll give them to Dikker. He can pretend they're fan mail."

"Here," I said, shoving them at her. "Good riddance."

"See you later, Dyllie," Joc said, her grin absolutely ear to ear as she tucked the construction-paper books into her purse. Then, without warning, she leaned forward and kissed me on the cheek.

"It's going to be completely and utterly fab, you know," she said, her nose one inch from mine. "Your display will make the day, even if I am slime-rhyming."

Then she got up, ejected *Feast on Scraps* from the stereo and headed out the door, leaving me with the sensation of her lips, still warm and slightly wet, on my cheek.

Early the next morning my bedroom door creaked slowly open, and feet tiptoed cautiously across the floor. The end of my mattress gave slightly as Keelie clambered onto it, and I lay holding myself stock still as she crawled to my shoulder and stared intently at my face. When she'd convinced herself that I was still asleep, she leaned in, flooding me with the scent of baby shampoo and her musty morning breath.

"Good morning, Dylan," she whispered into my ear. "The sun is waiting for us to get up so it can jump into the sky."

Reaching out an arm, I tugged her down beside me and we snuggled under the blankets, murmuring back and forth about important five-year-old things. Keelie had just started giving me a rundown on her favorite Quidditch tactics when I suddenly remembered what day it was. Sitting bolt upright, I glanced at my clock radio.

"Geeeeezus!" I yelped. "It's 8:30. I have to be at the Dief by 9:00."

Yesterday afternoon Ms. Fowler and I had agreed to meet this morning in the library so I could set up my genius idea in the display case. "Sorry Keelie," I said, climbing hastily over her. "I've got a zillion things to do before we go swimming this afternoon."

"Can I come, can I come?" she demanded, trotting after me.

"Uh-uh. They don't allow Quidditch maniacs where I'm going," I said, ruffling her hair.

As she took off out of the room, I pulled on some clothes and headed downstairs for a waffle. The breakfast thing over and done with, I rolled up the girl and boy silhouettes and tied them to my backpack, then checked through the book outlines Joc and I had cut out to make sure they were all there. Finally I took off for the Dief on my bike. It felt weird, zooming through the early morning streets without taking my usual detour toward Joc's house, but then I had passed the turnoff and was heading over the Dundurn Street bridge. Racing down a few more streets, I rounded the last corner, and the Dief came into view, a gray concrete outline that looked like several large shoe boxes shoved together. And there, standing at the east entrance, was Ms. Fowler, looking as rumpled, gray-haired and observant as ever. Underneath that quiet exterior hummed a hyper-alert mind. Ms. Fowler was a spy for the gods.

"Good morning, Dylan," she said, as I dismounted and locked my bike to a street sign. "Ready to go to work?"

"Got it all done last night," I grinned. "All I have to do now is staple it into place."

"That's lovely," she said, unlocking the school door. "Just let me know how I can assist you."

We walked quickly through the halls, the sound of our footsteps traveling ahead of us into the long emptiness. When we got to the library, Ms. Fowler let us in, then flicked the light switch, and the place lit up with endless books arranged on shelves, stacked on the check-out counter and piled into filing carts.

"As you can see, I've cleared out the display case," said Ms. Fowler, turning toward it. "I had one of the maintenance men bring in a stepladder so you could reach the top of the case, and the staple gun is right here on the check-out desk. Would you like me to help?"

"Um," I said, hesitating. I hadn't thought about it ahead of time, but now that I was about to start, the task of putting up the display felt private—like getting dressed or something.

Ms. Fowler clued in immediately. "Ah," she said, taking a step back. "Why don't I let you get on with it, and you can call me to observe the final product?"

With that she vanished into her office, and I got to work, climbing up the stepladder and stapling the girl and boy silhouettes into place. Then I began stapling each construction-paper book into position. Halfway through the job, I realized that I could have glued the individual books into the girl and boy silhouettes at home, shortening the process considerably, but even so I was really getting into it, watching the girl's body grow book by book, title by title: *Absolutely Normal Chaos* dead center in her forehead, *Harriet the Spy* riding her eyes, and *The Chocolate War* for her mouth. Next came *Color of Absence* as her throat. With slightly shaky hands, I stapled *The Egyptian Book of the Dead* into place as her heart. *Good Families Don't* went into her gut, and *Foxfire,* in an orange open-book shape, each side tilted upward like a flame, became her groin. Another slew of titles like *The*

Handmaid's Tale and *The God of Small Things* went into her legs and feet, and then I was ready for the boy silhouette.

Cirque du Freak hit him smack in the middle of the forehead, *Rats Saw God* took over his eyes, and with a grin I stapled *The Joy of Sex* into place as his mouth. Cam was going to love that. *The Giver* became his throat, *The Subtle Knife* his heart, *Tribute to Another Dead Rock* his gut, and *The Once and Future King* his groin. Just as I'd promised, I'd spent the last three days reading T. H. Whyte's book, and like Cam had said it was a soul book, a servant-king for your mind. Giving it a satisfied beam, I moved on to the silhouette's legs, and finished off the feet with *Hate You* and *Bad Boy*. Then I stapled the leftover titles into little thought clouds around the edge of the display: *Watership Down, Gone With the Wind, The Stone Angel, Never Trust a Dead Man*. Finally I put up the display's title, *The Small Words In My Body*, written inside a huge thought cloud, and backed down the stepladder. It was done now, whatever was up there was utter crap or halfway decent. Either way, it was about to make its multicolored construction-paper way into the eyes and minds of every student at the Dief.

"Why that's excellent, Dylan," said Ms. Fowler from behind me, her voice quiet as ever, but I could hear the pleasure in it. Slowly she approached the display, and I stood holding my breath as she ran her eyes over it.

"*The Chocolate War* for the mouth," she said slowly. "That's good. *Breathing Underwater* for the nose and *Color of Absence* for the voice—I like that." She paused a moment, her eyes fixed on the girl's heart, then continued on without comment. "*Foxfire*," she murmured suddenly. "How interesting. Very interesting."

As she glanced toward the boy silhouette, an actual grin flashed across her face. "*The Joy of Sex*," she said. "We'll have to see what Administration says about that. And *The Giver*. One of my favorites."

Her eyes traveled downward and widened. In that second I swear I actually felt her thought vibes quicken. "*The Once and Future King*," she murmured. "How very *very* interesting. Yes, Dylan, I think you have done a tremendous job here."

I could have whooped, but managed to keep a grip. "Thanks, Ms. Fowler," I said. "I loved doing it, I really did."

"Well," she said, turning toward me, her eyes fixing on a spot to the left of my face. "It's almost lunch. Shall I order in some pizza?"

"Oh, I can't," I said, dismayed. I mean, the uncertainty in her voice was obvious, something delicate and shy. "Mom asked me to take my little sister swimming at one."

"I see," said Ms. Fowler. For a second she stood blinking rapidly, then turned toward her office. "Well, that's all right," she said briskly. "I just wanted to express my appreciation for all your work."

"Ms. Fowler," I said quickly. "I'd really like to, sometime... have lunch with you, I mean."

She stopped, and I felt the pause in her. Then she turned slightly and glanced again at the space to the left of my head. "I'd like that too," she said quietly. "Perhaps sometime we will. Thank you again for your work."

Pulling her cloak of mystery quiet about her, she went into her office, and I headed outside to unlock my bike.

Chapter Twelve

That evening Cam and I went to a dance that was being held across town at Confederation Collegiate. Both of us knew kids there from summer sports leagues, and Cam had a friend in the school's Student Dance Security who looked the other way on selective alcohol infringements. So after parking the car in the student lot, we headed to the front door to get our hands stamped. A wall of sound hit us as we entered the auditorium, and for a second we just stood blinking in the strobe lights. The decorations theme was obviously outer space, and images of galaxies, aliens and laser guns were plastered everywhere. The entire stage had been converted to look like the inside of a spaceship, and some of the kids were dressed as alien Grays, with slanted insect-eye sunglasses. The effect was kind of eerie, enough to lift you out of your usual drift and get you looking at things from another dimension.

"They must've wrapped the whole place in tin foil," Cam yelled in my ear.

"Shiny side out," I yelled back.

He grinned, I bumped him with my hip, and we started dancing, kind of goofy. Cam liked to fool around on the dance floor, move however he felt. He didn't care what other people thought about his dancing, and when we first started going out, I wasn't sure how to react. I mean, rhythm wasn't Cam's thing, he didn't have a clue when it came to following a beat, but no one had as much fun dancing as he did. He'd jump up and down if he felt like it and usually came off the dance floor dripping sweat.

Tonight he was moving in what I can only describe as monkey-jiving—here, there and jibber-jabber everywhere, grabbing my hands and making me jive with him so I lost the tightness I'd brought onto the dance floor and began to let loose. Circling each other, we started bumping hips. Suddenly Cam gave me his ecstasy grin, lifted his arms and began shaking his chest. I must have split a gut laughing. All around us, kids were turning to stare.

After some more jibber-jabber jiving, we headed over to the refreshment table for a can of pop, then tracked down the kids we knew. As expected they were huddled in a back corner, slurping down a mixture of rum and Coke and critiquing the dancing technique of everyone in sight. For a second I cringed, hoping they hadn't seen us, but then someone called, "Hey Zeleny, I was wondering when you'd show." Someone else held out a bottle of rum, and Cam grinned as the dark liquid poured into his can. Next I got my dose. Sipping slowly, I stood beside Cam, watching kids on the dance floor twist and jive. As far as I could see, he and I appeared to be the only jumpers, but there were a few wild ones out there.

Without warning I saw her, the girl from the movie theater washroom, leaning against a nearby wall. Immediately a jolt of electricity ran through me, just like the one I'd felt last weekend when our eyes met in the mirror, and my hand jerked, slopping some Coke onto my runners. Swearing, I checked my clothes for damage, but I'd gotten off lucky—T-shirt still white, unstained, virginal.

"You okay?" asked Cam, leaning into me.

"Yeah," I said quickly. "My arm got bumped. No prob."

With a nod he went back to his conversation, and I glanced at the place the girl had been standing. It was empty now, she'd obviously moved, but I could feel her somewhere close. Turning, I scanned the crowd. In the thirty seconds since I'd seen her, everything had changed. Suddenly my heart was in massive overdrive, as if someone had flicked a switch and my entire body had come on, full heat. Lifting my Coke to my mouth, I drank steadily. I didn't usually do that with alcohol; slow and thoughtful was my rule. But in the last few seconds, something that had been asleep and unnoticed deep inside me had come awake—something huge, heated and irrevocable. The Coke and its burning slide down my throat just seemed to match the mood.

Setting the empty can on a nearby table, I edged away from Cam and his friends. No specific thoughts were in my mind, my body had simply morphed into an extreme pair of eyes, searching for the movie-theater girl. She was here and she was alone, I was sure of it—something about the way she'd been standing, leaning against the wall and watching, as if she would always be a watcher, never a dancer. Aloneness was her mystery cloak, like it was Ms. Fowler's.

Back to the auditorium wall, I stood scanning the crowd. I don't know why I was looking there, I should have known better, because when I finally caught sight of her, the girl wasn't on the dance floor but sitting with her legs dangling over the front of one of the large speakers that had been set up on the stage. Cautiously I edged closer, using the crowd for cover. I didn't want to be seen by her, just look her over, *observe* like Ms. Fowler.

If I watched her long enough, I figured I could pin down what had set off that mind-blowing spark between us.

Tonight her hair was pulled back into a barrette, revealing the smooth line of her neck. Her mouth was in a pout, her eyes restless and shadowy. Casually I let my gaze slide downward, inch by slow inch. And it hit me then the way I'd known it would, even though I was standing in the darkest part of the auditorium, even though I was alone and no one was observing *me*—a power blush, a wave of *Foxfire* heat and a heart so far into overdrive that I was verging on a near-death experience.

Something took hold of me, moved me out of the shadows by the wall and stood me directly in front of the speaker. Sound hit me full blast, I was riding a sheer throb of bass. As I stood there looking up at her, the girl glanced down and our eyes locked. For a second she just stared at me, her face in neutral. Then, swinging her legs to one side of the speaker, she slid to the stage and jumped down beside me, so close we were almost touching.

"Want a smoke?" she shouted. I nodded and she turned, weaving her way through the crowd. Pushing open a side door, she headed down a hall, then through another door. As we came out into the student parking lot, a cloud of cigarette smoke hit us. Without stopping to greet anyone, the movie-theater girl slipped through the small group of smokers that surrounded the exit and turned a corner to the back of the school. Abruptly, we were alone. Ahead stretched a parking lot of empty cars; behind us, dull sound throbbed through the school wall.

"Here," said the girl, lighting a cigarette and passing it to me.

"Thanks," I said. Taking a drag, I passed it back.

"You been here before?" she asked, her face a low glow as the cigarette ember flared in the dark.

"I know some kids who go here," I said, trying to fake casual, my eyes flicking everywhere but her face.

"You don't know me," she said.

That got me so jumpy, I almost took off. I mean, what the *fuck* did I think I was doing here? Nervously I turned to look out over the parking lot, and my eyes landed on Cam's Firebird.

"I've seen you around," I muttered, my eyes flicking away from that too.

"Yeah, I know *how* you've seen me," said the girl, and suddenly our eyes were locked, my heart pounding, just *pounding*. "You're like me," she added, then waited, letting the silence speak for her.

"Maybe," I said finally, "and maybe not."

"Then, why are you here?" she asked.

"For a smoke," I said, taking the cigarette from her hand and dragging on it. It was a shaky drag—she was watching me so close, I almost choked on it.

"Where there's smoke, there's fire," said the girl, taking the cigarette from my hand and dropping it to the pavement. Then she added, "By the way, my name's Sheila." Letting her eyes slide to my mouth, she leaned forward.

A surge of heat hit me, so intense I almost yelped, and then our lips were touching, touching again. We leaned closer, not just her leaning into me—I was right in on her, my hands in her hair as hers slid up my back. Sweet fire shot through me, so vivid I was lost in it—whirling, spaced-out, gasping-crazy, *hot*.

"Shit," I hissed, jerking away. "Shit, shit, *shit*."

Ahead of me the parking lot blurred in and out of focus, the rum and Coke putting in some special effects. Inches to my right Sheila stood silently, not moving, just breathing, quick and quiet in the dark. Ducking my head, I took a few steps away from her, then broke into a run, heading for the safety of the smoking crowd and the school entrance that loomed just beyond them.

Obviously I didn't spend much time Thanksgiving Sunday thinking about Cam. Or Joc. Or the math and history assignments I was supposed to have been working on. Instead I spent any time that I wasn't chowing down turkey and cranberry sauce and talking to my grandparents, lying in bed doing you-know-what while I relived that kiss behind Confederation Collegiate. Over and over I remembered Sheila saying, "Where there's smoke, there's fire" and leaning in, as unbelievable sensations flashed through me—I was an electric billboard plugged into overdrive, a supersonic strobe light, a maniac's scream. Sunday night I went at it again for hours and probably would have Monday afternoon too, if Julie Crozier hadn't called and asked me to go to the mall with her and Rachel.

For a second I hesitated. I mean, what would I rather have been doing? Besides, Julie and Rachel had a tendency to be acquisitional, as in they liked to acquire things and not always in the legal manner. As far as I was concerned, shoplifting was no thrill. I'd tried it several times in grade school, and the last time a hyperventilating store manager had come after me, screaming her head off as she chased me for several blocks. I'd gotten away but barely, and when the woman finally gave up, I realized that I'd been so scared, I'd peed my pants. I also realized that even if the store manager didn't know my name, she would damn well recognize me if I walked into her shop again. There was no way I could ever go back there, even to spend my weekly allowance, and it was enough to convince me that a life of crime wasn't my thing. Julie and Rachel, however, were still getting a rush off it, so whenever I went "shopping" with them, I stood as far away as possible in case they were caught.

Just after lunch Rachel picked me up in her car, and the three of us drove to the downtown mall. By mid-afternoon we'd cruised the Panhandler, the Gap and Mariposa, and were headed toward the Bay. Julie had managed to pocket a pair of earrings that had caught her fancy, but Rachel had been cheated out of a leather wallet by a sharp-eyed clerk. So as we made our way down the mall's central corridor, she was on a royal bitch, her eyes on the prowl for a victim—someone, *anyone* she could verbally attack, maul and mutilate.

"Look at that wiener girl by the A&W," she snapped, pointing at a girl standing on the other side of the food court. "I bet she hasn't eaten in a month. Her bum's flat as a paper napkin."

I glanced at the girl standing in front of the A&W. She was thin, but not that thin. Rachel was obviously desperate to unload some venom.

"Anorexia," singsonged Julie, rolling her eyes.

"Anor*ass*ia," Rachel replied.

"Yeah," snorted Julie. "Not like that girl at the Booster Juice. She's a chug-and-chuck. Bulimic, *obviously.*"

Obediently I glanced in the direction of her pointing finger, then sucked in my breath as my eyes landed on a familiar face— hot lips Sheila, star of approximately forty-two nonstop hours of my private fantasies, sitting alone at a table in front of the Booster Juice. As luck would have it, the second my gaze landed on her, she happened to look up and see me. Her eyes widened, her mouth came open, and she shot out of her seat like a jack-in-the-box.

I took off. No way, no way, no *way* was I having a chit-chat with the passion of Confederation Collegiate while Julie and Rachel stood nearby, listening in. I could just imagine it.

How are you today, Sheila?

Oh, fine. How are you? Still thinking about that kiss I gave you Saturday night?

Mmm, I gave it the odd thought, when I wasn't doing something important like washing the dishes.

I mean, even if Sheila didn't mention the kiss directly, she would be looking at me with a desperate hungry look on her face. I give Julie and Rachel two seconds in her presence and they would know, they would just *know*. Hot lips Sheila needed a lesson in subtlety, and she needed it bad. So without giving it a second thought, I took off down the mall's main corridor, in search of a place to hide. But as luck would have it again, there were only small stores in this area, every inch in them open to the most casual glance. It looked like I was going to have to leg it all the way across the mall to the Bay, where there was more floor space to lose myself in.

Why, oh *why*, did Sheila have to show up when I was putting in time with the phone patrol? After I'd taken off on her Saturday night, she'd left me alone, probably because she'd seen me head back to Cam. When she caught sight of me today, she must have thought we could talk because he wasn't around. Well, we couldn't. We couldn't talk now, later, or ever. Sure, the kiss behind Confed had been a rush, but so what? I was drunk and obviously not thinking straight. You don't turn your life upside-down over something you do when you're sloshed *stupid*.

Frantically I ducked into the Bay and headed down a side aisle. To my left was the teen department—too obvious, the place I would be expected to hang out. And to my right was men's socks. No camouflage there. So I headed farther into the store, searching for a department that sold king-sized beds, washing machines or cement trucks—something big enough to hide behind—but all I could see were slippers and perfume. About to start up the escalator, I glanced back at the entrance and saw Sheila enter the store. Just as I'd thought, a desperate hungry look was plastered all over her face. Ditching the escalator, I dived into the department to my left, and began pushing through racks of women's lingerie. Camisoles, lace-edged bras and frilly satin panties—this was the last place to go if you were looking for decent cover.

Trying not to freak, I grabbed something from the nearest rack and headed for the change rooms. Fortunately a woman was just coming out of a cubicle, so I didn't have to call a clerk to unlock one. Quickly I stepped inside, closed the door and leaned against the back wall, shutting my eyes. Within seconds, footsteps rushed through the change rooms' entrance. My heart stopped then, I mean *absolutely*. No question, I was on the verge of an utter freak. What if Sheila glanced through the open space under the cubicle door and recognized my runners? Would it be smart to take them off? But what if she noticed me doing that? For sure it would look suspicious.

A new thought hit me, along with a fresh wave of panic. Horror of horrors—what if Sheila decided to get down on her hands and knees and look under each cubicle door to check who was inside? Should I put on the lingerie that I'd grabbed off the rack and stand with my back to the door? Would that be enough of a disguise?

Grabbing the lingerie from its hanger, I looked it over. Black and lacy, it was wired to push your boobs to your chin. The label on the back said "Spider Lingerie."

Make that Black Widow Lingerie, I thought. All things considered, with the way I was acting, it would be no disguise at all.

But maybe I wouldn't need one. Outside my cubicle, I could hear footsteps heading slowly toward the change rooms' entrance. Next to my door, Sheila paused and gave a loud sigh. Then she walked out into the store. Still I held my breath, waiting.

Count to a hundred, I told myself. *No, a thousand. A zillion.*

After several more minutes, I opened my cubicle door and peeked out. No sign of anyone with a desperate hungry look in the immediate vicinity. Tiptoeing to the change rooms' entrance,

I scanned the store but didn't see Sheila anywhere. If she was still around, perhaps I would be able to sneak past her without being spotted if I stuck to the outer wall.

The trick then would be finding Julie and Rachel and coming up with an explanation for my sudden disappearance. An atomic bladder? A teeny-tiny voice whispering "Bay Day" inside my head? But what if they'd noticed Sheila take off down the mall after me? Even worse—what if she'd stopped to ask Julie and Rachel where I'd gone?

Just thinking about the possibilities was sending me into another near-death experience. With a long slow breath, I got a grip and headed out into the store.

Chapter Thirteen

When I went to bed that night, I kept my hands above my waist and concentrated on thinking *rationally*. As far as I could tell, the afternoon's catastrophe at the mall could now be downgraded to a semi-catastrophe. After leaving the Bay, I had tracked down Julie and Rachel stuffing their faces in the food court. To my surprise, they hadn't noticed Sheila take off after me and completely bought my story that I'd had to suddenly disappear because I'd seen a girl who'd bullied me last year in my ice-skating classes. When I'd said I would rather not bump into her again, Rachel had driven me home. That seemed to have solved any possible problems with Julie and Rachel and just left hot lips Sheila. And since she didn't know my name, there wasn't any way she could contact me. Except hang out at malls, of course, and the library, *and* the movie theaters and cafés. Which meant I was going to have to keep my eyes peeled, as well as come up with a few tactics for our next encounter—I mean, something better than absolutely losing my mind.

I couldn't get over how stupid I'd been. Why had I gone and kissed someone who was such an obvious problem—always alone like that and with massive emotional problems? I mean, most lesbians had friends they hung out with—other lesbians and straight kids—but Sheila was a reject. Why hadn't I seen it on time?

Because, I realized, turning over with a groan, *I was drunk. And also*, I added, after a reluctant pause, *because she shot me full of sparks.* Which, unfortunately, continued to be true. Even after what had happened today at the mall, I still felt it when I thought about Sheila—a sparkly hum deep inside. Well, I was just going to have to ditch that sparkly hum. I couldn't go around getting a lust on for someone with so many emotional problems. It wasn't...well, it just wasn't *convenient.*

With a sigh, I stared at the dark shadowy mound my body made under the blankets. There it was, the source of all my trouble. Softly, very softly, I muttered, "Hello, groin. You are a very confusing part of my body. If only you were more like my brain—y'know, reasonable, civilized. If only you wanted what the rest of me wanted, so the bottom half of my body was in sync with the top. Then everything wouldn't be so fucked up. It's your fault, y'know. It's all your fault."

Rolling over, I stared at nothing for what felt like hours until I finally fell asleep.

Tuesday morning I woke, still stuck in a funk, my homework not done, school two hours away and Keelie crouched over me whispering, "Good morning, Dylan. Mommy says we're late and you have to get up quick." For the first time in my life, instead of pulling her down for a hug, I almost pushed her away. But I managed to get a grip and fake enough big-sister-happy to convince her. Satisfied, she scampered out the door, and I headed downstairs for breakfast, where I piled about half a cup of sugar onto my oatmeal to get myself going.

Unfortunately, my sugar fix didn't last long. As I biked over to

Joc's, the streets felt as if they were all uphill. The weather had
once again turned colder, the trees had lost most of their leaves,
and the sky looked like a dull gray headache. Steering my bike
onto Joc's street, I wondered how her weekend had gone. She'd
been out of town, visiting relatives, and still hadn't gotten back
when I'd called last night. With everything that had happened
since Friday, it felt like I hadn't seen her for weeks.

Coasting into the curb in front of her house, I looked up to see
the front door open and Joc come bursting out, a grin all over
her face. The minute I saw her my tiredness vanished, and then
suddenly, without warning, all the feelings that I'd experienced
during the kiss with Sheila rushed over me again, just *screaming*
with sweetness. I mean, it was agony. Here I'd been hoping the
feelings I'd had for Joc would be gone now I'd kissed another
girl—that they would have somehow transferred themselves to
Sheila. Which meant, of course, that I wouldn't have to deal
with them anymore, since I was absolutely never going to speak
to her again. But instead, the feelings that I'd experienced with
Sheila seemed to have transferred themselves to Joc, and the rush
that came with them was so strong, all I could do was duck my
head and swear nonstop under my breath while she swung onto
the seat behind me.

"Holla bolla, moron," she said, bumping her forehead against
my back.

"Get thee to a nunnery," I mumbled, trying to ignore the
warmth of her arms tightening around my waist.

"Thanks a lot," she said as I pushed away from the curb. "I
spent practically the entire weekend in one. I haven't even talked
to Dikker since Friday. Hey, did you get your display done?"

For a second I drew a complete blank. So much had happened
since I'd put up the display Saturday morning that I'd completely
forgotten about it.

"Oh yeah!" I said. "I met Ms. Fowler at the library on Saturday morning, and I finished it then. C'mon, I'll show you."

Putting on a burst of speed, I zoomed over the Dundurn Street bridge. When we got to the Dief, I locked my bike, and we headed indoors to check out the display. As I wove through the crowded halls, I was pumped, everything going by in a blur. With a grin, Joc swung open the library door, and we practically ran toward the check-out desk. There it was—my display in all its construction-paper glory: *Absolutely Normal Chaos* for the girl's brain, *Color of Absence* for her throat, *The Egyptian Boo*—

My jaw dropped and I stood openmouthed, gaping at the display case. *Foxfire*—it was gone. The flaming orange, open-book shape that I'd stapled so carefully into position Saturday morning was now missing. In its place were three closed-book silhouettes, their titles written in precise block letters: *To Kill a Mockingbird*, *Stranger in a Strange Land* and *The Farthest Shore*. The handwriting was Ms. Fowler's; I recognized it immediately. Glancing at the boy silhouette, I saw *The Once and Future King* had been replaced with *A Separate Peace*. T. H. Whyte's book had been moved to the boy's mouth, and *The Joy of Sex* was nowhere to be seen.

"Hey," said Joc, her voice bewildered as she scanned the display. "Where's *The Joy of Sex?* I thought—"

"You thought right," I said grimly. Turning from the display case, I headed for Ms. Fowler's office. As expected, I found her doing paperwork at her desk, her head framed by the large globe on the counter behind her.

"Ms. Fowler," I croaked, coming to a halt in the doorway.

She looked up. "Dylan," she said, her eyes flitting across my face. She looked pale, dark shadows smudging the underside of her eyes.

"The display," I said, still croaking, half in shock. "Two books are gone, and one was moved. I—"

"It was Mr. Brennan," she said, rising from her chair. "He saw it this morning and said they had to be changed."

Mr. Brennan was the Dief's principal.

"Why?" I blurted.

Ms. Fowler hesitated, as if sifting through possible explanations. "He felt they weren't appropriate," she said finally.

"Appropriate?" I repeated, staring at her. The word did not compute. What did *appropriate* have to do with the display I'd just poured an entire week into—my gut, my *soul*? Backing out of Ms. Fowler's office, I took off for the library exit.

"Hey, Dyl, where are you going?" called Joc, but I kept going. I mean, I was *pumped*. By the time I reached the front office, I was verging on nuclear. Walking past the secretaries' desks, I headed straight for Mr. Brennan's office. The door was ajar, and as I approached I could see him through the gap, seated at his desk and talking on the phone. Without hesitating, I raised both hands and thumped them against the door, pushing it wide open. Then I stepped into his office.

Mr. Brennan looked up, raised his eyebrows and said, "I'm going to have to call you back. There's a student here I need to talk to." Setting down the phone, he motioned to a chair. "Dylan, sit down," he said. "I was hoping to get a chance to talk to you."

I did not sit. Sitting was not within the range of possible options, since every joint in my body had fused solid with rage. Instead I stood and glared while Mr. Brennan watched me carefully, trying to suss me out.

"Why?" I croaked finally.

"Sit down and I'll tell you," he said quietly. For a moment I hesitated, then forced myself into the nearest chair. A look of decided relief crossed Mr. Brennan's face, and he cleared his throat.

"You're here because of the display," he said.

I continued to glare at him without speaking, and his expression of relief faded. With a slight frown, he cleared his throat a second time, slowly and delicately.

"First," he said, leaning toward me, "let me tell you, Dylan, that I think your idea is wonderful, and the display itself is well done. It's a great metaphor for the way our identities are composed of the ideas we assimilate. I agree with Ms. Fowler entirely on those points."

Blah blah blah, I thought, slouching in my chair. This man had just gutted my soul. Trying to buy me off with compliments wasn't going to work. Still, from the sounds of it, there had at least been a discussion before the damage was inflicted. And Ms. Fowler had tried to defend me against this...this *mutilation*. Gripping the arms of my chair, I continued to glare at Mr. Brennan, who was admittedly a fairly decent guy, even if inclined to verbiage.

Shifting uncomfortably, he cleared his throat again. "The problem, Dylan," he said carefully, "is that we are a public institution. A public institution that serves fourteen- to eighteen-year-olds *and* their parents. This is a very diverse constituency, with a wide range of backgrounds. Whatever goes on display in this school has to take all of this into consideration."

"We studied *Foxfire* in class," I blurted.

"Yes, you did," he nodded. "With Mr. Cronk, in a *senior* English class. I had no problem with that title appearing in your display. It was the position in which you placed it."

"Why?" I spluttered. I mean, I was well past nuclear now. All across my brain, protons and neutrons were starting to fuse.

"It simply isn't appropriate for a display in a public high school," said Mr. Brennan. "For an art class assignment, yes.

For an English essay, fine. But not in the library, where every student is going to see it."

"But I was doing the human body," I protested. "Why is it okay to have a book title for an arm or a leg, but not…"

I faltered, and Mr. Brennan's gaze wavered slightly.

"Well, for the groin?" I managed finally.

"Not *Foxfire*," Mr. Brennan said grimly. "And not *The Once and Future King*."

"Have you read them?" I demanded.

"Yes, I have," he said. "They're both fine books. In fact, T. H. Whyte's book was one of my favorites when I was a kid."

"That was my boyfriend's idea," I said hotly. "The title *and* the position. He suggested it because of Lancelot's miracle. And because Arthur is a king, but he's so humble. Cam said that's what a guy needs to be in that part of his body—humble, a servant-king."

Shaking, I got to my feet, then added, "But don't expect me to tell you why I picked *Foxfire*, Mr. Brennan. You know why? Because you haven't asked me why I put it there. You judged my display and took down the most important parts without bothering to *ask* me what they meant. I've been in this room for five minutes now, and you still haven't asked why I put them there."

With that, I stormed out of his office. As I passed through the doorway, my hand knocked against the door, and without thinking I grabbed and slammed it. The sound of the crash tore through me, doubling my anger. Putting my face to the window in Mr. Brennan's door, I yelled, "You can kiss off!"

Mr. Brennan sat frozen at his desk. As we stared at each other through the window, I was suddenly reminded of the time I'd seen Joc and Dikker kiss the library doors. While I wasn't wearing scarlet lipstick like Joc had been, "Flaming Peach" was enough to leave a statement. Puckering my lips, I planted a kiss on the glass.

"Kiss off!" I yelled again, the words reverberating through me. "Just kiss off!"

Then I turned and stormed past the staring secretaries. As the outer office door swung closed behind me, I came to a halt in the hall and stood staring back into the room. Anger was still pounding through me. I mean, it was *pounding*.

"Hey, Dylan," called a girl standing nearby. "What's going on?"

It was Britney Sauder, a member of the senior soccer team. She looked slightly bug-eyed. I guess it wasn't every day that Dylan Kowolski came storming out of the Dief front office, yelling, "Kiss off!" at the top of her lungs.

"Brennan," I spat in her direction. "He wrecked my library display."

Then I stomped off down the hall. Fortunately it was empty, homeroom period about to start and only a few kids racing to make the bell. As I reached the library it went off, and for a moment everything was reduced to that harsh mechanical scream, cutting through the halls, the library, my head, *everything*.

Entering the library, I stood, once again staring at the display case. There it was, my carefully mutilated soul. No, not mutilated. Ms. Fowler had done her best. Just looking at it, no one would guess anything had been altered.

A soft rustling sounded behind me, and I turned to see her coming out of her office.

"Okay," I said grimly, before she could speak. "Here's the deal. Mr. Brennan changed my display without asking what it meant. So it's not mine anymore. It's his."

"Part of it, Dylan," Ms. Fowler said quickly.

"The most important part," I said. "So here's what happens."

I had to take a deep breath before I could continue. I was still shaking and my voice was wobbly, but Ms. Fowler listened without interrupting or trying to calm me down.

"Either the whole thing comes down," I said, watching her flinch, "or we put a big black censor strip through both their groins."

Surprise darted across Ms. Fowler's face, followed by something that was almost pleasure. "Exactly," she murmured, her eyes darting to the display. "Yes, exactly. If you'll wait a minute, Dylan, I'll call your homeroom teacher and let him know you're here, so you don't get a late demerit. Mr. Leakos, isn't it?"

I nodded, and she hurried into her office. When she came out again, she was holding the key to the display case, some black construction paper, a staple gun and a pair of scissors.

"You do the honors," she said, holding out the paper and the scissors. Then she opened the display case, and I placed a sheaf of construction paper against the girl silhouette's groin. Folding it lengthwise, I placed it there again.

"That'll do it," I said, and Ms. Fowler handed me the staple gun. Quickly I stapled the censor strip over the girl's groin, then repeated the process for the boy's. Taking a simultaneous step back, Ms. Fowler and I stood in silence, staring at the black strips. I mean, we were in awe.

"Yes," Ms. Fowler murmured again. "Exactly. *Exactly.*"

"Thanks, Ms. Fowler," I said. "I think I'll be okay now. I mean, I think I can probably stop with the revenge fantasies."

A tiny smile snuck onto Ms. Fowler's lips and she asked, "Do you want to do the boy's mouth too?"

I looked at *The Once and Future King* in its new position, speaking for Cam. "No," I said quietly. "It belongs there just as much. Thanks again, Ms. Fowler. I really appreciate what you just did. I mean, I *really* appreciate it."

Blinking rapidly, she nodded, and I turned and headed through the empty halls to homeroom.

Chapter Fourteen

Within minutes I was called back to Mr. Brennan's office, and we hashed it out again. He was actually fairly decent about the whole thing, and I could tell he felt badly about my being upset, but he wouldn't apologize for changing my display before asking me what I'd meant by it, so I refused to apologize for blowing up at him. And when he asked why I'd placed *Foxfire* in the girl silhouette's groin, I wouldn't tell him. He owed me an apology first, it was that simple. I figured I deserved it.

Because I also refused to clean my smooch mark off his office door, Mr. Brennan gave me a lunch and after-school detention. School policy required that parents be informed of all student detentions, so I had a lot of explaining to do later that evening, after Keelie had been put to bed. Mom and Dad heard me out, then sat quietly, floating in their thoughts. My guess was that they were slightly dumbfounded. I mean, they weren't exactly strangers to my temper, but I'd never thrown it at a school principal before.

"Well," said Mom, glancing at Dad, who was sitting beside her at the kitchen table. "I don't know what to say, really. I can see Mr. Brennan's point, but I can also see yours."

"It was really that important to you?" asked Dad, watching me carefully.

I nodded. Even now, twelve hours later, a rush of anger hit me when I thought about it.

"He didn't ask first," I said. "He just assumed it was dirty and obscene."

"Maybe he was concerned *other* people might think it was obscene," Mom said hesitantly.

"No, *he* thought it was obscene," I said decidedly. I was sure of it. "Maybe he changed his mind later, but that's the conclusion he jumped to right off."

"I wonder why Ms. Fowler didn't warn you this could happen," Dad said slowly. "She must have known there could be problems with it."

"She did, Dad," I said, not wanting her to get into trouble. "She said something about wondering what Administration would think of it, but I didn't really clue in. Because she understood what I meant by the display, I figured everyone would."

My parents sat quietly, still not sure what to make of it. And as I sat there watching them, I got a sudden warm burst of wanting to connect, wanting them to really *get* it.

"It's like everyone thinks that what goes on between a teenager's legs is dirty," I said, letting the words out in a rush. "I mean, whether you're having sex with someone or not. That part of your body is automatically indecent *because* you're a teenager, and everyone just assumes teenagers are wild and on the edge of losing control at every moment. You're never allowed to just *live* in that part of your body. It's a forbidden zone, a place you're never supposed to think about, and adults are always lecturing you about saving sex for marriage, or STDs and how they can shrivel your brain to a peanut. And the whole time you know half of *them* were having unsafe sex in the back of a car when *they* were teenagers. Anyway, why does that part of your body have to be treated like a wild animal that should be caged and controlled? Why can't it be about decency and honor and what's true and good?

"*And* wise," I added defiantly, crossing my arms over my chest. With a deep breath, I made myself look straight at Mom, then Dad. There, I'd said it. They would probably jump on me for it, but not too bad. They were pretty decent as far as the parent thing went. There would be some sighs, stern looks and mild finger-waving, and then a hug to round things off.

To my surprise, I saw tears in their eyes. They glanced at each other, and then Dad leaned toward me.

"Dylan, honey," he said quietly. "If there's anywhere in your body that I want you to feel truly wonderful about yourself and your whole life, it's in your groin. That's as important now, when you're young and still living with your family, as later on, when you'll be married and raising children of your own. The groin is a central part of life and love—we all come from there, don't we? And I can't tell you how important it has been to me to be loved by your mother."

He hesitated, then grinned sheepishly. "Well, I also had a few girlfriends before her," he added, glancing at Mom, who smiled wryly. "They were all important to me, and each one of them taught me something different. When you love someone, *truly* love them and are loved back, you learn so much about yourself, and life and what it's really all about. Your sexuality is a core part of that, whether you're sexually active or not. And you're right, you should feel completely free to live in that part of your body—you think and feel and *are* in your groin, just as much as in your heart and mind."

Stunned by his honesty, I just stared at him. Then I blurted, "So d'you think I was wrong? To get angry, I mean?"

Glancing again at Mom, Dad took a long thinking breath. "Anger isn't wrong, Dylan," he said. "It's an important warning signal that tells you when you're being crowded or invaded in some way. What you have to figure out is how to handle your anger, what's the best way to communicate it."

One of my power blushes kicked in and I ducked my head. "I guess I didn't really do that," I said, staring at my hands.

"Oh, you communicated," Dad said wryly.

"I was just so *mad*," I said, glancing at him, then away. "I still am."

Dad leaned across the table and took my hand, making me look at him. "I think you had a right to be," he said. "The display could've been covered until Mr. Brennan had a chance to talk to you. I'm sure he's thought of that since. He's probably learned as much from this as you have."

When he'd finished speaking, Dad continued to hold my hand, not letting go, making me feel his warmth and how much he loved me. I gripped his hand tightly and he squeezed back. Suddenly I wanted to bawl my head off.

"A picture," said Mom, her voice wavering as she wiped her eyes. "We have to get one of your display for our photo album."

"I'll take one for you," I said, freeing my hand from Dad's and rubbing my own eyes. "I'll bring the camera to school tomorrow and take a bunch before homeroom."

"No, I want to see it for myself," Dad said firmly. "I'll drive you to school and take a few pictures with you standing in front of the display. I can call into work and let them know I'll be late. I'll just go check the batteries in the camera."

Jumping to his feet, he hurried off to check, while I sat at the table thinking about what we'd discussed. Neither Dad or Mom had said straight out that I'd done the right thing, but they hadn't criticized me either. It left me feeling in limbo, sort of, but then I realized they were letting me work it out for myself. They were trusting me with it.

Taking a shaky breath, I smiled at Mom. She smiled back.

"Yup," said Dad, bustling into the kitchen with the camera. "The batteries are fine and the memory card is only half full. Should be able to get in quite a few pictures."

"Hey, can I be in one?" asked Danny, following him into the room. Right away I knew my brother had been listening in at an air vent in the upstairs hallway that was handy for eavesdropping on kitchen conversations. I raised an eyebrow, and he gave me a quick grin.

"Everyone's talking about it, y'know," he said. "The library's been crowded with kids looking at your display. I know some guys who'd absolutely love to get into a picture with those censor strips."

We all just split. I mean, after the tearful melodrama we'd been through, we needed it.

"Oh god," I spluttered. "Major Kodak moment."

And I was right. Danny must have gotten the word out later that evening on the phone because the next morning it looked as if half the school had shown up for the photo shoot. Dad was kept busy shooting pictures of Danny and his friends and the censor strips, Cam and his friends and the censor strips and Joc and Dikker and the censor strips. Then, of course, there had to be shots of the watching audience of kids and the censor strips. And finally, a few of Ms. Fowler and me, grinning our fool heads off as we stood under the now thoroughly photographed silhouettes and their infamous strips of black.

As Dad lowered his camera, the warning bell rang and the library began to clear. Joc, Cam and Danny waved goodbye and left for homeroom, and Dad and I also headed out of the library. But to my surprise, when we reached the hall he turned left instead of right, the direction of the parking lot.

"No, Dad, it's that way," I said, pointing.

He shook his head. "Pit stop on the way," he said, starting down the hall.

Immediately my radar went up. So *that* was why he was on the phone so long before we left the house. I'd assumed he was calling the city transit office where he worked.

"You're going to talk to Mr. Brennan," I accused, running after him. So much for my parents letting me work this out on my own.

With a smile, Dad put an arm around me. "Yes, I am," he said. "I'm your father, and I have some concerns about how this was handled. But I give you my word—I'll fill you in on everything we discuss, okay?"

A wave of relief hit me. So, my father really did think I had a right to be angry. I wasn't a complete zero.

"Okay," I said, bumping my forehead against his chest.

His arm tightened briefly. "Go on now," he said. "Or you'll be late for homeroom."

When I reached the end of the hall, I turned to see him standing in the same position, watching me. A grin crossed both our faces, and we raised a hand simultaneously to wave at each other. Then a rocket-launch burst of energy hit me and I took off through the empty halls, racing to beat the final bell.

Just as Danny had said, everyone was talking. For the rest of the day I couldn't go anywhere without getting comments—in the halls, my classes, or catching a smoke with Joc at midmorning break. I hadn't realized yesterday what a stir the censor strips were causing because I'd spent so much time in detention, but today I was a free woman and everyone I met seemed to

have something to say. The guesses kids made about the censored titles were mind-boggling: *The Titanic. The Encyclopedia
Britannica. The Edible Woman. Freddy the Pig Goes to Mars. On
the Brighter Side, I am Now the Girlfriend of a Sex God. Hamlet.*
(I bumped into Dikker again between classes.) And, of course,
everyone wanted to know what the actual offending titles had
been, even Cam's buddies. Well, especially Cam's buddies.
When I sat down with the senior jock crowd in the cafeteria at
lunch, the comments didn't let up.

"*Harry Potter and the Chamber of Secrets,*" suggested Julie,
and everyone snickered.

"*Temptation,*" said Deirdre. "Or how about *The Tycoon's
Virgin Bride?*"

"*The Tycoon's Virgin Bride?*" repeated Len. Letting his jaw
drop, he bugged his eyes at her. In two seconds flat, Deirdre
was severely rattled.

"Duh, let me guess," Len added smugly. "Harlequin,
right?"

"I read it last week," Deirdre said defensively, throwing a
french fry at him. "And stop looking at me like that. Some of
the scenes were pretty hot."

Len rolled his eyes, then opened his mouth, about to reply,
but was interrupted.

"*Superman,*" crowed Gary, stretching out his arms and pretending to fly. "You put my favorite book right over the guy's
dick, and Brennan saw it and got pissed."

As screeches of approval erupted from Julie and Rachel, a
girl at a nearby table turned to look at us. A flash of guilt hit
me as I saw that it was Michelle Allen, who obviously should
have been sitting at this table, laughing at Gary's comment
along with the rest of the jock crowd. But she wasn't; in fact
she hadn't sat with us for weeks—not since the first few days

after she'd made the senior girls volleyball team. It looked like Julie and Rachel had found a way to make it *very* clear that she wasn't welcome.

Completely oblivious, Cam pulled a sandwich out of his lunch bag. "She couldn't use *Superman*, Feeb Brain," he grinned at Gary. "It had to be a real book with real words. Y'know, more than POW, BAM, SLAM and exclamation marks."

"Superman Pooperman," agreed Len, turning his gaze on me. "It was probably *War and Peace*. Now that would really jerk Brennan's chain."

"Maybe," I shrugged, ducking a direct reply. All morning I'd been answering kids' questions the same way—with a shrug and a grin. Let everyone think what they wanted. The only people who knew the actual titles were Mr. Brennan, Ms. Fowler, my parents, Danny and Cam, and obviously they hadn't let anyone else in on the secret. Even Joc didn't know what I'd placed into the girl silhouette's groin, because she'd left my house last Friday before I'd finished writing all my titles onto their construction-paper outlines.

"*Treasure Island*," persisted Len, between guzzles of Pepsi. "And *Sweet Valley High*. C'mon, Dylan—admit it. You used my suggestions, and Brennan pulled them."

About to manufacture another shrug, I was saved by Joc. "Hey, Dyl," she called from the end of the table where she was standing with Dikker, and I waved them in to sit in the open space across from me.

As they squeezed into place, Gary reached across Rachel and punched Dikker's shoulder. "What's the matter, Dik?" he smirked. "Too cold in your car?"

Dikker gave him a slow grin. Most of his reputation came from his nickname, and the rest lay in that grin. I mean, no one could have survived the number of lays he was rumored to have pulled off. At least not *and* eat, sleep and get in a few favorite TV shows.

"Hillo, ho, ho," he said mysteriously. "We are arrant knaves all, believe none of us."

"Oh, shut up about Hamlet," moaned Joc, giving him a shove. "And yes, Gary, for your information, the car's heating system is broken."

"What's the matter?" drawled Len. "Can't you make your own heat?"

Joc shrugged. "I'm sensitive," she said, rubbing her cheek against Dikker's shoulder.

Gary snorted loudly. "That's not what I hear," he said.

A raucous guffaw swept the entire group. "Hey, just a sec," I said, seeing Joc stiffen, but she was way ahead of me.

"Just because I'm getting it more regular than you are," she snapped, looking Gary right in the eye. "*And* in better company."

Gary straightened, about to shoot something back, but then Cam broke in with an uneasy, "Okay guys, knock it off." After a few more snorts and giggles, everyone calmed down. In the ensuing quiet, I glanced sideways at Cam, studying his face. I mean, the question was there in my mind—whether he'd intervened because Gary had been picking on Joc, or because I happened to be sitting right next to him and he'd realized that I'd seen him laughing with the others.

But then I ditched the thought. Everyone laughed without thinking sometimes, and he'd stood up for Joc as soon as he'd seen that she was uncomfortable. Anyway, it was more than Dikker had done. Right now he was digging into a hamburger and fries as if nothing had happened, and Joc was sitting there watching him, a kind of sadness floating across her face. Then abruptly she switched gears and started hogging his fries.

Soon they were feeding each other and putting on their usual show. As the rest of the group watched appreciatively, Len turned to me, his eyes honing in.

"So c'mon, Dyl," he said. "Give us the scoop. What did you put under those censor strips that made Brennan take such a major flip?"

Everyone's eyes zeroed in on me. And right away I saw they weren't joking around; this time they expected an answer. These guys weren't like the rest of the school—an air of mystery wouldn't keep them at bay forever. Deep in my gut a dull thud started up, and my hands went prickly with sweat. At the same time I felt Cam stiffen as he went into diplomatic gear, simultaneously trying to figure out why I wasn't just answering straight out, and how to ward off Len's question without being obvious.

Taking a quick breath, I said, "Whatever you want it to be. I mean, that's the point, isn't it? Everything gets censored, even *Huckleberry Finn*. So give it whatever title you want."

"Uh-uh," said Len, leaning forward intently. "We've already told you what *we* thought. Now we want to know what *you* put up there."

FOXFIRE, FOXFIRE. The title screamed itself, huge and hypersonic, across my brain, and without warning I was once again behind Confederation Collegiate in my mind, Sheila pressed tight against me, her lips on mine. Instantly I was hit by a wave of blowtorch heat and my gaze wavered, flicking away from Len's. But not before I saw his eyes narrow, as if catching sight of something unexpected.

Forcing my gaze back to his, I said, "That's censorship for you. You'll never know what I put up there, because Brennan censored it."

A moment of stunned silence followed as the group just stared at me.

"I guess," Len said reluctantly, and the others looked at each other and shrugged. As they finally let go of it, I heard Cam let out a small sigh, and the thud in my gut eased a little. But then I glanced across the table and saw Joc watching me, her eyes narrowed and speculative like Len's. Had she figured it out? I thought quickly. She'd worked on the boy's silhouette, not the girl's, but she might have seen *Foxfire* in the girl's master plan.

Our eyes locked, and in that second I could have sworn I saw disappointment on her face. Then, with a shrug, she turned to Dikker, picked up one of his french fries and began feeding it to him.

"Something," said Dikker, chewing agreeably, "is rotten in the state of Denmark."

No one noticed me freeze, and the conversation shifted to other things while I sat, momentarily forgotten. Face in neutral, I swallowed repeatedly, forcing down a heated ugliness that was creeping up my throat. Why, oh why, hadn't I just said *Foxfire* the first time Len asked? I mean, it wouldn't have been a big deal, not with Cam sitting next to me. If I'd been willing to include the title in the display last Saturday, why was I backing away from it now?

But that had been before the dance at Confed, the kiss with Sheila, and the nuclear fantasies that had taken over my life since. The word *Foxfire* now had a thousand times more meaning than it had had last Saturday morning. I mean, it was *loaded*. There was no way I could have said it without a radioactive glow taking over my face.

So instead of just telling the truth, I'd choked. And the worst part of it, I realized grimly as I mulled it over, was that I was actually relieved Mr. Brennan had done what he'd done. As long as Cam and Danny kept quiet about the censored titles, no one else would ever find out what they'd been. I was more than sure Cam would never tell, and I knew Danny would promise not to if I asked. And so the problem, once again, appeared to be solved.

Unless Joc figured it out and talked, I thought, glancing at her. But she wouldn't, I could trust her for that. Or could I?

At that moment Joc happened to glance from Dikker to me, and I saw it again in her eyes, definite this time—disappointment. Then her gaze flicked back to Dikker, but not before it had told me what I needed to know. She had figured out that *Foxfire* was one of the censored titles. Not only that, she'd read the novel, had probably already finished it the day I'd said justice was like sex in our English class. And I was pretty sure she'd read it in one sitting the way I had, her eyes racing from page to page while heat pounded softly, *softly,* through her entire body.

Sensing my gaze on her, she glanced at me again. Her eyes were a bit glazed, almost frightened, and I could just *feel* what she was thinking—the way her body was soft and full of heat. I'd never seen her like this with Dikker, not once, and then suddenly, as we stared at each other across the table, a flash of electricity passed between us—shimmering, dancing, singing. Joc's lips parted, as if in astonishment, and a flush swept her face. Getting to her feet, she grabbed Dikker by the arm.

"C'mon," she said. "I'm tired of this place. Let's go have a smoke."

"Hillo, ho, ho, my lord," Dikker said cheerfully. Without a backward glance, they headed out of the cafeteria, Joc clinging tightly to his right arm.

Chapter Fifteen

After school, Joc headed off somewhere with Dikker. Since I didn't have to double-ride her home, I decided to spend some time watching Cam's football practice. As luck would have it, that afternoon's senior girls' volleyball practice had been canceled because the coach, Ms. Harada, was ill, and some of the girls were also hanging around the field, watching the football teams run laps and drills. Sitting down beside them, I watched guy after guy run full tilt into a row of sandbags that had been positioned at the far end of the field. Even without the number 19 on his jersey, it would have been easy to pick Cam out of the group. Like everything else in his life, he went after those sandbags in hyperdrive. I swear he actually lifted off the ground and flew toward his target, and his third slam into a sandbag had me cringing. I mean, it looked as if he'd splintered every bone in his neck, but Coach Gonie immediately hollered, "Atta boy, Zeleny! Way to kill, way to kill!"

Pumping his fist in the air, Cam trotted to the back of the line, but as soon as the coach had focused on someone else, he started rubbing his neck. Like I'd thought, he was going at it too hard.

Something was bugging him—*bad*—and a sick hook in my gut told me what it probably was.

"You're quiet," Rachel said abruptly, her eyes zeroing in on me. "Something wrong?"

Warnings ran softly up my back. I mean, it wasn't like Rachel to express concern for anything except her makeup.

"I dunno," I said quickly. "Cam's going at it too hard. He's going to hurt his neck."

"He's always like that," Julie said dismissively. "Nuclear missile." She smiled. "Not like Len, the big oaf."

"Maybe," I said. "But he doesn't usually rub his neck after."

"Coach likes it," Deirdre shrugged. "If Cam keeps it up, he might get bumped up to offence."

"Maybe," I said again, keeping my eyes on the field.

"He's just got too much energy," Rachel said with a grin. "Not like Len. We know where he's putting it, don't we, Julie?"

Julie gave her an answering grin. "You bet," she said. "That man is like, nonstop."

Heat rose in my face as if I'd been slapped. There it was again—the *knowing*. Every chance they got, the phone patrol had to rub the fact that Cam and I weren't having sex in my face. A couple of weeks ago, Julie and Len had started going out. Who knew how far they'd gone in the backseat of his car—my guess was Julie was more talk than action. But suddenly it got to me, the way they thought about Cam and me, and dating, and the whole girl-guy thing—as if it was all just about sex. All the time Cam and I had spent talking, the books we'd told each other about, the way he practically showed me his *soul* sometimes—as far as the phone patrol was concerned, it was all just a game Cam and I were playing in order to get laid.

"Yeah, well," I snapped, so goddamn mad I didn't stop to think. "I guess I'd wait longer than two weeks before I let Len

Schroeder put his dick-that's-been-everywhere between my legs."

The words were a grenade going off, absolutely blowing everyone's minds. Mouths open, the phone patrol turned en masse to stare at me.

"What…did you say?" Julie faltered.

"Nothing," I muttered, realizing how unbelievably stupid I'd been. "I didn't mean anything by it. Just forget it, okay?"

"Forget it?" said Julie, her eyes narrowing. "Just because you're so above us, Dylan—too goody-goody to get it on with Cam. What's the matter with you? Waiting for Prince Will?"

Above us. Prince. There it was again, the queen bullshit. I *wasn't* a queen. Taking a deep breath, I made myself keep a grip.

"Hey," shrugged Deirdre, turning to Julie. "You never know. Maybe she's just scared of getting preggers."

"She wasn't scared when she was doing it with Paul Bohner, was she?" spat Julie, her eyes bright and hard, the hurt mixed in with the venom.

"Look," I said, forcing myself to hold her gaze. "I'm sorry I said that. It's none of my business and I didn't mean it. Dumb thing to say. *Really* dumb."

"Yeah," said Julie, but her gaze didn't soften. For a moment the entire group sat silently, eyes fixed on the field as we waited for the tension to subside. Then Deirdre carefully cleared her throat.

"So why…are you waiting so long with Cam, Dylan?" she asked, slanting me a glance.

Instantly a cold eagerness leapt onto everyone's faces. And even though I knew the question was there, hiding out in their minds, I was surprised at the look of it when it hit the surface—the bare hard meanness of it.

A soft panic settled onto me, fluttery and delicate. "It's private," I said, my eyes slipping from theirs.

"I bet it is," Julie said coolly.

The panic got more fluttery, more delicate. "Why does it matter?" I asked hoarsely, staring across the field. "I mean, why is it important?"

As if on cue, Cam took another run at the sandbags, hurling himself headfirst through the air. "WAY TO GO, ZELENY!" roared Coach Gonie as he lay stunned, then clambered slowly to his feet.

Sniggering softly, Rachel said, "Man, has that guy got energy to burn."

Without a word, I stood and headed for my bike.

When I got home, I found Dad and Keelie washing the family station wagon in the driveway, and remembered that it was my night to make a salad. Because both Mom and Dad worked, we all took turns cooking and washing up—even Danny, who'd complained at first, saying cooking was faggy. But Dad had just asked, "Is it faggy to eat?", and Danny had gotten the message. In fact he'd gotten it so well that he was getting quite handy at making meat loaf...and more meat loaf...and *more* meat loaf. But tonight Dad was the main chef and I was on salad and clean-up, so we were meat loaf-free. After giving Keelie a hug, I stashed my bike in the garage, went inside and got to work. As the smell of Dad's tuna casserole filled the kitchen, I washed and diced vegetables, my thoughts keeping time with the rhythm of the knife: *Idiot. Moron. Very* very *dead meat. Hail, Basti, who comest forth from wisdom and the gods and all that stuff, I do not have what you would call a basic functioning brain.*

I wasn't kidding myself. I knew the look of girls who had *their* brains in high gear. As soon as they got home, the phone patrol would go into action, and tomorrow the story would be all over the Dief: *Dylan Kowolski is keeping her legs crossed and locked, even though she knows it's killing her boyfriend. And she had the nerve to criticize Julie Crozier for just wanting to show* her *sweetie some love. There's something odd about Dylan, don't you think? She's unnatural, tight-assed. What d'you think, could she possibly—*

Caught up in my thoughts, I wasn't watching carefully enough and cut into the tip of my finger. As I howled in pain, Dad whirled around with the hose and stared at the kitchen window. Quickly I leaned into the glass and waved to let him know that I was all right. Then I ran cold water over my finger and examined it. Not bad, just a surface cut. Fetching a band-aid from the bathroom, I got back to work. Through the window I could see Keelie stalking importantly around the car, pointing out imaginary flecks of dirt while Dad followed with a lopsided grin, dutifully washing them off.

Just for a sec, I stood and watched him. It hadn't taken me long growing up to clue into the fact that my father was unusual. He had a quiet place inside him that most dads didn't have, a watching place like Ms. Fowler's, but stronger, more connected to the people around him. Ms. Fowler watched everyone like a shy quiet bird, an angel for your mind. But Dad was right there with you in the thick of things, a close warm presence you knew would listen until he understood. He wasn't good-looking—even though he was big-boned, he still managed to look nerdish when he put on his glasses. Still, I knew Mom, who was drop-dead gorgeous, thought she was damn lucky to have gotten him. Right now I could see her idling her car at the end of the drive, a huge smile on her face as she watched Keelie sternly lecture Dad about a speck of non-existent mud on the headlights.

When Dad spotted her, he turned the hose on her car, and Mom rolled up her window and sat waiting him out. Racing toward the soaked car, Keelie ran around it shrieking wildly until Dad finally laid off. Then Mom got out and gave Keelie a hug.

As they walked hand-in-hand toward Dad, I leaned into the window to keep them all in sight. There they were, the typical Canadian family—Mr. and Ms. Heterosexual, and their rambunctious squealing offspring. How many couples like them were coming home from work at this very minute, parking their cars and giving each other an after-work kiss?

As I watched, Dad picked up his sponge and went back to work, soaping the car. Without warning an arc of water hit him in the butt, and I realized that Mom had picked up the hose and turned it on him. Dad whirled around, earning himself a full-frontal soaker, then charged Mom and wrestled the hose from her. A moment later she was also drenched, her office clothes plastered, her blouse completely transparent. The effect on Dad was immediate. The hose dropped to the ground, his arms went around her, and my parents started making out in the driveway like two teenagers in a wet bathing-suit contest.

Okay, I thought, watching until they broke off. So maybe they weren't *exactly* your typical Ms. and Mr. Canada. But they were definitely not a scene out of *Foxfire* either. *Foxfire* was a great book, but that was all it was—a story—whereas the scene in front of me was real life, where I belonged. If I worked hard at it and kept my stupid queen mouth shut, that scene in the driveway could be me and Cam in ten years.

Picking up the knife, I got back to work. No matter how much it bugged me, I thought grimly as I chopped away, those censor strips were just going to have to remain in place over the library display *and* my mouth. No matter how much other kids got on my case, wanting to know what the original titles had been, from this point on my best course of action was silence and a mystery smile. Yeah, that was it, I thought, my head coming up—a silent mysterious grin. Before going to bed, I would put in some time with my dresser mirror and figure out the exact angle of mystery to put into my smiling lips when refusing to answer a question about the censored titles.

I would also have to work harder at holding the gaze of other kids, so my eyes didn't flick away the way they had with Len's. Looking away was a dead giveaway. It meant you had something to hide, and what I had to impress upon everyone right now was that I was squeaky clean. I had no secrets, no skeletons in my closet. Yeah, look inside me and I was virtually empty.

Hail, Basti, who comest forth from nothing, even my heart was eaten.

After supper, Dad gave me a rundown on his discussion with Mr. Brennan while we stacked the dishwasher. Basically Brennan had agreed with Dad—he should have covered the display and talked to me before any changes were made. I was certainly welcome to return to his office and talk about it again if I wanted, he'd said, and he wasn't bothered by the censor strips. In fact, he'd told Dad that he thought they were an intelligent response, and he respected it. At the same time he was adamant that Ms. Fowler's substitute titles remain in place. Neither *Foxfire* or *The Once and Future King* could appear in the silhouettes' groins, and that was where he and Dad had left it.

It took me all of two seconds to shrug off Mr. Brennan's invitation to rehash things. Why bother, if it wouldn't change anything? Besides, the last thing I wanted to do right now was discuss my reasons for putting *Foxfire* into the girl silhouette's groin with anyone, much less my school principal. I was starting to wish I'd never heard of that crazy girls' gang. Why hadn't Mr. Cronk assigned us a normal, average, run-of-the-mill book to read like *Lord of the Flies*?

Grumpily I scrubbed off the burnt bits stuck to Dad's casserole dish and put it into the dishwasher. Then I started down the hall, intending to head upstairs to my room and get to work on some homework. But as I passed the living room doorway, I overheard Keelie say something that brought me to a dead halt.

"Who's that guy, Danny?" she asked, pointing at the TV. A weekly sitcom was on, one she normally wouldn't have been watching. By now she was usually in the tub, singing to her rubber duck—because of Dad and Mom's garden-hose frolic, things were a little behind schedule.

"Which guy?" asked Danny, so absorbed in the show that he was only half-listening. Or not listening at all. Because it was obvious which character Keelie was asking about—a gay architect who lived next door to the main character.

"*That* guy," said Keelie, pointing again at the screen.

"Oh," said Danny. "He's a faggot."

"A what?" asked Keelie, screwing up her nose.

"A fag, Keelie," said Danny, half-glancing at her. "That means he likes guys."

"Oh," said Keelie. A confused frown settled onto her face and she stared at the TV.

"C'mon, Danny," I said, stepping into the room. "You can't talk to her like that. How's she supposed to know what it means?"

Danny shrugged easily. "You explain it," he said, without glancing away from the screen.

For a second I hesitated, then sat down beside Keelie. She gave a little wriggle, working her way in against my arm, then looked up at me with an expectant wide-open expression on her face. Whatever I told her next was important, I realized. She was going to take it deep into herself and believe it completely.

Foxfire, I thought, looking down at her. *Will you ever read that book? Will it screw up your life as much as it's screwed up mine?*

"'Fag' isn't the right word, Keelie," I said, thinking my way slowly into what I wanted to say. "It's 'gay.' And what 'gay' means is…," I took a deep breath. "Well, it's what Danny said. It's when a guy falls in love with a guy, or a girl falls in love with a girl. The word for two guys who are in love with each other is 'gay,' and the word for two girls is…"

Pausing, I took another deep breath. "Well," I added reluctantly, "it's 'lesbian.'"

One of my power blushes kicked in, eating up my face, but Keelie didn't seem to notice.

"Lesbean?" she demanded, staring up at me. Beside her, Danny gave a muffled snort.

"Not lesbean," I said, trying to *think* down the temperature of my face. "LesbiAN."

"LesbiAN," Keelie echoed loudly. She repeated it just as loudly several times, then looked up at me again and said, "That's two girls?"

"Uh-huh," I said, feeling my face heat up a few more degrees.

"And they're like Mommy and Daddy?" she asked.

"Sort of," I said. "A mommy and a mommy, I guess."

Another confused frown appeared on Keelie's face. "But how can they make a baby without a penis and a vagina?" she asked, putting her hand on my arm.

A gurgling sound came from Danny and he shot me a grin. "That question is definitely yours," he said.

"Well," I said helplessly. I knew Mom and Dad had given Keelie the basic facts on baby production. Obviously they hadn't gotten around to cluing her in on the gay scene yet. "Gay and lesbian couples don't make babies," I said carefully. "They just live together and love each other."

Keelie's dark eyes bored into mine. "Do they sleep in the same bed?" she asked.

"Probably," I said.

She tapped her toes together thoughtfully. "But Mommy and Daddy loved each other to make me," she said slowly. "Daddy told me he put his penis into Mommy's vagina and his sperm found Mommy's egg, and then I growed into a baby and got born."

"Yeah," I said, "that's true. But lots of times Mommy and Daddy love each other without making a baby. They just love each other because they like doing it."

Danny gave a loud unhelpful snort and grinned at the TV.

"Like kissing and hugging?" asked Keelie, ignoring him.

"Yeah," I said quickly. Finally, a *G*-rated question.

"And putting his penis into her vagina?" Keelie added.

"Yeah," I said reluctantly. "Except it's different when there are two daddies or two mommies."

"They do something different?" asked Keelie.

"Yes," I sighed. I was going to have to figure out how to put the brakes on here. I mean, Keelie was taking us down the road to sheer and utter pornography at breakneck speed.

"WHAT?" she demanded loudly, getting to her knees and poking her face into mine. At the other end of the couch, Danny let loose with a howl of laughter. I wanted to slug him.

"Whatever...they want," I said finally. Reaching around Keelie, I gave Danny a shove.

"Ooooooooooooooooh," Keelie said thoughtfully. I could almost see the gears spinning in her brain. Hundreds of questions were forming there—eager, hungry, detail-specific questions.

"Mom," I shouted, getting up hastily from the couch. "Is Keelie's bathwater ready yet?"

"Send her up," called Mom. Quickly I lifted Keelie down from the couch, and she took off like a shot, hollering at the top of her lungs.

"Mommy, Mommy," she bellowed as she climbed the stairs.

"Dylan just told me about lesbiAN and gay. It means there's a mommy and a mommy, or a daddy and a daddy, and there's no penis and vagina, they do whatever they want."

"Oh," said Mom in a startled voice and I dropped back onto the couch, horrified at the mishmash Keelie had made of my explanation. Beside me there was a thud as Danny rolled off the couch and hit the floor, howling in glee. Grabbing a throw cushion, I began bashing him mercilessly about the head.

"No penis and vagina," he spluttered, clutching his stomach. "They do whatever they want." More howls claimed him. "Wait 'til Cam hears this one," he moaned.

Instantly my body went cold. "No," I said, leaning into his face. "Don't tell Cam, okay?"

"Okay," said Danny, going quiet. Rolling onto his back, he studied me curiously. "If you want. But what's the big deal? He'd get a real kick out of it. You should tell him, he'd—"

"No," I repeated firmly, getting to my feet. "Just don't tell him. And y'know those titles that used to be under the censor strips? You haven't told anyone what they were, have you?"

"No," said Danny. "It's your secret. Guys have been bugging me, but I kept mum."

"Thanks," I said, flashing him a relieved smile. "Just keep on keeping mum, okay?"

"Okay," he said, obviously bewildered.

My eyes slid from his and I started for the door. "Thanks again," I added lamely. "I really appreciate it, Danny."

With that, I headed to my room. The stairs to the second floor seemed longer than usual, and the air kind of heavy, in a way I hadn't noticed before. But I managed to shrug it off, and got to work on a history assignment that was due the next day. When I finished, I spent some time practicing my mystery smile in front of the dresser mirror. Then I crawled into bed, but though

I lay waiting for the phone to ring, Cam didn't call. This wasn't unusual. He didn't call every night, and if he didn't call me, I didn't always call him. There was a natural rhythm to it, sort of like breathing, something I'd taken for granted. Tonight, however, I lay in the dark, waiting out the silence and willing him to call. My whole mind formed itself into a hook, trying to snag him with my thoughts.

C'mon, Cam, I kept thinking. *Call me, man-of-my-life. Please, just call.*

Several times I reached for the phone, but my hand always stopped midair. About me the silence deepened, and the darkness grew more intense. Finally, with my hands above my waist and my pajama bottoms firmly tied, I fell asleep.

Chapter Sixteen

Just as I'd figured, the phone patrol had been active last night. I got a rundown on their basic chitchat from Joc when I picked her up the next morning.

"Caitlin van Doer called me last night," she said, hanging on tightly as I pushed off from the curb. "She said you said something about Len Schroeder's dick having been everywhere, and you'd wait longer than five minutes before letting him stick you with every STD known to the human race."

"Actually," I said, pedaling grimly down the street, "I said two weeks. And I didn't say anything about STDs. Lucky for me, Caitlin didn't think of leprosy and the mad cow virus too."

Joc gave me a sympathetic forehead thump on the back. "Don't take a hairy," she said. "The STDs were my extra little bit, just to perk you up."

"I'm feeling quite perky already, thanks," I said, turning onto the Dundurn Street bridge. "And would you mind terribly much keeping that extra little bit to yourself from now on? I'm in enough shit with Julie Crozier already, without your creative additions getting back to her. Why didn't you call me last night and tell me about this?"

"Because you would've started freaking out, just like you're freaking out now," Joc said reasonably. "And then you wouldn't have slept a wink and been a very grumpy owl all day today. Besides, Dikker called right after Caitlin hung up. We had things we needed to discuss."

Dikker had called Joc, but Cam hadn't called me. A sick feeling oozed through my gut.

"I am in such deep shit," I moaned. "I apologized twice to Julie, but she's never going to forgive me. Never ever *ever*. She likes holding grudges. It's like a badge of honor to her."

"So what?" said Joc. "You're such a worrywart, Dyl. Y'know what I told Caitlin when she told me what you'd said to Julie? I said, 'Three cheers for Dylan. It's about time someone put Len Creep-Meister in his place.'"

As usual, Joc wasn't *getting* it. "For your information," I said heavily, "Len Creep-Meister happens to be Cam's friend. So is Julie."

Gloomily I swerved my bike onto Diefenbaker Avenue and the Dief came into view, looming ominously at the end of the block. "Well, I suppose Julie and Len are my friends too," I added reluctantly. "Sort of, because I'm going out with Cam. Otherwise they wouldn't bother."

"Pack of werewolves," muttered Joc. "Vampires. Soul suckers."

"Yeah, well, my parents like them," I said, coasting up to the bike racks. "And anyway, since when is Dikker's rep any better than Len's?"

"That's just talk," snapped Joc, sliding off the seat. "At least *he* doesn't hang around with fucking pricks the way your boyfriend does."

With that she took off, leaving me standing openmouthed by my bike. *Fucking pricks?* I thought, watching her stalk into the surrounding crowd. Maybe a *little* overdone—as an in-depth character sketch, that is. But, as with most things Joc said when angry, it bordered on the truth.

The question that begged was, of course: *Then why does Cam hang around with them?* But I just brushed it off. Who else was he supposed to hang around with—the chess team?

Locking my bike, I joined the crowd streaming toward the Dief. *Head up*, I reminded myself firmly as I flashed a practice mystery smile at a nearby garbage pail. *Remember—it doesn't matter what the phone patrol is saying about you. What's important is how kids* see *you acting. So make sure you look them in the eye, but not challenging or mad, as if you've got something to hide. YOU'VE GOT NOTHING TO HIDE.*

Still, when I pulled open the school door and stepped inside, I couldn't help holding my breath. I don't know what I was expecting—a horde of vampires coming for my throat or a herd of wild-eyed boogeldy bears—but to my relief as I started down the hall, no one, absolutely NO ONE, paid me the slightest attention. Everywhere kids were yakking at each other or walking along quietly, carrying gym bags and school band instruments, and no one was giving me a second glance. Or even a snickering first one. Either the phone patrol hadn't reached that many kids last night, or most of the students at the Dief simply didn't care what I thought about Len Schroeder's dick.

"Hey Dylan, liked your library display," called a voice to my right, and I turned to see Ewen Busse, the Dief's yearbook editor, standing at his locker. "Can I get a picture of you with those censor strips for the yearbook?" he asked, focusing an imaginary camera on me.

"Sure," I said, giving him a Kodak smile. "Just tell me when."

"Lunch, 12:15?" he asked, and I nodded, then headed on down the hall, a grin ruling my face. Had I ever been wrong about things? Like Joc said, so what if Julie never forgave me? I'd said something stupid, but I'd apologized. Temporary stupidity wasn't a crime, there was no need to go on and on, banging my head against—

Turning into the hallway that led to my locker, I ducked a group of yakking second years and almost ran smack into Maria Gonzales and several of her friends. Maria was Rachel's younger sister, and their personalities had definitely crawled out of the same gene pool. Huddled together, she and her friends were snickering among themselves as they stood observing a piece of foolscap that had been taped to someone's locker.

No, not someone's locker, I realized, as cold dread oozed over me. *My locker.*

As if on cue, Maria glanced around and caught sight of me. With a smirk she elbowed her friends, and they whirled en masse to gawk at me. Then they all took off down the hall. Stunned, I watched them go, then turned slowly to face my locker.

This is it, I thought, as my knees melted down my legs. *The phone patrol has figured out my secret and decided to announce it to the entire world on the front of my locker. It's all over—Cam, Joc, life, the universe, everything.*

Cautiously I took a few wobbly steps forward, then stopped about five feet from my locker and studied the piece of foolscap taped to the front. Across the top someone had written "VIRGIN QUEEN" in large block letters, then drawn a nun underneath with a giant censor strip over her groin. Disbelieving, I stared at the crude sketch. There was that word again—*queen*, but why "virgin"? The phone patrol knew that category didn't apply to me. Was it possible they hadn't figured out the truth, and had decided that I was just being frigid and uptight?

As I stood stock still in the middle of the hall trying to make sense of things, kids kept streaming by. Snorts and comments floated back to me, and some guy patted my shoulder and said, "I can help you with that if you'd like, Dylan." Stuck in a funk, my eyes glued to the sketch, I didn't even bother turning to see who it was. Then, as I continued to stand, still frozen, a hand reached out from my left and started fumbling with the tape that held the sketch in place.

"That's okay," I said, snapping out of my funk and stepping forward. "I can handle it."

The hand jerked back. "Oh, sorry," said Andy Lambard, a guy whose locker stood two over from mine. "I didn't see you there, Dylan."

Andy was a minor niner, a shy skinny kid like Tracey Stillman. I'd seen him here at his locker almost every day this year, but so far I'd never spoken to him.

"I tried to take it down five minutes ago," he stammered awkwardly, his eyes lowered as he turned back to his locker. "But they made me put it up again."

"They?" I asked quickly.

Andy's eyes went vague. "Uh, y'know," he said. "Luke Pankratz and his friends. Those guys."

Luke Pankratz was Gary's younger brother. *So*, I thought grimly, *the entire junior jock crowd has been sicced on me.* The ooze feeling in my gut was definitely getting oozier. Slowly I pulled the sketch off my locker.

"Virgin Queen," I said shakily to Andy, making myself say the words out loud, feel them in my mouth. "What d'you think—is it me?"

Holding up the sketch, I tried to smile.

Andy's eyes slid from the sketch to my face, then dropped to his feet. "I'm still a virgin," he shrugged. "Most of the kids in this school are. If that's who they want to pick on, they've got lots of targets."

All of a sudden his skinny pimply face was the sanest, *wisest* thing I'd seen all week. "You are so right, Andy," I said, crumpling the sketch into a ball. "This is prime bullshit, isn't it?"

"Uh-huh," said Andy, a flush of pleasure riding his face.

"And you tried to take it down, even after Luke told you not to?" I asked. Patting his shoulder, I watched his flush go into overdrive. "Y'know what?" I added, almost kissing him. "You've got guts."

He shrugged again, trying to fake casual, but not enough to dislodge my hand from his shoulder. "Not bad for a Virgin King, eh?" he said shyly.

A shout of laughter came out of me. "Not bad, Andy," I said. "Not bad at all."

Grinning like fools, we high-fived each other, and then I ditched my jacket and the balled-up sketch into the bottom of my locker, grabbed my history books and headed for homeroom.

Fortunately Julie and Rachel weren't in either of my morning classes, and I didn't run into them in the halls. I did get a few smirks from some of Maria's friends as I was heading to history, but after my conversation with Andy, it didn't seem to matter. In fact, even seeing Gary Pankratz in algebra didn't phase me—at least, not much. As soon as I sat down, he leaned across the aisle, locked eyes with me and said, "Seen any virgin queens lately, Dylan?"

But I managed to keep a grip, shrug and say, "I dunno. I don't hang around with royalty."

A blank look crossed Gary's face and he just stared at me. Abruptly he swiveled around in his seat and started talking to the guy behind him. For a moment I continued to sit, staring at the back of his head, wondering if I'd missed something. Then a tiny grin crept onto my mouth as I realized that nothing was missing, I simply hadn't allowed something to happen. Andy Lambard, the Virgin King, was right—*this wasn't important.* If I could just leave it alone and not let the phone patrol provoke me into picking up my end of the fight, the whole thing would have to die out.

For the rest of algebra Gary strenuously ignored me, which was fine with me. When the lunch bell rang, I headed to the library to meet Ewen and pose for my yearbook picture with the censor strips. After he left, Ms. Fowler asked me to fill in at the check-out desk because her regular Thursday lunch-hour volunteer hadn't shown. So though I was getting anxious to see Cam, I settled in behind the desk. The library was the usual scene—kids yakking quietly across the work tables, the fluorescent lighting buzzing overhead. Some guys came by with books to sign out, and one of them started bugging me about the censor strips, but I flashed my well-practiced mystery smile and that kept him at bay.

After he left, however, I started working my way into one of my funks, thinking about Cam eating lunch in the cafeteria without me. Was he sitting beside Len? Or worse, was he trapped between Julie and Rachel while the entire group made jokes about virgin queens? Biting my lip, I considered. No, Cam wouldn't let them do that. He might moan about not having a sex life to Len and Gary, but he wouldn't let anyone else joke about it. He would defend me, I knew he would.

But what if he got tired of waiting for me? Or what if he started to get suspicious? I mean, he knew what had originally been under those censor strips. Miserably I glared at the display case with its two multicolored figures. *Damn those censor strips,* I thought. If I'd just had some common sense and put *Anne of Green Gables* into the girl silhouette's groin, none of this would have happened.

Turning toward the filing carts, I got to work, organizing them for reshelving. The library had hit the lull it often got into around 12:30—no one coming or going, everyone settled into research or a good book. On my knees beside a filing cart, I was alphabetizing the bottom shelf when I heard someone humming on the other side of the check-out desk. The tune sounded familiar, but I couldn't place it, so I got to my feet to ask what it was.

As my head surfaced above the counter, I saw Joc standing with her back to me. She had obviously come in while I was crouched down behind the desk and didn't know I was there. Dikker was nowhere to be seen, and she didn't seem to be doing anything in particular, just standing around and humming.

Abruptly I realized that she was doing something, she was studying the two silhouettes in the display case. At the same moment I recognized the song she was humming—"Fear of Bliss" by Alanis Morissette.

The second I realized these two things, the entire universe seemed to suck in its breath. Sweet heat hit me like a blowtorch and I could have been in bed, doing you-know-what—the sensations were hitting me that hard, I was that helpless, that *gone*.

Foxfire, was all I could think as I stared at the long gleaming fall of hair down Joc's back. *Foxfire, Foxfire, Foxfire.*

Footsteps sounded to my left, and I jerked myself out of my massive moment of lust to see Tracey Stillman walking up to the check-out desk with a book in her hand. Immediately I realized that she'd *seen*. In the second I'd turned toward her, her eyes had darted between Joc and me, and a kind of knowing had flashed across her face. Instant panic swept me and I was hit with images of myself machine-gunning Tracey Stillman to bits, throttling Tracey Stillman to bits and machete-chopping Tracey Stillman to bits. That, or taking up life permanently as a carpet fiber.

Fortunately I managed to get a grip.

"Hey, Tracey," I said, forcing a smile. "Look what you inspired—the October library display. I got the idea from that poetry book you showed me."

At the sound of my voice Joc stiffened, then turned slowly to face me. Our eyes met, and to my surprise I found myself looking directly into fear. It was a soft lonely kind of fear, something I'd never seen Joc feeling, and it was only there for a second before she shut it down. But in that second I realized fear was always with her the way it was always with me, and she was as good at hiding it as I was. Better even.

Again, Tracey's eyes flicked between us. "Yeah," she said, so quietly I could barely hear her. "I like what you did. Except..."

She hesitated.

"Except what?" I asked, keeping my eyes fixed carefully on her face.

"Except...well...," she mumbled, looking down, then glanced at me quickly. "Why won't you tell anyone what's under the censor strips?"

I could feel a major power blush coming on, but managed to keep my voice steady. "Because the titles I put up aren't there anymore," I said. "Brennan made Ms. Fowler take them down. The censor strips are covering the new titles she put up."

"Oh," said Tracey. She stood for a moment, studying her hands, then asked hesitantly, "Okay, so what *was* there, before Brennan made her change them?"

Without answering, I took the book she was holding and read the title—*Land to Light On*, another book of poetry by a woman named Dionne Brand.

"I haven't been telling anyone," I said slowly, "because that's the point of censorship, right? When something's censored, it's gone. You don't get a chance to know what it was. But since you inspired the display, I'll tell you. *If* you promise to keep it to yourself."

Tracey nodded, her eyes glimmering with interest.

"The book in the boy's groin was *The Once and Future King*," I said. "Ms. Fowler moved it to his mouth. And the book in the girl's groin was *Foxfire*."

For a second, after I'd said it, I just stood there in surprise. I mean, when I stopped fighting and simply let it, the title walked easily out of my mouth.

"Have you read it?" I asked Tracey.

She shook her head.

"It's a damn good book," I said, taking her ID card and signing out *Land to Light On*. "Read it sometime."

"Okay," said Tracey, a smile flickering across her face. For a moment she looked delicate, almost pretty. Then, as if this was too much for her, she flushed and ducked her head.

Andy Lambard, I thought. *This is a girl for the Virgin King.* But then I thought, *Hey, who knows? Maybe she needs a Virgin Queen.*

"Have yourself a truly superb day, Tracey," I said as she pushed through the turnstile and headed toward the exit.

"You too," she called over her shoulder, and then she was gone and there was no way to avoid it anymore—the gaze of my absolutely best, my *very* best friend.

Joc was still standing there, watching me silently, her purplish blue eyes flat on me. "So, where's Dikker?" I asked, trying to keep my voice light.

"*Hamlet* shit," Joc shrugged. "He's decided now he's going to spend his lunch hours helping to build sets."

Our eyes were doing an odd kind of dance—meeting, then flitting away, then meeting again. Flit flit flit—we could have been late-season mosquitoes.

"How come you're not helping him?" I asked, pulling a book off a filing cart, then putting it back again. As usual, I was in a funk. Everywhere I touched, I left a trail of sweaty guilty fingerprints.

Get a grip, I thought. *This is, like, your best friend since grade three.*

Joc shrugged again. "I don't *want* to build sets for Hamlet the Turd," she said. "What're you doing after school?"

Our eyes did another flit-flit.

"Nothing," I shrugged back.

"Come over," she said. "There's leftover pizza—ham and anchovies, your fave. We'll put on Morissette and get jagged. Unless…"

She hesitated, then added, "You have to meet Cam, of course."

"He's got practice," I said. "I don't."

"Yeah," grinned Joc. "That's what I figured. Dikker's got *Hamlet*, me NOT."

As I grinned back, the warning bell rang, practically sending us both leaping out of our skins.

"Oh god," I moaned, glancing at the clock. "Ms. Fowler isn't back, and I have to get to my locker before English."

"Wing it," said Joc. "We're still doing *Foxfire,* and you've got the whole book memorized, don't you?"

An electric vibe passed between us, so tangible I could almost touch it.

"Have you read it yet?" I asked, my eyes flitting past hers.

"Maybe," she grinned, then pushed through the turnstile, out the library door and into the crowded hall.

Chapter Seventeen

I made it from my locker to English in twelve seconds flat, just beating the bell, and dropped into my seat in time to hear Mr. Cronk inform the class that the next two days were to be spent working in preassigned discussion groups. I guess he figured Joc and I already spent enough class time together in discussion, because he placed us in different groups. So when we met up at the bike racks after school, we hadn't had a chance to talk since lunch. And of course, I'd spent the entire afternoon inside my head, trying to work out every possible angle on our short conversation in front of the library display case. Which meant that by the time I got to my bike, I was a supersonic bundle of nerves. I mean, I was in a dead sweat just trying to keep my heartbeat somewhere *near* normal.

"Hey," said Joc, coming up behind me.

"Hey," I replied, hoping the sudden heat wave sweeping my face was not as obvious as it obviously was.

Our eyes did some more of the flit-flit thing, and then I just started pushing my bike toward the street. At the curb there was an awkward moment as Joc got on behind me and I pushed off and started pedaling. Then she hooked a finger through one of my belt loops and started waving with her free hand, calling out to kids we were passing. As usual, I was doing the legwork, and she was being the social butterfly.

"Tim might be home," she hollered as I pedaled over the Dundurn Street bridge. "I hope he hasn't gulped all the pizza."

"If he has, we'll give him super-nuggies," I hollered back. Nuggies were a form of mild torture that Tim had taught us in grade three. According to his version you got someone down, then dug your knuckles into his arm and twisted until he hollered, "Spaghetti and barf on the barbecue!" It had to be exactly those words—nothing else would do. Tim figured it was a bigger concession than "Uncle."

"Agreed," said Joc as I swerved onto her street. Coasting up the driveway, I braked beside Tim's Chev and let her get off, then locked my bike to the porch rail. As I straightened, she was opening the front door, her eyes flitting delicately around my head.

"C'mon, Goofus," she said and went in. Following her through the doorway, I was hit with the usual combo of cigarette smoke and blaring TV. "Hey Rambo," called Joc, kicking off her shoes and heading into the living room. "Did you leave any pizza for us?"

"Pizza?" demanded Tim, sitting up as we entered. His hair was mashed oddly from lying on the couch, and he still looked oily and greasy from work. "Did I hear you say pizza?" he grinned.

"Yup," said Joc. "And I also said stereo. As in *loud*. As in we're sending messages to Mars."

"The Martians will be pleased," said Tim. "In fact, they're beaming an important message to you right now." Putting both hands to his head, he waggled his fingers and intoned dramatically, "This is the message: Your mother is at work until nine, and she wants, nay, *orders* you to eat ALL the pizza."

With a whoop, Joc ditched her jacket and headed into the kitchen while Tim hauled himself off the couch and turned off the TV. "What's your fix, Dylan?" he asked as I hung up my jacket. "What d'you want to hear?"

"Something jagged," hollered Joc through the kitchen doorway.

"Got any Alanis?" I shrugged at Tim.

"Morissette?" said Tim. Agreeably he flipped through the CD rack. "Let's see...*Jagged Little Pill, Supposed Former*—"

"*Feast on Scraps* is in my room," yelled Joc. "In my CD player."

"I'll get it," I called. Taking off down the hall, I angled a perfect slide through her doorway that ended several inches from her CD player. With a satisfied grin, I ejected *Feast on Scraps*, then took off in another perfectly executed slide that took me all the way down the hall. When I got back to the living room, Joc's and my eyes started doing the flit-flit thing again, so I just handed her the CD without saying anything. Quickly she slid it into the stereo and pushed play. Slow reverb heartbeats began filling the room, and then the first notes of "Fear of Bliss" came on, loud and pulsing.

"C'mon, let's get the pizza," said Joc. Following her into the kitchen, I watched as she took several sizzling slices out of the microwave. Then she opened the fridge and beckoned to me.

"What d'you think?" she asked, pointing to a twelve-pack of beer at the back.

A vision of my mother, frowning strenuously, loomed inside my head. *School night,* I heard her say sternly. *You've got to be home soon for supper.*

But all I said was, "Whose is it?"

"Tim, we want some of your beer," Joc yelled over her shoulder.

"You want it, you pay for it," Tim yelled back. "A looney a can. Fetch me one too."

With a triumphant grin, Joc pulled three cans out of the pack. Tim was usually pretty possessive with his beer, telling us he wasn't into corrupting minors and if he caught us stealing any, he would super-nuggie us into a state of absolute terror. That had been enough to convince us to keep our hands off, but today he was obviously in a different mood. Piling the beer and pizza onto two trays, Joc and I carried it into the living room. A second later we were parked on the couch, scarfing down pizza at an unbelievable rate.

"Yeah," said Joc, holding up her can of beer. "Pizza and beer. Perfect combo, don't you think?"

I didn't, actually, and was fighting off a burst of beer fizzies in my nose from swallowing too quickly. But again, I didn't say anything. To tell the truth, the whole scene had me on edge. Whenever you bring beer into a situation, kids start acting differently. For someone who's underage, beer is a symbol—of independence, defiance, pushing boundaries. And sometimes, it has to be said, of sheer stupidity. So, like I mentioned before, when drinking beer, slow and thoughtful was my rule. I usually faded back into the crowd and watched other kids drink more than I drank myself.

But this afternoon there was nowhere to fade to. And with all the questions I had revving around my head about Joc, and the way the music was pounding away, and with Tim sprawled oily and greasy on one side and Joc on the other, her leg brushing mine, it was no wonder half my beer was already gone. Tim had completely finished his, and Joc was right on his tail.

"C'mon, Dylan," said Tim, getting to his feet. "I'm itching for a dance partner." Grabbing my hand, he pulled me up from the couch.

"You too," I said, taking Joc's hand, and a second later the three of us were jigging around the room, riding Alanis' huge throb of sound.

"More!" yelled Joc, turning to the stereo and hitting the stop and play buttons. "I want more 'Fear of Bliss'!"

Once again the giant heartbeat came on, reverberating through the room. Right away Tim starting twisting like a maniac, jumping all over the beat, and then Joc kicked in, slower but with an all-body movement, as if her entire being was a single thought. Keeping my head down, I jigged along with them, but I was still feeling on edge. The three of us had done this before, jacked up the living room stereo when their mom wasn't home and danced until our clothes were plastered. But there hadn't been any beer then, and I'd spent the entire time completely and absolutely ignoring my feelings for Joc while I danced with Tim.

Today those feelings refused to be ignored. Heated and shifting, they were like part of the music. Even though I was facing Tim, my eyes kept turning toward Joc, watching the way she swung her hair as she moved, pulsing it to the beat. Several times already she'd brushed against me—maybe by accident, maybe not.

"I'm dying here," gasped Tim as a song ended. Sweat beaded his forehead and his T-shirt was plastered. "I'm going for some water," he added. "Catch you later."

With a wave he headed down the hall, leaving Joc and me standing in the middle of the room. For a moment I was almost afraid to move. There I was, finally, alone with Joc and practically vibrating out of my skin. I mean, the air around me felt *huge*, electric with possibility.

Before I could say anything, Joc ducked past me and pushed the stereo's stop and play buttons. Immediately the great reverb heartbeat from "Fear of Bliss" began filling the room. As Joc turned to face me, I could tell she was a bit tipsy, her cheeks flushed. Sweat had dampened the front of her shirt and she pulled it out of her jeans, grinning at me as she flapped it. Then, without speaking, we started dancing several feet apart, as if the space between us was a conversation we were having, a question, a held breath. Gradually, very gradually, we moved closer. Joc's arm touched mine, a moment later my hip brushed hers. Each time we connected, it was like touching the impossible, a mild shock, a velvet electric dream.

"Fear of Bliss" ended, and Joc darted to the stereo and hit the repeat button. Then, without saying anything, she walked up to me, slid both arms around my waist, and laid her head on my shoulder. Stunned, I stood absolutely still, absorbing the sweet shock of it, and then the impossibility of the moment vanished, the line had been crossed and I let my body take over, sliding my arms around Joc and moving with her to the music. By now the beer I'd drunk was kicking in, and I was lost in the warm buzz of it, my face buried in Joc's hair. So I just let my mind do whatever it wanted, while I concentrated on breathing in that familiar coconut scent.

Then, just as my thoughts were really starting to heat up, Joc lifted her head from my shoulder. Startled, I took a step back, but she kept her arms locked around my waist. For a moment we just stood and looked at each other. Joc's lips were parted slightly, revealing a soft wetness along the inside of the lower one. And I was glued to the sight of that wetness. All I could do was stand there, imagining myself leaning forward and ki—

Taking a quick breath, Joc said, "Dyllie, I—"

Without warning, "Fear of Bliss" cut off mid-note. The change was so sudden, the music ending so abruptly, it was as if a fist of silence had slammed down onto the room. Instantly Joc jerked away from me, and we turned to see Tim standing by the stereo, staring at us.

"Whooooa girls," he said, his eyes narrowing. "What is going on here?"

A flush swept Joc's face, but she raised her chin defiantly. "Just fooling around," she said. "What's it to you?"

"Me?" demanded Tim, his chin jutting back at her in a mirror image. "What would your *boyfriends* say if they saw the two of you like this?"

"It's just dancing," protested Joc. "Dikker and I always dance with other people at parties. We dance with whoever we want."

"You call that dancing?" said Tim, his voice skyrocketing. "Why—because your clothes are still on? I don't know what you're thinking, Joc, but there's no fagging around in this house."

For a second Joc just stared at him. Then she darted forward and shoved him hard in the gut.

"Fuck you!" she shouted. "Just fuck you!"

Taking off down the hall, she slammed the door to her room so hard, the walls shook. In the silence that followed I stood frozen, staring at Tim who was bent double, hugging his gut and moaning.

"I think you'd better go now, Dylan," he wheezed, dragging himself to the couch and sinking down onto it.

Turning, I stared down the hall, but the door to Joc's room remained closed. As I stood there stunned, not knowing what to do, I felt it everywhere—silence all over the house, people curled into themselves, no one moving or speaking, just Tim wheezing on the couch. Suddenly then, I was afraid—skin-melting, radio-active, nuclear-gut afraid. Without speaking, I pulled on my jacket and shoes, pushed open the front door, unlocked my bike and took off down the driveway for home.

By the time I got home, most of the beer had worn off, and I managed to brush my teeth before anyone smelled it on my breath. Then I tried to call Joc, but the line was busy. Before I could try a second time, Mom called me for supper. It was Danny's night to cook, and for some reason he'd ditched his usual meat loaf in favor of chili. Except he obviously had no idea *whatsoever* of the impact a hot chili pepper can have on the inside of the human mouth. Fortunately I'd eaten so much pizza I wasn't hungry, and everyone else's attention was too taken up with surviving the food on their plates to notice my mood. As soon as I finished eating, I took off for my room and called Joc again, but the line rang continually busy. Finally, at 8:20, Tim answered, and I just hung up. I didn't think in advance, *If Tim answers, I'm ditching this.* I just heard his voice, jerked the receiver from my ear and slammed it into the cradle.

Then I sat there shaking while I relived the whole thing—the music cutting off, Tim's expression of utter disbelief and his "Whoooa girls." I mean, he'd looked as if he'd thought the Martians actually had landed. *There's no fagging around in this house,* I heard him say again in my head. *No fagging around in this house, no fagging around…*

I guess what made it so surreal was that I never would have seen it coming from Tim. Sure, he was a bit of a roughneck, but more in a daredevil sense than a mean one. He'd never tried to boss Joc around, at least not much, and he'd never struck me as the kind of guy who got off on authority trips. More than that, I couldn't remember him ever going on about fags or dykes, except for the occasional comment, and *everyone* did that. Even I used those words sometimes. Not to attack anyone, but as a joke, as in, "Hey, you look like a fag when you do that." Or, "You're wearing your dyke shirt today." No big deal, just joking around.

So that was why this thing with Tim really blew me away.

I mean, all Joc and I had been doing was *dancing*. Lots of girls danced together at school dances. If Tim jumped all over us for doing a simple thing like dancing together, how would he react if he saw us holding hands? Or kissing? How would Len Schroeder and the phone patrol? Not that I was thinking of dancing down the school halls with Joc or anything, but this afternoon's incident with Tim underlined how important it was to maintain my reputation as Cam Zeleny's loyal and devoted girlfriend. Maybe, all things considered, I should stop being sexually unattainable. If I concentrated, I mean, *really* worked on it, I could probably figure out how to fake liking sex with him. So what if I didn't feel much? It would make Cam happy, he would tell his friends we'd finally made it, and the phone patrol would lay off on the pressure. Besides, if Cam was happy, I was happy, right? It might even make him stop trying to break his neck in football practice.

Reaching for my phone, I dialed Cam's number. It had been a day and a half since I'd talked to him, and suddenly I had to hear his voice, I just *had* to.

"Hi," he said at the other end of the line, and my whole body went limp with relief.

"What're you doing?" I asked and listened to his quiet intake of breath.

"Dyllie," he said. "I was just going to call you."

Tears stung my eyes, I wanted to bury my face in my pillow and bawl. "Oh yeah," I said hoarsely. "What about?"

"Nothing much," he said. "Saturday, I guess. What d'you want to do—go see a flick? Cruise the mall?"

"Whatever," I said. "As long as it's just us. I'm tired of everyone always bugging me about those censor strips. I wish I'd never done that goddamn display."

There was a short pause and then Cam said, "Why don't you just tell them, Dyl? What's the big secret?"

"I dunno," I mumbled, riding out a wave of panic. I had to be careful here—this had to convince him utterly. "At first," I said slowly, "I thought not telling anyone would emphasize what Brennan did, y'know? Censorship means you don't get to know what someone else wanted to say, period. If I told everyone what Brennan censored, then it would be as if there was no censorship, right?"

I held my breath. Big, fucking, *obvious* lie. Would Cam suss it out?

"I guess," he said quietly.

"But then, because I wouldn't tell anyone," I continued, fighting a tightening in my throat, "well, the whole thing just got so loaded, right? I mean, everyone thinks *Foxfire* is a book about dykes, instead of a story about justice and independence and thinking for yourself. And I started to feel…"

I hesitated. At the other end of the phone I could hear Cam breathing steadily, waiting me out.

"Well," I said finally, "I didn't want everyone to think I was a dyke, that's all. Because I'm not, I'm really not. You know that, don't you, Cam?"

I was clenching the phone so tightly, my hand hurt. In the short silence that followed, Cam let out a long slow breath.

"Course you're not," he said firmly. "I always knew that, Dyllie. It's just got to be right for you. You're the kind of girl who's got to feel right about it."

"Yeah," I said, my heart thundering with relief. I mean, it was *booming*, I was shaking with each thud. "And it'll be right for me soon, I promise," I blurted. "I'm getting there Cam, I can feel it. I really can."

"Sweet," he said softly, and I could feel him smiling. "Sweet sweet Dyllie, you're my queen, right?"

"Right," I said, and a wave of utter hopelessness washed over me. Cam had just bought my lie, or was trying to convince himself to. Even though he knew something was wrong, even though he knew that *I* knew he knew something was wrong. Cam Zeleny was making himself believe my lie because it made him feel safer. He was one of the best guys on the planet, but for some reason in his relationship with me he was afraid. What exactly he was afraid of, I didn't know. I mean, it couldn't have been a fear of losing me. Who was I but Queen Dylan, and Queen Dylan was nothing more than a very good liar.

"Read any more about parallel universes?" I asked, twisting the phone cord around my finger.

"Yeah," he said, his voice quickening. "I told you particles are also waves, right?"

"Right," I said.

"And theoretically," he continued, "because they're waves, they can be everywhere at once…"

Curling my body around the phone, I listened to him talk.

Chapter Eighteen

I woke to the sound of steady drumming on the roof and water sluicing down the windowpane. Rain—I could smell it, the air heavy with wetness and a deep earth smell. Rolling onto my side, I reached for the venetian blind, intending to push it up and look out, and bumped into something large and warm lying next to me. Startled, I almost let out a shout, then realized that it was Keelie, curled in tight and facing me. She must have woken early and thought it was time to come wake me, then fallen asleep when she climbed onto the bed. But she'd managed to work her way thoroughly in under the blankets first.

Kids, I thought. Looking down at her flushed sleeping face, I just had to smile. The first thing people always said when they met her was, "You look so much like Dylan!" And Keelie always beamed, she always said, "Yes, Dylan's my BIG sister." I'd never met anyone else who gave off such a constant glow of happiness. It made me want to shrink her to the size of a pebble, put her into a pocket and carry her everywhere like an amulet.

Unfortunately she wasn't enough of an amulet to protect me from what had happened yesterday. Even as I was still smiling down at her, memories came flooding into my brain—Joc and

I dancing, Tim's reaction, last night's unsuccessful phone calls. With a groan, I sank back onto the bed. What in the world was I going to say to Joc when I saw her today? The rain meant I couldn't double-ride her on my bike. On days like this she usually called Dikker for a ride, but maybe I could get Dad to pick her up when he drove Danny and me to school.

Climbing carefully over Keelie, I tiptoed down the hall and knocked on my parents' door. Bedsprings squeaked, there was some muffled muttering, and then Mom said sleepily, "What is it?"

"It's raining," I said into the door. "Is it okay if Dad drives me and Danny to school, and picks up Joc on the way?"

More muffled muttering followed, and then Mom said, "Dylan, it's 5:30. Go back to bed."

"Oh," I whispered, embarrassed. "Sorry."

Tiptoeing back to my room, I pulled up the venetian blind, then crawled over Keelie and lay staring out at the rain. No way was I going to be able to fall asleep now, not with yesterday on my mind. I mean, something enormous had happened between Joc and I, or almost happened, and I didn't have a clue what she was thinking about it. The situation between us was getting so complicated, so flat out *twisted*, it was enough to send any sane person over the deep end. Why didn't she call me last night? Tim couldn't possibly have been on the phone the entire evening. And what about my phone call with Cam? For sure we were still going out, and I'd virtually promised I would make it with him sometime soon.

So what did that mean for me and Joc? Would it be best to just tell her straight out? *Joc, it was all a mistake. I'm sorry, I was drunk and I didn't know what I was doing. And you know I'm Cam's girl, he's the best guy on the planet and he has my whole heart. The part I haven't eaten, of course, but still...*

With another groan, I rolled over and stared at the wall. *Not a good scene*, I thought miserably. Joc knew me better than Cam, she would suss out that lie before I even opened my mouth. That is, I reminded myself heavily, *if* she was thinking what I thought she was thinking—about us, I mean. Because, realistically speaking, I didn't actually *know* what was going through her head. After all, Tim had interrupted her before she'd finished speaking. So it was entirely possible that I was assuming the wrong things. My brain had been fuzzy with beer—it would have been easy enough to misread the scene. All things considered, that was probably the reason Joc had taken off down the hall. When she'd heard Tim's accusation, she'd realized how I might be misinterpreting things and hadn't known how to handle it.

Which meant that the best way to deal with the situation was to ignore it. Taking a deep breath, I rode out a shuddery wave of relief. *Okay*, I thought. *As usual, Queen Dylan is in a funk over nothing.* I mean, once I got a grip and started thinking rationally, it became overwhelmingly clear that I was misreading the whole scene. Like Joc said, girls often danced with each other. It didn't have to mean anything. It was ridiculous, really, to even wonder if she was like me. She was so obviously hetero—she turned on to Dikker and their sex life was definitely happening. She'd just gotten tipsy yesterday, and her usual physically friendly self had gotten friendlier than normal. No big deal, no need to get radioactive about it.

Another hour and a half went by as I lay awake, watching the rain come down and wondering what to say to Joc the next time I saw her. But in the end I didn't meet up with her that morning. When I called at 8:00 AM her phone was busy, and when Dad drove by her house to see if she needed a ride to school, her mom told me that Dikker had already picked her up. Then, when

I went looking for her at lunch hour, she was nowhere to be found. I even tracked down Dikker painting sets in the drama room, but he said he hadn't seen her since school had started. He didn't seem concerned and obviously hadn't noticed anything odd about her that morning, but after lunch she didn't show up for English. And when I went to her house after school, no one answered the door.

Just to be sure I went around to her bedroom window, pushed through the soaking wet hedge underneath and looked in, but the room was empty. A scared feeling came over me then—I mean, with all the rain and cold and wet dark trees, it felt as if someone had *died*. And suddenly I just didn't know what to do anymore, how to *manage* things. I mean, all I wanted was to be close to Joc, to be *with* her. Why did friendship have to be so complicated?

Returning to the front of the house, I sat on the porch and watched cars go by. But none of them stopped, no derelict Honda came revving up to the curb. With all the rain coming down and cars slushing past, the street looked dismal and gray, and after a while tears started slipping down my face. Joc and I had had a lot of fights over the years, but none of them felt like this—a huge yawning ache, too big to even begin wrapping my mind around. I mean, technically we weren't even having a fight. Neither of us had done anything stupid, it wasn't as if I could say, *Hey, I'm sorry I was a jerk,* and everything could go back to normal.

No, this time there was no normal to go back to, I realized with a fresh rush of tears. When Tim had made his accusation yesterday afternoon, Joc had finally had to face what she'd suspected about me for years, and now she was avoiding me because she didn't know how to deal with it. As usual, everything came down to my goddamn hormones.

With all the crying I was doing, I knew I couldn't go home yet.

Someone would notice, and I would have to lie, or explain things I didn't know how to explain. So after a while I got up from the porch and wandered off down the sidewalk. The Dundurn Street bridge was close by, and soon I was leaning against the rail and staring down at the river, watching the water flow past. Only that got me thinking about last month's gigantic bubble bath, and the way Joc had taken off her clothes and I'd refused to take off mine. And *that* just got me started on all the crazy mixed-up possibilities again.

That was when I saw Joc. Crouched on the riverbank, she was partway under the bridge, trailing a stick in the water and watching the rain come down. I couldn't see her face, but her clothes and hair were soaked, and I realized that she must have been out in the rain for hours, skipping school and walking around the way I was now, thinking her own lonely thoughts.

What were those lonely thoughts about? I wondered as I watched her. If I went down there now and we talked, what would she tell me? Would we be able to be honest, say the things we each needed to say, and work out how things were going to be between us? But if that was what Joc wanted, why was she here all alone, hiding out under the bridge? It could only be because she didn't want to talk to me, because she was so completely and utterly embarrassed by the things Tim had said that she wasn't taking even the slightest chance of running into me.

Fear reared up through me then, and a sadness so huge, I could barely breathe through it. Because I wasn't ready to hear Joc say something like that, not in the middle of a cold gloomy rain, with both of us upset the way we were. It would be too absolute, too final. I mean, I just wanted things to go back to the way they'd been yesterday afternoon before Tim's accusation—secret, shimmering and in-between, where I could play with ideas in my head without having to do anything about them.

As quietly as possible I moved away from the rail and started walking back over the bridge. My legs had gone stiff from standing still for so long so I was walking slowly, my head down, full of a damp emptiness. Then, halfway over the bridge, a new thought hit me. What if Joc came climbing up the riverbank right now and saw me walking away like this? She would know that I'd seen her down there and hadn't talked to her, hadn't even bothered to say hello. Our friendship would be over for sure then, nothing would ever bring us together after that.

Without looking back I took off, running full out into the rain.

Saturday evening Cam picked me up at 6:30 and we headed to the mall. The movie we wanted to see started at 7:30, so we hung around the arcade for a while, playing Streetfighter, Cam's favorite game. He was in a good mood—I was wearing a sweater he liked, a light green crew neck with pale yellow flowers worked across the front, and his face had lit up when he'd seen it. So we were holding hands and leaning against each other a lot, and the whole thing could have been really fun if it hadn't been for the cold I was coming down with due to being out in yesterday's rain. And, of course, I kept thinking about Joc crouched alone on the riverbank, watching the water go by. Watching her thoughts go by. Just watching the sadness all go by.

"C'mon, Dyl," said Cam, turning toward me. "You have a go at it."

With a grin he stepped back from the controls, and I moved into the player's position. But just as he leaned forward to drop a looney into the slot, I glanced around the room and who did I see but hot lips Sheila, the passion of Confederation Collegiate, standing in the entrance to the arcade. Immediately I froze, watching as her eyes traveled the dimly lit room. She appeared to be looking for someone, and a sick feeling in my gut told me who it probably was. Would she be able to see me from the entrance, I wondered frantically. Cam and I were at the rear of the room, partially hidden by several junior high boys at the next machine, but as I watched, Sheila's eyes focused in on me and she stiffened. Yes, she'd seen me, and there was that familiar desperate hungry look again, erupting all over her face.

"Uh, Cam," I said, every nerve in my body going into red alert. "I've gotta go to the can, actually. C'mon."

"Hey, I don't have to pee," Cam grinned. "You go and I'll wait here."

"Okay, fine," I said, ducked around the junior high boys and took off through the crowd. Across the arcade I could see Sheila steaming down the far aisle, probably headed for Streetfighter. If I stuck to the aisle I was in, I would reach the entrance without a direct encounter—if Sheila didn't suddenly start leaping over the rows of video games that separated us, that is.

That left the question of how long she would hang around Streetfighter, watching Cam play once she'd realized that I was gone, but there was no point in worrying about it now. Barreling out of the arcade, I headed down the mall at light speed toward the food court and the nearest girls washroom. A small private space, that was what I needed—something I could close myself inside, get my head together and *think*. Fortunately the lineup waiting at the washroom entrance was short, and I got into a cubicle quickly. Without even checking the toilet seat to make sure it was clean, I sat down and buried my face in my hands. I could feel it coming—another extraterrestrial funk. Mad chaos was taking over my brain, and all I could think about was how much I wanted a smoke. A smoke with Joc. Where was she now? What was she doing? Was she sick in bed with a head cold, from being out in yesterday's rain? Or was she with Dikker, working her way through a six-pack and not even thinking about me?

Miserably I glanced at my watch. Fifteen minutes had gone by. Would Sheila have given up looking for me in the arcade and headed off somewhere else? And Cam must be wondering what was taking me so long. Reluctantly I stood up, flushed the toilet and stepped out of the cubicle. A quick scan of the waiting lineup revealed no one with a desperate hungry look on her face. But as I approached the sinks my eyes fell on a familiar figure, half-hidden behind several women and leaning against the paper-towel dispenser.

Hot lips Sheila. Waiting for me. Obviously.

"Uh-uh," she said grimly, ducking behind me and cutting off my escape. I had to give her credit—she moved fast, faster than I could *think*. Turning to face me, she added sarcastically, "Don't you want to wash your hands?"

"That's my business," I snapped, trying to step around her, but she moved with me, cutting me off again.

"Fine," I said, trying to keep a grip as I turned back to the sinks. "I will wash them."

Soaping my hands carefully, I held them under the tap and watched the water sluice off each and every soap bubble. Under no circumstances was I looking at Sheila, the line of gawking women behind her, or the mirror and my beet-red, obviously guilty expression. With a grim dead-end feeling, I dried my hands and tossed the paper towel into the garbage. Then I turned toward Sheila and fixed my eyes on her left shoulder.

"There," I said coldly. "Satisfied?"

She shrugged, then said, "Are you?"

I wanted to slug her. I mean, why didn't she just *get* it? Didn't she ever fuck up? Had she never made the slightest itsy-bitsy little mistake?

"What business is it of yours?" I demanded. "What business is anything I do of yours?"

"It is when you kiss me," she replied, her voice calm and deadly clear.

Panic swept me and I almost clapped a hand over her mouth. "I did NOT...kiss you," I spluttered, taking a step back. "I was *drunk*. I wasn't *kissing* you, I was *drunk*."

By now every woman in the lineup had forgotten her need to pee and was eyeballing us frantically. Fortunately they were all complete strangers. With any luck, I would never see them again. Arms crossed, Sheila was also ignoring the row of fascinated expressions, her dark eyes flat on me, bright and full of hurt—hurt that had undeniably been caused by me, hurt that I was continuing to cause. Well, that was her fault, really. If she hadn't come in here, looking for me when I so obviously didn't want to see *her*, this conversation wouldn't be happening.

"I just want to talk to you," she said softly, her eyes getting even brighter. Then she started blinking rapidly, and I realized that she was trying to keep herself from crying. "Just...talk," she added, her voice trailing off.

"Yeah, well," I said, my eyes flitting everywhere but her face. "I don't want to talk, okay?"

This time when I moved toward the door, she let me pass. The lineup of waiting women stepped back quickly, creating a path, and then I was out of there and letting the washroom door swing closed behind me. With a deep breath, I turned to head back to the arcade and saw Cam leaning against a nearby wall, a concerned expression on his face.

"There you are," he said, coming toward me. "A girl asked me where you went and I told her, but you were taking so long I got worried."

Behind me the washroom door opened and Sheila came bursting out. Hurt still glimmered in her eyes, but the desperate hungry expression was back and she looked very determined.

Walking up to me, she held out a slip of paper. When I didn't take it, she jammed it into the left front pocket of my jeans.

"Call me," she said, leaning so close I could feel her breath on my face. Then she turned and strode off across the food court.

"That's the girl who asked about you in the arcade," said Cam, watching her go. "Who is she? What did she want?"

"Just someone I met at the Confed dance," I said quickly. "It's not important."

"Confed?" asked Cam, looking startled.

"Yeah," I said, shooting him a glance. "Why?"

His eyes dropped. "Nothing," he said, but he seemed uneasy. "Hey, the movie's about to start. We'd better get in line."

I held out my hand and for a second, just the flicker of a heartbeat, he hesitated. Then he reached out, our hands connected and we were in sync again, headed down the mall toward the movie theater.

Chapter Nineteen

I spent Sunday in bed, riding out my cold and working my way through a box of Kleenex. Every now and then Mom or Dad would come into my room with some tea or chicken broth, and Keelie thudded in regularly on her Quidditch broom. Outside my window rain poured steadily down, and the phone beside my bed remained quiet. As the hours dragged by, Joc didn't call me and I didn't call her. Inside and out, everything felt the same— thick, gray and cold, like something out of *The Egyptian Book of the Dead*: *Hail, Basti, I have not, did not, am not.*

Mid-afternoon, I dragged myself downstairs for a grilled cheese sandwich. As I was going back up, I noticed a dog-eared copy of *Hamlet* sitting on the top shelf of the hallway bookcase. Pulling it out, I took it to my room and crawled into bed. When I opened the front cover, I found Dad's name written on the overleaf—Daniel Brian Kowolski. The book was obviously one of his university texts and it got me thinking about him, trying to imagine him in his twenties, going to classes and hanging out with his friends. His girlfriends. How many had he had? What had they been like? What if one of *them* had become my mother? It would have meant an entirely different set of genes contributing to my makeup, and a very different me. Maybe then I would have turned out hetero. Maybe then I wouldn't have been so fucked up.

But then I remembered that it was Dad who had the questionable uncle and sister. So having a different mother wouldn't have solved the faulty gene problem. If only Dad had been infertile, and Mom had resorted to a sperm bank.

With a sigh I opened *Hamlet* to Act I, scene i, and started reading. The story was definitely geared for a head cold and a rainy day—poison, ghosts, insanity and talking to skulls. *If,* that is, you could understand half of what you were reading. Like Joc said, it was almost a foreign language. After looking up twenty or so ancient words in the dictionary, I gave up on all that *to be or not to be*-ing, closed the book and just lay in bed, listening to the air whistle through my stuffed nose. After a bit I realized that by blowing harder or softer, I could whistle different notes. It took a lot of concentration, but I'd managed to work my way through half of "Mary Had A Little Lamb" when my phone rang, interrupting my musical masterpiece.

Joc! I thought, and all thoughts of Mary and her lamb exploded out of the top of my head. Petrified, I lay staring at the phone. My sinuses were tap dancing and my heart doing absolute reggae. On the fifth ring I finally got it together, leaned over and picked up the phone.

"Hewwo?" I asked cautiously.

"Dyl—is that you?" asked Cam.

At the sound of his voice my heart took a sky dive, then slowly picked itself up. "Yeah, it's me," I said, trying to pull my voice down out of my nose. "My code is worse, and I'm sig in bed."

Cam laughed softly. "You sound like it," he said. "I caught a bit of the sniffles off you, but not that bad."

"Mage sure you eat lots of chiggen soub," I said, trying to be helpful, then lay there listening while Cam went off into howls of laughter. It sounded as if he would be enjoying himself for a while, so I reached for another Kleenex and tried to blow some of the haze out of my head. But that just set him off again. Finally he calmed down and started telling me about a CFL game he and Len had watched that afternoon.

"So, uh, what did she say?" he asked, changing the subject so abruptly that for a moment I didn't know what he was talking about.

"What did who say?" I asked slowly.

"On the note," said Cam. "The girl at the mall, remember?"

"Oh," I said, my eyes darting to the jeans I'd worn yesterday. After taking them off last night, I'd thrown them across the back of a chair and climbed straight into bed. I'd felt so sick, I hadn't even bothered to check the note.

"Nothing," I said carefully. "I haven't looked at it, actually."

Cam paused, as if thinking, then said, "Well, look at it now."

Again my eyes darted to my jeans. Why was Cam so interested in this? After last night's run-in with Sheila outside the girls washroom, he hadn't mentioned her for the rest of the evening.

"Uh, I can't," I stammered, trying to ignore the guilt heating up my face. It was so hard to *think* with a head cold. "I threw the jeans into the laundry this morning. I guess I forgot about the note. Like I said, it wasn't important."

Silence stretched out on the other end of the line. "Cam," I said nervously, "are you there?"

"Yeah," he said quickly. "Are you?"

"Of course, I am," I said indignantly, fighting a flash of panic. "Why are you asking me that? And why is this such a big deal to you? I don't even know her name."

Well, not her last name, I added guiltily inside my head.

Cam took a long breath, then let it out slowly. "It's not a big deal," he said quietly. "At least...Oh, never mind."

"Never mind what?" I demanded, sitting up in bed. Suddenly my head felt ten times worse and my heart had graduated to a kick-ass thud. Power funk time, definitely.

"See," said Cam. "Now you're making a big deal out of it."

"Okay, okay," I said, glancing nervously at my jeans. "Hey, wait a minute," I added, trying to keep my voice casual. "There's something on the floor. Maybe the note fell out of my pocket when I took off my jeans last night."

Placing the phone on the bed, I got up and pulled the note out of my jeans pocket. Then I climbed back into bed and picked up the phone.

"Here it is," I said, spreading out the crumpled paper. "It's just her name and phone number. Sheila Warren. Do you want me to give you her number?"

Cam gave a short laugh. "Hardly," he said. "Why would I want to call her?"

"Exactly," I said. "And why would I?"

"I dunno, Dyl," he said. "She seemed to think you would."

"Ah, she's just got some crazy ideas in her head," I muttered. "She needs a reality check, big-time."

"What kind of crazy ideas?" Cam asked quickly.

"I dunno," I said. "They're her ideas, not mine. It wasn't *me* chasing *her* around the mall, was it?"

In the long pause that followed, I listened to Cam breathe. "No," he said finally. "I guess it wasn't. Look, I'm tired, and I've got a Physics test tomorrow. I'd better hit the sack."

"Yeah, okay," I said, relieved. All this ducking around the truth was way too much work for my sick head. "See you at lunch tomorrow?"

"Yeah," he said quietly. "Tomorrow. If you're not too sick. Bye."

The phone went dead, and I lay for a while, holding it as I imagined Cam lying motionless in the darkness of his room, both hands above his waist until he fell asleep.

Overnight my cold improved, so when Mom pushed me to spend another day in bed, I told her I couldn't afford to miss an algebra class right now because I had a major test later in the week. Since math had admittedly never been one of my priorities, she gave me a suspicious look but let me out the door, and I biked straight over to Joc's place. The morning was dismal and gray, and after a few blocks a thick, burning sensation in my sinuses told me that my head cold hadn't improved as much as I'd hoped. Worse than that, my thoughts were absolutely all over the place. What in the world was I going to say to Joc? Would she even be home? It wasn't raining today, but she might have asked Dikker to pick her up again, like last Friday. Since grade nine, when she'd started going out with him, it had been an unspoken thing between us—I double-rode her to school every morning until the snow fell, and then Dikker started picking her up.

But maybe since Thursday afternoon, that had changed. And maybe, when I knocked on the door, Tim would make sure he answered it just so he could deliver that essential bit of information to my face.

As usual I was going into a funk and also as usual, I needn't have bothered. Just as I pulled up to the curb, the Hersches' front door flew open, and Joc came jogging across the lawn. In spite of the cold day her jacket was flapping open and her hair looked half-combed, as if I'd caught her in the middle of getting ready. But all she said as she slid onto the seat behind me was, "Boot it quick, before big brother gets his grumpy ass to the door."

So I took off down the street, my whole mind glued to the fact that this morning her hands were barely touching me—just her fingertips, and those just enough to keep herself balanced. Several blocks went by with neither of us speaking. Finally I worked my way past the burning in my throat and croaked, "You weren't in English on Friday."

Half a block away the Dundurn Street bridge came into view, and then we were coasting over it and leaving it behind.

"No," said Joc, her voice flat, and left it at that.

"So...what did you do all weekend?" I asked.

Up ahead was the corner that would take us onto Diefenbaker Avenue. Reluctantly I veered around it.

"Nothing much," said Joc.

"See Dikker?" I asked casually.

"Yup," she said.

So it was as I'd thought—I'd completely misinterpreted her actions last Thursday, and she was as tight as ever with Dikker. And today she was being distant with me because she was afraid I wouldn't get that. Well, unlike hot lips Sheila, I *did* get it. And, more than anything, I wanted Joc to know that I got it.

Coasting up to the bike racks, I braked and let her slide off behind me. Then, before she could take off for Dikker's locker, I said, "Hey, what're you doing at lunch?"

"Dunno," she shrugged, her eyes flicking across mine. With a start I saw they were red-rimmed and heavy-looking, as if she'd been crying. Turning toward the Dief, she stood fiddling with the zipper on her jacket. "Dikker's working on stage props," she added, not looking at me. "And, well...I don't want to."

This was my chance, I thought, my heart quickening. Now was the moment to prove to her that I understood completely.

"Come sit with me and Cam in the cafeteria," I said, smiling at her. "I promised I'd eat with him, but you can joi—"

Joc's eyes cut across my face, almost startled-looking, and the words died on my lips. "Nah," she said, looking away again. "Not today, Dyl. I mean, Cam's okay most of the time, but his friends…". With a shrug, she started toward the school.

"Okay, see you in English," I called after her, fighting a wave of panic. Walking away casually was just Joc's way of showing me that Tim had been wrong. No big deal, I understood that. I *got* it. I *wasn't* a hot lips Sheila.

"Oh yeah," said Joc, glancing back at me. "We're starting a new book today, aren't we? *1984*. I'm already halfway through it."

Turning, she disappeared into the crowd.

The morning went by like thick glue. My head was so woozy it felt upside down, and all I wanted was to crawl into a dark hole and let the world go by. But that would have been a catastrophe. If I went home sick now, opting out of things for a few days, Joc was sure to grow even more distant. And there was no question—I had to see Cam as soon as possible. At the end of our phone call last night his voice had sounded so heavy, as if he was having second thoughts about us…as if he was ready to give up. He couldn't give up, not now. Not when I was in the middle of this massive misunderstanding with Joc. I mean, what if I lost them *both*—the two most important people in my life—at the very same time? It couldn't happen, it just *couldn't*.

So in spite of the fact that my head cold was growing steadily worse, I sat through my morning classes, then headed to the cafeteria for lunch. To my surprise, as soon as he caught sight of me Cam broke into a smile and slid over to make room. And I was so relieved that at first I didn't catch it, the change in the air. I don't think Cam had gotten it either—the quick looks or the whispering between Rachel, Julie and Len. But then I was doing my very best to occupy all his attention, leaning against him while he fed me one of his ham sandwiches. His mom made the best sandwiches, they were like an art form, but my cold was so bad I could barely taste anything.

"Hey, Dyl," Len said casually as Cam offered me another bite. "I was talking to your brother earlier today."

"Oh yeah?" I said, flicking my eyes across his. Right away the hair went up on the back of my neck. I mean, Len's gaze was too focused, too intent. He was onto something.

"Yeah," said Len, leaning forward, his eyes honing in. "We were talking in the hall by his locker, and he told me the title under the girl's censor strip is *Foxfire*."

It was instant flamethrower. I mean, I just wasn't expecting the secret to get out now—the display had been up for weeks, and the questions and comments had pretty much died off. And with my head cold and everything, I had no strength to *think*. So there I was, stuck in the middle of absolute hell—flamethrower face, the power blush of power blushes. And there was no way to hide it, all that ugly red evidence shouting out its truth.

Beside me Cam stiffened, staring at my face. Julie let out a long low snicker.

Get a grip, I thought. *Just fucking get a grip.*

"Oh yeah?" I faltered, trying to nail Len with my eyes. But the damn things wouldn't cooperate, just kept flitting here, there and everywhere.

Danny, I thought savagely. When I got home that afternoon, I was going to murder him. He'd promised me, he'd *promised*.

"Yeah," said Len, his voice casual, his eyes two killing points. "I mean, isn't *Foxfire* a book about dykes?"

In the sudden silence everyone heard my quick intake of breath. "Not necessarily," I stammered, trying to keep a grip. "Some of the characters might be, but at the end of the book at least four of them get married. None of them ever have sex with each other, and—"

"Yeah, but they take off their shirts and rub boobs," Julie said quickly. "That's a dyke thing to do, if you ask me."

"Yeah," agreed Rachel. "And they rent a house together, way off in the middle of nowhere. And they always attack men as their victims."

"They went after *jerks*," I protested. "So what if they were all men?"

"They were dykes," interrupted Gary. "Even if they didn't have sex with each other, they were thinking it."

"It's a book about justice," I said hoarsely, my eyes skipping across their grinning faces. "And thinking for yourself."

Desperate, I sounded desperate. Quietly, without speaking, Cam put down his sandwich and stared at it.

"So what if they were an all-girl gang?" I said, trying to ignore his silence. "They were just *people* trying to bring justice into the world. What's wrong with that?"

"They were dykes, Dyl," Len said evenly, erasing everything I'd just said with his tone. "And you put *Foxfire* between the girl's legs. You could've put it anywhere—her hand or her foot, or in one of those little thought clouds floating around her head. But you put it right between her legs."

"Yeah, okay," I said, my eyes skittering around the edge of his face. "So what?"

"Well, it's kind of a dykish thing to do, isn't it?" he said carefully. "I mean, for *you* to do?"

Our eyes locked, and I sat trapped in a dead stare with him. So here it was, finally, the accusation I'd been dreading for years. Heat deepened in my face, I was burning up with it—burning up with the shame, the ache, the need of *Foxfire*.

"I put it there," I began, then stopped, searching for the right thoughts, the right words, *anything* that would take the gloat out of Len's eyes.

Abruptly Cam broke in. "Leave her alone," he said, lifting his head and glaring at Len. "She can put whatever she wants between the girl's legs, got it? It's okay because I say it's okay, and you're going to drop it right now."

He was flushed, his cheeks as red as mine, the pain all over his face. Stunned, everyone stared at him, and Len jerked slightly, as if struck. For a second I saw regret in his eyes, real regret.

"Okay, bud," he said quickly. "If you say so."

"I do," said Cam, holding his gaze, "say so."

"Then that's the way it is," said Len. Their gaze held for a few more seconds, and then Len broke it off, and everyone sat staring at the table.

"Hey, what did you think of the game yesterday?" Gary asked uneasily. "Roughriders plowed the Stampeders. I think they've got a good chance at the Cup."

"Roughriders?" Len said quickly. "Nah. They'll make the western final, but—"

Conversation kicked in, quick and relieved, smoothing things over. Beside me I felt Cam begin to relax, easing himself back into a normal state of affairs. Without looking at me, he moved his hand slowly over mine, took hold and squeezed gently—in front of everyone, just like that. Briefly conversation halted, and everyone's gaze fixed on our hands. Then they started talking again while Cam and I sat silent and motionless, not looking at each other as it all went on around us.

Chapter Twenty

After lunch I biked straight home and crawled into bed. Then I lay there, sniffing the afternoon away while I counted the minutes and waited for Danny. When I finally heard him coming upstairs, I threw off the blankets and tore out of my room. Racing down the hall, I grabbed the front of his shirt and backed him into the nearest wall.

"You shit!" I hissed into his startled face. "You *told*. D'you have any idea how much trouble you've caused me?"

"Take it easy," said Danny, fending me off. "I didn't tell anyone until today. And that was only because they got my arm up behind my back."

"They *what*?" I demanded, still hanging onto his shirt.

"They twisted my arm behind my back," said Danny. Lifting his right hand, he waved it emphatically in my face. "*This* arm. I was at my locker and they were bugging me—Len, Gary and a few other guys. They kept asking what was under the censor strips and I kept ducking it. So they took a quick look down the hall to make sure no teachers were around, then put me in a headlock and got my arm up behind my back." Danny grimaced. "I was shitting acid, it hurt so bad. I couldn't write all morning."

A deep, shocked feeling poured through me. "They hurt you?" I said, letting go of his shirt.

"It's all right now," Danny said hastily. "I can write and stuff. But that's the only reason I told, honest. It *really* hurt. And someone kept jamming my head into Len's crotch, saying I was a fag to keep a girl's secrets, and—"

"Say *what*?" I interrupted, my jaw dropping.

"Yeah," Danny shrugged. "Weird, eh? Then Len said he knew I wanted to eat his dick, and he was going to feed it to me real good."

"Jeeeeeeezus," I gasped, and for a long moment we just stared at each other. "Hey," I said finally, "I'm sorry for going after you like that. I should've known something like this happened. I know you would never tell on me unless…"

My voice trailed off, and again we stood and stared at each other.

"Well," Danny said. "At least now you know for sure."

A flush hit me and I nodded. Danny was right—I should have known better. But before I could start working myself into one of my funks, he added, "The weirdest thing was the way kids looked at me after—kids who had lockers near mine and were watching. I mean, I'm no fag. They know that. But suddenly they were all looking at me as if I'd been hiding something from them."

"That's crazy," I said angrily, trying to ignore his use of the word "fag." "I can't believe they would stand there and let those guys do that to you. I can't believe Len and Gary…"

Again my voice trailed off as I saw the dubious look on Danny's face. "Well," I added slowly, "maybe I can. Len is a shit. I've always known that. Joc can't stand him. Or Gary."

"Yeah," said Danny. "I guess Cam hangs around with them because they're on the team."

I nodded, then said, "Y'know, Danny—I'm so sick of them,

their stupid jokes and beer-and-belch stories. If you ever make the football team, don't act like that, okay?"

"Uh-uh," said Danny. "I'm going to be like Cam, the guy who ties little girls' shoes. But hey, Dyl—what's the big secret about *Foxfire* and *The Once and Future King*? Why don't you just tell everyone they're the censored titles?"

Right away I got a quick breathy feeling in my chest. But then I thought, *Get a grip, Goofus. This is just Danny. He's not out to get you.*

"D'you know what *Foxfire* is about?" I asked.

Danny shook his head.

"Okay," I said, taking a deep breath. "It's about a gang of girls in the fifties, who do a Robin Hood thing and start robbing the rich to help the poor. We studied it this year in English. And, well, a lot of kids think the girls in the story are dykes."

Danny's eyes widened. "And you put *that* title," he said softly, then paused. "Well…you know where."

I shrugged. "Yeah," I said, grinning slightly. "And then Brennan saw it and flipped."

Danny whistled softly. "No wonder Len howled when I said *Foxfire*," he said. "It was as if he'd struck pure gold."

A sinking feeling took over my gut. "Yeah, I know," I said dully.

Danny studied my face quietly. "Well, why did you do it?" he asked. "You must've known something like this could happen."

I shrugged again. "You have to read the book," I said. "It's awesome, it made me feel like I could do things, be someone important. I mean, those girls thought for themselves and did what they thought was right. What does it matter if they were dykes or straights? Why does that matter?"

Danny shrugged back. "Okay," he said agreeably. "I'll read it. Have you got a copy?"

"Yeah," I said, turning toward my room. "I've got my copy from English. I'll get it for you. And Danny..."

I paused, looking back at him. "I'm really *really* sorry for jumping you like that," I said fervently. "I should've known better."

Danny nodded slowly. "Now you do," he said, his dark eyes holding mine.

"Yeah," I said, taking a quick breath. "I do."

After giving Danny my copy of *Foxfire*, I went to my room, sat down on the bed and stared at the phone. As usual, my heart was doing its kick-ass thing, and my brain felt like the bell of doom, repeatedly tolling out a single thought: *LEN, LEN, LEN*. I mean, I had to call him, it was obvious. No way could I let what he did to Danny pass without comment, and no way did I want to have to make that comment to him in front of a watching audience at the Dief.

Slowly I reached for the phone, and just as slowly I pulled my hand back. *No point in rushing things*, I thought grimly. Not until I had what I wanted to say really clear in my mind.

Hugging myself tightly, I tried to figure out what that was, but the only thing my brain seemed to be picking up on was the megasonic thud of my heart. And the longer I sat, trying to come up with something specifically brilliant to say to Len, the more megasonic my heart became.

It's kind of a dykish thing to do, isn't it? I remembered him saying while Julie grinned at me smugly. *I mean, for* you *to do.*

Even though it was just a memory, my cheeks burned. It wasn't so much what Len had said that was the problem now, it was the way he'd said it—so matter of fact and conclusive. As if there was no argument about it, the situation was case closed and nothing I could do, say or *feel* would ever change anything. And what made things worse was the fact that, technically speaking, his accusation had been correct. Len Schroeder was the one who'd told the truth today at lunch, and I was the one who'd lied. But that didn't give him the right to attack my brother. Danny had been standing up for me whether I deserved it or not, and now it was my turn to do the same for him. Because there was no question about it—*he* deserved it.

Hands shaking, I picked up my address book and flipped to Len's name. Then I dialed his number. On the fourth ring his mom answered and called him to the phone. Footsteps thudded in the background, I heard a mumbled "Thanks" as Len picked up the phone, and then he was breathing into the mouthpiece.

"Hello," he said.

"This is Dylan," I said, fighting a tremble in my voice. "Dylan Kowolski. As in Danny Kowolski's older sister."

There was a pause at the other end of the line and then Len said carefully, "I know who you are, Dylan."

"Good," I said, trying to ride out the massive slam-hammering of my heart. "Because I want you to know exactly who's saying this to you and why. Listen closely. If you *ever* go near my brother again, I will tell everyone in the entire fucking Dief that you told Danny to eat your dick. Just before one of your buddies practically twisted his arm off, that is. You got that, Len?"

He breathed in and out, in and out. "Yeah," he said finally. "I've got it."

Takes one to know one, I thought, staring at the phone in my hand. *A coward, that is.*

I hung up. Then I just sat there for a while, staring at nothing while a hugeness raged around inside me. It wasn't anything I could define, just a gigantic kind of energy, roaring away—a mix of gladness and sadness, pride, fear and absolute hysteria, making me feel ten times my actual body size.

Well, I thought grimly, at least one thing was clear. In spite of all the twisted crap going on in my life, my heart wasn't stuck living inside *The Egyptian Book of the Dead* anymore.

With a tiny crouching smile, I went downstairs to help with supper.

The following morning was pretty much like the previous one, a *hello-how-are-you-I'm-fine-see-you-later* bike ride to school with Joc, then three endless hours in class, watching the wall clocks go round. Finally the lunch bell rang, and I headed to the library to do my weekly volunteer shift.

"There you are, Dylan," said Ms. Fowler as I walked up to the check-out desk. "I'm so glad you're on time. I have a meeting with the tutoring club in my office at twelve, and most of them are already here."

"No prob," I said. "No detention today—I haven't been kissing any doors lately."

Flashing me a small grin, Ms. Fowler went into her office, and I took up position behind the desk. The library was the usual scene—kids yakking over the tops of study carrels, the fluorescent lights buzzing overhead. Crouched down beside a filing cart, I was heavily involved in the alphabetizing process when someone let out a low whistle behind me. Turning, I saw Dikker standing on the other side of the check-out desk, holding a book.

"Hey, Dylan," he grinned, setting it on the counter. "Sign me out this book, pronto."

Reluctantly I got to my feet, swiveled the book around and looked at the title: *The Stage in Shakespeare's Time.* "You can't be serious," I said. "This book has words in it, lots of them."

"Mr. Tyrrell sent me down to get it for him," Dikker shrugged. "Anyway, don't pick on me. I'm already bleeding."

"Bleeding?" I said, surprised at his plaintive tone. "Why? Did the book give you a paper cut?"

A bewildered look crossed Dikker's face. "Paper cut!" he said. "Come on—more like my heart. It's been three days and I'm still hemorrhaging."

"Hemorrhaging?" I repeated. Now it was my turn to look confused. "Why would you be hemorrhaging?"

Dikker's jaw dropped, and then he said, "She didn't tell you? But you two are like glue."

"No," I said, swallowing hard. "She hasn't told me, whatever it is."

"She dumped me," Dikker said flatly. "Last Saturday night. I haven't talked to her since."

Stunned, I stood staring at him while he stared back at me. "Oh," I said finally, then got myself into gear, signed out his book and handed it over.

"Did she...happen to say why?" I asked cautiously.

"Not really," said Dikker, taking the book. "Just that she wanted to think about things for a while. I dunno, stuff like that." He looked around helplessly. "What's there to think about all of a sudden? We went out for a year and a half without thinking. In that whole time I didn't cheat on her, I swear I never cheated on her once. So why would she be gung-ho for me one day and suddenly break up with me the next?"

Again we stood staring at each other, except this time my eyes kept flicking to the display case behind him.

"I don't know," I said finally. "Like I said, Joc hasn't talked to me about it."

"Weird," said Dikker. He sighed heavily, then gave me a lopsided grin. "'The frailty of women,'" he quoted emphatically.

"Yeah right," I said. "Joc is hardly Ophelia. No way would

you catch her drowning herself over some turd who treated her the way Hamlet treated Ophelia."

For a moment Dikker just stood there blinking at me. "Okay," he said, "but it's still a great line. And here's another one."

Staggering backward with one hand pressed to his heart, he said, "'What should fellows as I do crawling between earth and heaven?'"

Hamlet seemed to be perking him up quite rapidly. With a half-grin, I said, "Watch out for broken glass, I guess."

Slowly Dikker lowered his hand, his playfulness vanishing. "I really would've thought she'd've told you," he said. "She was always closer to you than me. It bugged me, that thing between you two, as if the rest of the world was just...well, extra."

His eyes held my face for a moment, as if trying to read something in it, and then he turned and walked out of the library. Watching him go, I almost called after him, but then I thought, *What could I tell him? I'm the last person who would know what Joc is thinking.*

At that moment the door to Ms. Fowler's office opened, and the tutoring club came pouring out. On their heels, Ms. Fowler walked up to the check-out desk and said, "Thank you so much, Dylan. You're one of my most reliable volunteers. I don't suppose..."

Hesitantly she glanced at the display case. "Well," she added wistfully, "you haven't been struck with a genius idea for next month's display, have you?"

"Uh *no*," I said, aiming for a tone between definite and polite. Another display was absolutely the last thing I needed right now. Glancing at the infamous construction-paper silhouettes, I studied them for about the zillionth time, and that was when it hit me. The three titles Ms. Fowler had put in the girl's groin—*To Kill A Mockingbird, Stranger In A Strange Land* and *The Farthest*

Shore—she'd chosen them for a reason. They were a kind of code, clues that said something about *her*.

I wanted to ask her then, oh how I wanted to ask her straight out. Instead, I went at it deviously.

"Ms. Fowler," I asked. "Are you married?"

"No," she said, giving me a startled glance. "No, I never have been."

"Do you have kids?" I asked.

A brief sadness passed through her face, and she shook her head. "No," she said quietly. "I don't."

"Are you happy?" I asked, watching her carefully.

"Happy?" she repeated, as if astounded. "I don't know about *happy*." Eyes narrowed, she stared off across the library. "I don't know if I would say life is about being happy, Dylan," she said finally. "But I'm alive, and aware, and learning. And yes, every now and then I am actually happy."

For a moment we just looked at each other, a kind of unspoken meaning there in the air between us. Then Ms. Fowler gave a small shrug and said, "It's the seventeenth of October, and I'm going to have to put up a new display soon. Put on your thinking cap and see if you can come up with another brilliant idea, why don't you?"

"Maybe," I said cautiously. "I'll think about it."

And we left it at that.

Chapter Twenty-one

When I got to English after lunch, I put on my best terminally bored expression, dropped into my seat and tried to glance casually at Joc. But instead of glancing back, she continued to sit, eyes closed, and leaned against the wall with an equally terminally bored expression on her face. *I am stuck here in neutral for the rest of my life*—the thought was written all over her. And my having just walked into the room obviously hadn't changed that for her. Last Thursday afternoon was beginning to look more and more like something that belonged in a parallel universe.

Holding up my copy of *1984,* I said, "You've read half of this already? What's happened to your love life?"

Joc's terminally bored expression didn't waver. Looking me dead in the eye, she said, "I get Dikker to read it to me. Then I can pay attention."

"Oh," I said weakly, my eyes flicking away. Then, of course, I got hit with another neurotic power blush.

Blushing! I thought furiously. *Why the hell am* I *blushing? I'm not the one lying here.*

Grimly I forced my gaze back to Joc's to find her still watching me, her eyes tired and dull-looking, but with something glimmering in behind the dullness. I had to hand it to her—of the two of us, she was the much better faker.

"You mean he's not quoting *Hamlet* at you anymore?" I asked, watching for a change in her expression, a brief flicker in her gaze, but she just shrugged.

"I wanted to tell you," she said coolly. "I've decided to start walking to school in the morning. I'm getting fat and I need the exercise."

Panic hit me full force. "What d'you mean?" I asked, my voice going up into a squeak. "The last thing you are is fat. I wish I was as thi—"

"Dikker said I was," Joc said flatly, cutting me off. Again, her gaze didn't waver, but mine did. I mean, in all the years that I'd known Joc, I'd never figured she would flat out lie to me. And I had the feeling she knew that I knew she was lying. So how come *I* was the one who felt guilty about it?

"Okay," I said helplessly. And then, because there didn't seem to be anything else to say, I turned around in my desk and sat facing the front of the room. The clock over the door stood at two minutes to one, and all across the classroom kids were yakking, getting in that last bit of gossip before the bell went. Even Mr. Cronk was talking to a couple of front-row keeners at his desk. Usually Joc and I were the last ones to break off conversation when the bell rang, in fact it was probably more realistic to say that we never actually broke off talking, just took a few breathers here and there. But today, as the last minute ran down on the clock, we sat side by side, deadly quiet. Never before had I realized how lonely air could feel.

Finally the bell went, launching Mr. Cronk into *1984*. Stuck in a funk, I barely heard a word he said. *Why is she doing this to me?* I kept thinking. *Why would she lie about Dikker? And why, all of a sudden, would she want to start walking to school? Does she hate me that much?*

No, I thought, getting an infinitesimal grip. *Joc would never hate me*. But if she thought I was attracted to her and she wasn't to me, she would go out of her way to tell me in every way possible.

So how did I prove to her *absolutely* that I was hetero? As the classroom clock ticked off the seconds, I tried frantically to come up with the perfect, drop-dead, hysterically funny one-liner that would completely terminate all of her doubts. But my brain was like a blender, turning all my thoughts into mush. And when the bell finally went, Joc shot out of her seat before I could even turn toward her.

"See you," she mumbled and headed for the door. I don't think she even looked at me.

"Yeah," I whispered, watching her go. "See you, I guess."

That was the way it went for the rest of the week—cold lonely bike rides in the morning and one-liner, deep-freeze conversations in English. To make things worse, Cam had volunteered to ref the lunch-hour volleyball intra-murals that had just started, and with his after-school football practices I hardly saw him. Suddenly, everywhere I looked the school felt…empty. So when my intra-murals team didn't have a game, I put in time shelving books for Ms. Fowler in the library and otherwise sat tight and waited for Joc to work her way through whatever it was that she was working her way through.

Then, Friday lunch hour as I was trudging drearily through the cafeteria en route to the library to shelve more books, someone called my name. Turning, I saw a grade ten girl named Arlene Heidt get to her feet at a nearby table and wave at me. Easy to pick out of any crowd, Arlene had triple-dyed hair (green, orange and pink), a stud in her nose and right cheek, and was the Dief's best trumpet player. She also happened to be one of its five official lesbians.

"Hey, Dylan," she called again, and without thinking I started toward her. At that moment my eyes fell on the couple sitting across from her—Joyce Dueck and Lucy Settee, two of the Dief's other known lesbians. Not only were Joyce and Lucy holding hands in a way that broadcast their relationship far and wide, but they were both looking right at me. That was when it hit me: I was in direct transit toward three dykes who obviously had something to say to me, and I was immediately blasted with that familiar flamethrower feeling.

"Uh, hi," I said, coming to a halt at the end of their table.

"Hi yourself," said Arlene, giving me a wide grin. "I just wanted to tell you that I really like your display."

Across the table Joyce and Lucy nodded enthusiastically. "I heard you put *Foxfire* under the girl's censor strip," said Lucy. "Is that true?"

"Yeah," I shrugged. The word about *Foxfire* and *The Once and Future King* had been out for several days now. To my surprise it hadn't been that big a deal. A few kids had asked me why I'd used *Foxfire*, but when I'd told them it was a book about justice and courage, they'd simply bought it. But then that might have had something to do with the fact that my face didn't go fireball red when they asked me about it. I guess, after what had been happening lately with Joc, my kiss with Sheila felt like ancient history. So *Foxfire* didn't have that overloaded meaning anymore. In the end it was just a story about a group of girls from another century.

"Sweet," said Arlene, brightening. "I love that book."

"Thanks," I said quickly. Grabbing at a chance to end the conversation, I turned toward the exit.

"*And*," said Arlene, raising her voice so I either had to turn back or listen to her shout at me from halfway across the cafeteria, "I have a message for you. From a friend."

The flamethrower feeling was back, full force. "Oh yeah?" I said, turning slowly to face her.

"Yeah," said Arlene, her eyes flat on me. "Her name's Sheila. Sheila Warren. Remember her?"

As if on cue, Joyce, Lucy and the entire table honed in on me—kids from the drama club, the creative writing club, the junior and senior bands.

"Um...yeah," I said, focusing on a zit that sat dead center on Arlene's forehead. "I met her a while ago at Confed."

"You sure did," said Arlene, her grin growing wider. "Anyway, she asked me to say hi."

"Great," I said, forcing myself not to turn and run screaming for the exit. "Well, thanks, I guess."

"Anytime," said Arlene. "Want to sit down? Join us?"

Jeeeeezus! I thought, but managed to keep a grip. "Really, I can't," I mumbled. "Things to do, y'know? Gotta go."

This time I did take off for the door, but not before I saw a knowing grin pass between Arlene, Joyce and Lucy. Then I was out of the cafeteria and heading down the hall, my thoughts in absolute chaos. They *knew*, damn it. The Dief's official lesbians *knew*. And if they saw my dumb stupid drunken mistake with Sheila Warren as the hilarious joke they so obviously thought it was, they would be more than likely to pass it on to someone else. Wasn't everyone always ready for a good laugh?

I had to get a grip and think about this, just get a grip and *think*. So instead of going to the library as planned, I grabbed my jacket out of my locker and went for a walk. The wind was in a nasty mood, ripping and tearing the last of the leaves from the trees, but that suited me fine and I walked straight into it with my head down, letting its cold twisting emptiness blow

right through me. *Bitch*, I kept thinking. *That Sheila Warren
is such a bitch.* I mean, why did she have to tell Arlene Heidt, a
dyke from my school, of all people? Why couldn't she just keep
it to herself? This was about both of us, after all. What right did
she have to spread stories about what had so obviously been a
private moment?

Blurry block after blurry block passed, my eyes stinging with
tears. Gradually, very gradually, my funk began to wear off. I
could have kept it pumped, telling myself how much I hated
Sheila and how I was going to get her back, absolutely bury her
in an avalanche of rumors and lies. I mean, I knew how that
worked—hadn't I been observing the phone patrol in operation,
up close and personal, for almost a year? All I had to do was feed
them a few tidbits and they would be on their phones, spreading
the dirt with glee. That kind of thing was a real rush for them.

But what would be the point? Sure, it would cover my ass for
a while, but Sheila didn't deserve that. Besides, my ass was getting pretty lonely these days. I seemed to have developed quite
a knack for convincing my closest friends that they didn't want
to spend time with me. If only I could figure out where I'd gone
wrong. If only I knew how to get inside Joc's head and figure out
what she was thinking, so I would know the best thing to say to
her, the exact way she wanted me to be. That was all I wanted
really—for last Thursday afternoon to be forgotten as if it had
never happened and to have my best *best* friend back again.

Getting my lonely ass into gear, I turned around and headed
back to the Dief.

That evening Cam and I went to a house party at Gary
Pankratz's. Gary's family was well off; he lived in a gated com-
munity, and his dad was frequently out of town on business. That
left his mom in charge of things, or rather, not in charge. I mean,

the last thing Ms. Pankratz could be called was domineering. She basically doted on her two sons, and when they had friends over she pretty much let anything go. Not that their parties were bedlam—Ms. Pankratz didn't let us wreck the place—but there were several empty bedrooms and a lot of dark corners, with only an ancient German shepherd to supervise. So, all things considered, a party at Gary's place was a parallel universe to a party at Deirdre Buffone's.

When Cam and I knocked, Gary's brother Luke answered the door. We followed him into the rec room to see that it was pretty much the usual—kids sprawled on the couch and floor watching a video, a pool game going on in one corner and Ms. Pankratz sticking her head in every now and then, glancing quickly around the room and heading back to another TV at the other end of the house. The expected group was there—Len, the phone patrol, your basic jock social club. Room was made on the couch, and I sat down, leaving a space for Cam, but he grinned and said he was going over to check out the pool game. For a second I almost jumped up and scurried after him—something about Gary's place had me constantly riding my nerves—but I managed to get a grip.

C'mon, bozo, I thought. *Half the kids at the Dief would kill to be in your shoes right now. Act like you know it.*

"Hey, Dylan," said Rachel, leaning over and whacking me on the leg. "Listen up. You are getting a scoop here. Monday morning before homeroom, you are to march your ass down to the gym and tell Harada you're available to play ball."

Confused, I just looked at her. The volleyball season had been underway for weeks, and as far as I knew no players had died recently. Then, as Rachel sat there, continuing to grin at me, I started to get it. An enormous sinking feeling took over my gut.

"Why would I do that?" I asked slowly.

On either side of Rachel, Julie and Deirdre broke into snickers. Rachel's grin widened.

"Because we snagged a spot for you," she said dramatically. "*Just* for you. After we made the dyke e-*vic*-tion, that is."

Julie's and Deirdre's snickers escalated into guffaws, and they collapsed against Rachel in a hysterical seizure. With a condescending smirk, she patted them on the head.

Weed, I thought. *Or the punch is spiked.*

Then I thought, *Not once.* I mean, school had been on for a month and a half, and not once had I stopped Michelle Allen in the hall to ask how things were going. She was in grade twelve and I didn't know her that well, but still…

"What d'you mean, eviction?" I asked carefully.

"Michelle quit," Rachel said smugly. "It took an entire month to convince her, but she's finally seen the light. Apparently it happened today. Harada told me after school. Michelle's quit the team, she's quit the Dief, and she's gone back to Confed where she belongs. So right away, of course, I told Harada *you'd* be more than happy to take Michelle's place. And the team would be happy to see you take it too, because…well, because we know *you're*…safe."

Suddenly Rachel was also splitting a gut and collapsing on top of Julie and Deirdre. Eyes narrowed, I sat watching the merriment and trying to ignore the massive heat crawling across my face. Rachel Gonzales had a real knack for confusing a compliment with a knife in the back.

"I dunno," I hedged. "I'm not really in shape. I'd be too far behind the rest of you."

"You'll catch up," said Rachel, straightening. "Mind over matter, that's all it takes. And now you'll finally be part of the team the way you should've been in the first place. Unless…"

She paused, eyeing me significantly, then added, "You're too busy reading *Foxfire*, that is."

Stiffening, I sat trapped within the kick-ass thud of my heart as Rachel lost it to further hilarity. Things had been quiet on the *Foxfire* front since Cam had laid down the law earlier in the week, but illegal chemicals had a way of bringing out the uglies in people.

"Mind over matter," wheezed Rachel, grinning at me. "Fox over fire, fox over fire."

Silently I gritted my teeth and settled in for the long haul. If there was one thing last Monday's lunch in the cafeteria had taught me, it was that protesting would only be interpreted as a sign of guilt. Fortunately, before Rachel could recover enough to get in another jab, Cam sat down beside me and handed me a glass of Coke. Then he held up a bottle of vodka that was obviously making the rounds.

"The moon or Mars?" he asked, giving me our private code on how much liquor to add.

"Mars," I said grimly. As he tilted the bottle over my glass, I leaned into him, bumping his arm so extra vodka poured in. He looked at me, eyebrows raised, and I shrugged, so he shrugged back.

"Okay," he said. "But make sure you're walking straight when I take you home."

He turned to pass the bottle to someone else, and I quickly lifted my glass and downed half the contents. Then I leaned back against the couch to ride out the burn in my stomach. I'd never drunk vodka before, and at first I wondered if Cam had been fooling me by adding water to my drink because all I could taste was Coke. But soon things started to feel warm and fuzzy, and I knew the vodka was kicking in. Which was fine with me—warm and fuzzy had a way of making Rachel's predatory face seem almost...well, *nice*.

Laying my head on Cam's shoulder, I watched the general goings-on. Kids were leaving the room at frequent intervals, searching out dark private corners or looking for the can. As usual Gary was playing Mr. Hook-Up Man, swaggering around with his bedroom key and handing it over to privileged couples along with a time limit. I mean, it was the ultimate power trip, his shining moment of glory. Len and Julie were the first to land the key, of course, and when they returned forty minutes later, they were both smiling like the cat's meow.

But then, I thought, studying Julie's face, how else *could* they look? I mean, with everyone watching like boogeldy-eyed bears?

Probably inspired by Len's smirk, Gary retrieved his key and disappeared down the hall with a girl from the Confed volleyball team. But twenty minutes later he was back, patrolling the party and grandly doling out time in his bed to the next eager couple of his choice.

"Hey, Dylan," he said, stopping in front of Cam and I. "You look like you're falling asleep."

"Uh-uh," I said, squinting up at him. Things were a little blurrier than I'd realized. "I'm not sleeeepeeee," I said, letting my voice coast dreamily through vowels. "I'm haaaappeeee."

"Cam, Cam," said Gary in mock sternness. "What did I tell you about bringing drunk damsels to my party?"

"She's not drunk," said Cam, grinning at me. "Like she said, she's happy. Right, Dyl?"

"Uh-huh," I said, bouncing my chin up and down. Up and down, Up And Down, UP AND DOWN. Snickers broke out around me, but I couldn't seem to stop. Or rather, I didn't want to. It wasn't that I was *that* drunk, but it felt safer somehow, fooling everyone into thinking I was. I mean, someone who was stupid-drunk couldn't be expected to engage in meaningful conversation. Stupid-drunk wasn't worth picking on.

Grabbing my head, Cam held onto it firmly. "Whoa, girl," he said.

"Haaaappeeee, haaaappeeee," I singsonged brainlessly. Around us, an audience was starting to gather. Everywhere I looked, kids were sporting wide grins. Without intending to, Dylan Kowolski had suddenly become popular.

"Haaaappeeee," I singsonged again. "I'm haaaappeeee, haaaap-peeee."

"Happy to the third power?" asked someone behind me, and then Len leaned over the back of the couch and grinned down at me. "That's real happy, Gary," he said. "A girl that happy deserves a chance at the key, don't you think?"

"The key?" said Gary, faking astonishment. "What a great idea, Len! Here you go, Cam—the key to bliss." Holding it out, he added, "But remember—you're in my bed, so don't get too excited. I have to sleep on those springs tonight."

For a long moment Cam and I sat frozen, just staring at Gary's hand. Up to now, there had been some kind of unspoken agreement between Cam and his guy friends. While they sometimes teased me about the fact that we weren't having sex, they generally respected it. In the three previous parties that I'd been to at Gary's house, it had never even been suggested that Cam take the key.

All across the room conversations were dying off as kids tuned into what was happening. Soon the only sounds were those coming from the TV—gunfire, running, screaming. At least the movie wasn't in the middle of a sex scene, I thought grimly. Beside me, Cam seemed to have gone into complete shutdown, not a flicker of emotion crossing his face. Then slowly, unbelievably, he reached out and took the key. Getting to his feet, he grabbed my hand and pulled me up.

"C'mon," he said quietly, not looking at me. "Can you walk straight?"

My foot bumped a glass someone had left on the floor and I stumbled, but Cam tightened his grip, keeping me upright.

I'm haaaappeeee, I thought silently, hanging onto his arm. *Haaaappeeee, haaaappeeee.*

"Hey, Cam," called Len as we reached the doorway. "Better lock the door behind you, bud. Everyone's hot for the Virgin Queen."

Guffaws erupted, jolting me out of the dull blur in my head. Pulling free of Cam's hand, I turned and looked at the kids who were watching from all over the room. Silently, smirks riding their faces, they stared back. Here and there I thought I saw a flash of sympathy, but nothing obvious. Nothing anyone could be held accountable for.

That was when it hit me—this had been planned in advance. Gary and Len, maybe Rachel and Julie and Deirdre, had actually sat down and worked out a scenario that would place Cam and I in a bedroom alone together. A scenario that neither of us could wriggle out of without being absolutely obvious about it.

What's the matter with them? I thought incredulously. *Why is it so important that we be exactly like they are?*

Then Cam's arm came around me again, and we were walking through the doorway and down a dimly lit hall.

"It's this door here," he muttered, fumbling with the key. As the bedroom door swung open, I glanced down the hall to see Gary and Len watching us from the other end. Quickly, before they could say anything, Cam pulled me into the room and locked the door.

"He'll have another key," I said. "Pull something across it."

Flicking on the light, Cam dragged a dresser across the door and flicked the light off again. Then he put both arms around me and started walking me backward toward the bed.

"Is this what you want?" I mumbled into his neck. A zillion miles away from my brain, my voice felt as if it was floating up by the ceiling. "I mean really, Cam? Really?"

Cam tipped me carefully onto the bed, then lay on top of me and buried his face in my hair. For a while we remained like that, completely motionless. Up by the ceiling, far away from my brain, my voice just kept talking.

"I guess I never thought it would happen to us like this," it said, kind of singsongy. Vodka chitchat. "I mean in *Gary's* bed. Think of how many times he's jerked off here, Cam. Think of what he was *thinking* about. Think of Len and Julie, and everyone else who's been here tonight."

"If it was good enough for them, why isn't it good enough for us?" asked Cam, his face still buried in my hair.

"Is that all you want?" I asked. "What's good enough for *them*?"

We lay there for a while longer, not talking, just breathing. Then Cam said, "We could go back and pretend we did it."

"Pretend?" I demanded. Finally, *finally* the blur in my head was starting to clear. "Why should we pretend for them?"

"I guess," said Cam. Getting off me, he sat on the edge of the bed, his head in his hands.

"Let's get out of here," I said, staring at the ceiling. "Unless you want to go back, I mean."

"They're watching the hall," he said, still not looking at me. "To congratulate us when we come out."

For a second all I could do was stare at him. So he'd been in on the advance planning too.

"We're on the first floor," I said finally. "Let's use the window. And make sure you ditch the key somewhere Gary will never find it."

It took Cam all of thirty seconds to shove up the window and slide out the screen. Then we were climbing through the opening, out into the cold October air. My feet hit the ground and abruptly I was sober—stone cold sober.

"Shit," I said. "It's freezing. And we left our jackets inside."

"They're in the front hall. I'll get them," said Cam and took off along the side of the house. Following more slowly, I waited on the porch until he came back out and handed me my jacket. Then we headed down the street toward his car. The moon was out, three-quarters full, and a few specks of snow were spiraling down through the air. When we got to the Firebird, Cam unlocked my door first like he always did. Then we got in and sat shivering, waiting for the car to warm up.

"I can't believe I did that," said Cam. Shoulders slumped, he sat staring straight ahead. "I can't believe I was actually considering..."

"It's my fault too," I said weakly.

Immediately my heart started in fast and hard, doing its kick-ass thing. I mean, there was no going back now. It was coming. Finally it was almost on us.

"How can you say that?" asked Cam, still staring down the street. "I'm the one—"

"I'm the one," I said, putting a hand on his arm. For a long moment neither of us moved. Then, slowly, Cam turned to look at me. And there it was, the question he'd never dared ask, taking shape on his face.

"It's me," I said, swallowing hard. "The problem here is me. If I wasn't the way I was, you never would've thought about going along with that tonight."

"You don't have to have sex if you don't want to," exploded Cam.

"No," I said miserably. "That's not it, Cam. At least, not all of it. You know it and I know it."

He got really quiet then, staring at me, his breath rasping in his throat. "So what're you saying, Dyl?" he asked, and I knew we were flat up against it—the point at which we were both so sick of our fear that we were finally willing to face it.

What was the best, the truest word—*dyke, lez, lesbiAN?* None of them felt right, none of them felt like *me.*

"I love you, Cam," I blurted. "With my whole mind and my whole heart. But my body…"

My voice wobbled and trailed off into the silence. "Jeeeeezus," I whispered, hugging myself. This was so hard, harder than anything I'd ever had to do.

"Well," I said finally, "I guess my brain and heart love you, but my body likes girls."

Rigid and silent, Cam stared at me. "I heard," he said finally, "something about you kissing a girl—Sheila Warren, I guess—at the Confed dance. Some kids said they saw you. I just brushed it off. I thought it was *crazy.*"

"Did you?" I asked. "Really, Cam?"

With a sigh he laid his head on the steering wheel. "I dunno," he whispered, so quietly I had to lean forward to hear him. "Maybe not. I've wondered, I guess, if you might…"

He hesitated, then added fiercely, "But I never thought it straight out."

"Cam," I said hoarsely, "I never *ever* two-timed on you. There was just Sheila at Confed, and I didn't mean anything by it. She was coming on to me, and I was drunk. It happened, I guess, because I've been fighting it so hard, trying to keep it all down inside me so no one could tell. And when she came onto me, it all just sort of exploded."

I paused, waiting for him to say something, *anything*, but he just sat there with his eyes closed.

"I know…I should've been stronger," I said, forcing myself to keep talking. "I should've been honest with you and everyone else and just come out and said it a long time ago. I mean, no one was going to pulverize me over it. That stuff happens at some schools, but probably not at the Dief, I know that. But kids still look at you funny. And there's the hidden stuff, really *mean* crap—like the way they evicted Michelle Allen from the volleyball team because they thought she was a dyke."

Cam nodded without opening his eyes. "I heard," he said, his voice wobbling slightly.

That wobble just about broke my heart. "That's why I quit volleyball and soccer this year," I said quickly, desperate to fight off the enormous heaviness I could feel coming down around him. "Locker rooms, y'know—everyone with their clothes off. And the feelings, the way I get them now…Well, they're a lot stronger than last year. And sometimes I go so *red*. There's no way to hide it then, just no way. I was afraid Julie and Rachel would figure it out and come after me. Y'know—the way they went after Michelle."

I paused, swallowing hard, but again Cam didn't speak or open his eyes. I mean, it felt as if he was going to sit there like that *forever*. Taking a deep breath, I tried to think of what he needed to hear more than anything—the *truest* words.

"The hardest thing about this whole thing has been you, Cam," I said quietly. "You don't know how much I've been working at it, trying to turn onto you. Because I love you, I think you're the best guy on the planet, just the best. I really *want* to turn onto you."

After that I just shut up and sat with my head down, not knowing what else to say. And that was when I realized that Cam was sobbing quietly, his shoulders shaking, his forehead in tight against the steering wheel. When I tried to hug him, he pushed me away, and I had to sit there and wait while he sobbed for what seemed like eternity.

Finally he straightened. Without looking at me, he turned on the ignition and put the car into gear. "Well," he said quietly. "I guess I'll take you home now."

At the first intersection he opened his window and threw out the key to Gary's bedroom. Then, without speaking he drove to my place, watched as I walked up to the front door and unlocked it, and took off, tires squealing, into the night.

Chapter Twenty-two

That night sleep was a long time coming. I kept hearing Cam crying in my head and remembering the way he'd tried to keep the sound inside himself, curving his body around it. Without meaning to I'd hurt him deeply, and there didn't seem to be anything I could do to change that. I fell asleep crying about it and woke early Saturday morning to a feeling of dull stretched-out aloneness. At first I couldn't think of why, and then it hit me—Cam was now out of my life…and so was Joc. Everything I'd worked so hard to prevent had happened anyway, and the heaviness that came down on me as I realized this was so great, I seemed to stop breathing.

For a while I simply lay there, not moving, not thinking, not *being*. When the door to my room opened and Keelie started tip-toeing toward the bed, I didn't even try to play along, just rolled over and gave her my back. Her careful footsteps came to a halt, I heard her breathe in-out, in-out, and then, without speaking she turned and ran from the room.

It was hours before I got up and when I did it was to a world that had gone slow-mo with sadness. I thought constantly about calling Cam but decided that having to talk to me again was the last thing he needed. So after cleaning my room, I slumped down onto the window seat and sat staring out at the backyard. It was raining, large drops plopping steadily against the glass. Putting my hand to the pane, I watched the water run down the other side of the window. Happiness—that rain was my happiness and as usual it was out of reach, pouring down the opposite side of wherever I happened to be.

The heavy inner dullness gave way then, and the tears started. It was over, finally—the long charade, Queen Dylan, everything. By the time I got to school Monday morning, half the Dief would know that Cam and I had broken up. Cam would talk to Len, Len would tell Julie, and Julie would get the phone patrol into gear, revving with *Foxfire* rumors. Cam wouldn't tell Len the reason we'd split, I knew I could trust him for that, but it wouldn't help much. With him out of my life, there would be no reason for the phone patrol to show mercy and they would let loose, following their natural instincts.

Face pressed to the window, I cried harder than ever. Sweet sixteen absolutely sucked. Two months into grade eleven and my life was over. I mean, it was *over*.

Gradually the window fogged up and the front of my T-shirt grew damp with tears. Still I kept crying. Sniffs and sobs came out of me, then a couple of straight-out wails. This time there was no stopping it—I couldn't seem to get anywhere *close* to a grip, and soon my body ached from crying, I was raw from the inside out. At some point I felt something touch my knee and looked down to see Keelie staring up at me, wide-eyed. A little later Dad came into the room, sat down on the window seat and put an arm around me. That felt okay so I scooted closer, and he put his other arm around me too. Then I just kept crying. Mom brought me some green tea, but by that time I was so tired that my hand was too shaky to hold the mug. So Dad took it and blew on it to cool it, while I leaned against his chest and sobbed some more. When I'd finally calmed down enough, he held the mug to my lips, and I was astonished at how smooth and warm the tea felt sliding down my throat.

"This is amazing," I croaked.

"I asked your mom to put lots of honey in it," said Dad.

Slowly I slurped down the rest of it, then lay my head on his shoulder and snuffled my runny nose against his sleeve. With all the tears and gunk I was leaving on his shirt, he was going to have major laundry to do. Sighing heavily I glanced past him, out the window. To my surprise it was dark, which meant Dad had to have been sitting here with me for at least an hour, completely clueless as to what was going on, just waiting while I cried myself out. And now that I was finished he was still here, waiting for an explanation.

What should I tell him? Should I make something up, use the experience as a practice run for the story I was going to have to start spinning Monday at school? But this was my *dad*, not the phone patrol. And he was here, sitting beside me in the dark, not even complaining about missing his supper because he loved me so much. Maybe I could tell him something…part of the truth, a little tiny *teeny* bit of it.

Burying my face in his shoulder, I mumbled, "Cam and I broke up."

Dad's arm tightened briefly around me and he asked, "Why?"

"Because…," I muttered, working my way slowly through various options and ditching them one by one. "Well…," I said, still hanging on to being in between, nobody knowing. "Because…well…"

"Because, well…why?" prompted Dad.

Deep inside I could feel something untwisting itself in a long gulping sigh—something that wanted to breathe easier, something that wanted *space*.

"Well, because," I repeated, letting it untwist a little farther, then farther yet. "Because...I'm a dyke, that's why."

Dad sucked in his breath, and I could almost feel his thoughts moving carefully in the silence. Finally he laid his cheek against the top of my head.

"Good for you," he said quietly. "It took courage to say that."

Emphatically I nodded. *Monster courage*, I thought, blinking back a fresh batch of tears. *The mother of all courage.*

"Don't worry," I muttered into his shirt. "Danny will give you lots of grandkids. So will Keelie, probably."

Dad gave a short laugh. "Grandkids!" he said. "Heck, I'm too busy trying to keep up with my kids to worry about grandkids."

"Well, I wanted to have kids," I said. "With Cam. And he's upset. I hurt him really bad."

"How did you hurt him?" asked Dad.

With a sigh I pulled back, and Dad took his arm from my shoulder. The cool air came in around my face, patting it like gentle hands, and I sat staring out the window into the dark, thinking my way word to word.

"I lied to him," I said hoarsely. "I should've told him a lot sooner. I mean, I've known the way I am since—y'know, since my body started changing and all that. But I pretended, I dunno, because I wanted to be like everyone else. I wanted to be like you and Mom, and get married, and have kids, and be happy. How can I be happy if I'm a dyke? And Cam's so great, he would've been a great father, and—"

"Dylan," said Dad. Taking my face in his hands, he turned it toward him. "Listen to me, sweetie," he said. "This isn't all your fault. It's partly mine and your mother's. When we first told you about sex, we didn't mention the possibility that you might be lesbian, and we should have. We should've mentioned it right at the start, so you had that possibility in your mind from the very beginning. No one ever talks about being lesbian or gay in this house, do they?"

I shook my head.

"Well, I can see how that would make you want to hide it," said Dad. "It's completely understandable. And don't you worry too much about Cam. Lots of couples break up in high school. He's a smart strong boy, he'll work his way through it. No matter how much you cared about each other—"

"*Care* about each other," I interrupted.

"Yes, you do," Dad said firmly. "But you probably wouldn't have ended up marrying Cam even if you were straight. People rarely marry their high school sweethearts. They go on to university and meet someone else, or get out and do some traveling and come back changed. I had several girlfriends before I met your mother, remember? Dating different people is an important way of finding out who you are and what you like. It's not wise to marry your first serious boyfriend."

He paused, then added quickly, "Or girlfriend."

"Oh," I said weakly. Then I just sat there, staring at his soggy shirt. I mean, it had never occurred to me that Cam and I might have broken up for *another* reason—that if I'd been straight, we still might not have gotten married. A weight lifted off me then, and I glanced quickly at Dad's face. It was shadowy, but I could see him smiling at me.

"I feel like such a shit," I said, my voice wobbling. "Like no one else will ever love me as much as Cam did."

"Just you wait," said Dad. "They'll be lining up. You'll be fighting them off."

I had to smile a bit at that. I mean, he was obviously still thinking guys, not girls.

"So you're not…disappointed because I won't give you grand-kids?" I asked.

"Sweetie," he said, touching my cheek. "I'm going to get to meet some very wonderful girlfriends that you're going to bring home to meet your family. If there's one thing I know about you, it's that you have great taste in dating partners. And I think you're going to lead an unusual life, different from most people. An important life and a unique one. And I'm going to be right here watching you live it."

Jeeeezus, he was really making me want to bawl now. But I didn't. Instead I took a shaky breath and got a grip.

An unusual life, I thought, staring out the window. *Important and unique. That sounds interesting.*

Slowly I stood up, wincing at the stiffness in my muscles. Then I reached down and took Dad's hand.

"This important and unique person is very hungry," I said. "Let's go eat."

Dad grinned, then made a face. "Fair warning," he said. "It's Danny's night to cook. Maybe we should stop in at the bathroom and dose up on some Alka-Seltzer before we go down."

He waited outside the door while I washed my face and did my thing. Then, giggling like two maniacs, we opened the medicine cabinet and snuck a few Alka-Seltzer tablets into our pockets. And *then* Dad put his arm around me, and we went downstairs to join the rest of the family for supper.

For a week I didn't do much of anything except sleep, eat and stare out my bedroom window. If there were *Foxfire* rumors going around at school I didn't hear them, but that was probably because I was avoiding *everyone*. No way was I going anywhere near Cam's usual haunts, and when it came time for English, I slouched down in my seat and kept my eyes fixed on whatever page we happened to be on in *1984*. The hurt inside me was too big, I guess—I needed to go deep into myself and just be there for a while, waiting the whole thing out. Sometimes it's important to let yourself hurt and find out what sadness means.

But not forever. Gradually, as Tuesday and then Wednesday plodded by, the dullness began to lift. My body didn't feel like such a dead weight anymore, and it no longer seemed impossible to pick up my hairbrush. By Thursday food had a taste again, and I could smell the air coming into my nose. So when I woke Saturday morning to find Keelie's face poked into mine, her little voice saying, "Wake up, Dylan. It's going to be a busy *busy* day today," a tiny crouching smile crawled onto my face and I actually felt like getting out of bed.

Keelie sure noticed the difference because she stuck around while I got dressed, chattering like mad as she picked out socks and a T-shirt for me to wear. Then, when I was dressed to her satisfaction, she led me triumphantly downstairs and pulled out a chair, saying, "Sit here, Dylan. I'm going to make your breakfast now."

Well, I was willing to trust her with my socks, but not my french toast. So we did a quick role reversal, and I plunked her into the chair and tied a bib around her neck. Soon she was chowing down some fairly decent french toast, and the smell was dragging everyone else downstairs, still sleepy-eyed and mumbling. As I fried them up a few slices, I could feel Mom and Dad watching me carefully, obvious relief on their faces. Even Danny kept giving me ear-to-ear grins and actually volunteered to do clean-up.

So I left him to it, threw on my jacket and went outside. Over the past week I'd been too depressed to pay attention to the weather, but now I noticed that it had gotten noticeably warmer. For a moment I just stood with my jacket open, looking around the yard. After my week in the land of the dead, it felt as if I was coming back to a place I hadn't been in quite a while. And during that week, while I was lost wandering around in my thoughts, things seemed to have changed in some mysterious way. I mean, the sun was up in the sky the way it always was and the trees were growing in the same places, but at the same time everything felt completely new. Moving slowly around the yard, I started touching things—a tree, a large rock, even the side of the house—just feeling how alive the world was, how it opened to color and softness.

Abruptly the back screen door slammed open and Keelie came tearing down the porch steps. Hurtling around the yard, she started hollering at the top of her lungs. "I want to go swimming!" she yelled, spinning a pirouette. "I want to go to the zoo, I want to fly Daddy's big kite."

As I watched her spin another pirouette, bellowing about all the things she wanted to do in the next five seconds, it hit me— the million dollar question: *What do* I *want to do? In the next five seconds, the next three hours—what do* I *want, more than anything in the world, to do?*

The answer was as obvious as heartbeat. Quickly, before I lost my nerve, I hauled open the door, called Keelie back inside, and told Mom that I was going for a bike ride. Then I grabbed my bike out of the garage and took off down the driveway. As I sped along the street, the neighborhood was just a smudge of colors going by. So I didn't have time for second thoughts before pulling up at the curb in front of the Hersches' place, and the relief that hit me when I saw Tim's car was gone was massive. I mean, we're talking sky-wide here.

"Thank you, thank you. Whoever you are, I love you God," I whispered. Still, to be on the safe side, I wheeled my bike around the side of the house and locked it to the back fence. Then I ran up the front porch steps and knocked on the door.

Ms. Hersch answered, a newspaper in one hand and a lit cigarette in the other. "Dylan," she smiled. "I haven't seen you for ages."

"Is Joc here?" I asked, trying not to pant absolutely all over her.

"In her room," said her mom. "She's had breakfast, so she should be civil."

Kicking off my shoes, I took off down the hall. And then, suddenly, I was standing in front of Joc's closed door, wondering what to do next. I mean, I could do *anything*.

With a deep breath I knocked on the door, and when there was no answer, eased it open. The curtains were still drawn, but in the dim morning light I could see Joc lying on her bed, wearing headphones. Her eyes were closed, her lips moving, and she was balancing a lit cigarette on an ashtray that sat on her stomach.

A wave of longing hit me. I mean, we're talking hypersonic sweetness here. So I waited, riding it out, then slipped into the room. As I closed the door Joc's eyes didn't open, but it would have been impossible to hear anything over the volume she had going on those headphones. Taking hold of her dresser, I shoved it slowly across the door. When I'd gotten it levered into place, I turned toward the bed to see that she'd finally opened her eyes and was watching me.

She wasn't smiling, but she was definitely interested. For a long moment we stayed like that, just looking at each other. Then, without saying anything I walked across the room, climbed onto the bed, and straddled her hips. Joc still didn't smile, just quirked an eyebrow and held up her cigarette, offering me a drag.

Shaking my head, I leaned forward and took off her head-phones. Sound blasted from them, vibrating my hands. Just like I'd thought, it was "Fear of Bliss."

"I quit," I said, keeping my expression in neutral, to match Joc's. "I figured that would make me healthier, and *that* would improve my sex drive."

Joc raised her other eyebrow, but didn't say anything.

"Are you drunk?" I asked, leaning forward slightly.

Joc's eyes glimmered. She shook her head.

"Are you stoned?" I asked, leaning forward a little more.

Again, she shook her head.

"When was the last time you brushed your teeth?" I asked, and finally, *finally* a grin hooked one corner of her mouth.

"Fifteen minutes ago," she said. "Nature's Gate toothpaste. Wintergreen flavor." Pursing her lips, she puffed some air at me.

"Wintergreen," I said. "My fave." Then I leaned through the last few inches that separated us and kissed her. It was a soft slow kiss, a whispering, wanting, question-mark kind of kiss, and Joc definitely answered the question, her lips opening gently against mine. So when we finished that kiss, we started another and another. After the fifth, Joc put a finger to my lips and pushed me away. Stubbing out her cigarette, she set the ashtray on the floor.

"C'mon," she said, pulling back the bedcovers. "It's warmer in here."

Right away—gut reaction—I stiffened. "Uh," I mumbled uneasily. "Joc, uh…"

I could feel it, a goddamn kick-ass power blush taking over every inch of my face.

Eyes narrowed, Joc collapsed onto her back and stared up at me. "What is this, Dyl?" she asked, her voice very cool. "You come over here to jerk me around?"

"No!" I said, my flush deepening. "I wouldn't do that, you know that."

"Then what?" she asked, her expression softening.

"Well," I said, then stopped. Why is it always so hard to *think* when you need to? "I *want* to…," I muttered nervously, "you know…"

Before I could stop them, my eyes slid to Joc's chest. Still in the T-shirt she'd worn for sleeping, she obviously wasn't wearing a bra.

"Well," I said again, stammering a little. "I mean, I *want* to touch you, but…"

"So touch me, Goofus," said Joc, smiling at me.

I took a very long, very shaky breath. Slowly, the way you reach out in a dream, I placed a hand on one of Joc's breasts. The sweetness I felt then—well, you can forget heartbeat, this was *heatbeat*. Joc's eyes closed, her lips parted slightly, and I just had to lean forward and kiss her again.

Then I took my hand away.

"No, Dyl," said Joc, opening her eyes. "That's not the way it goes. C'mere." Taking hold of my wrists, she tried to pull me down on top of her.

"Wait," I said, pulling back. "Can we just wait with that for a bit?"

"What—you don't want to?" asked Joc, staring at me in bewilderment.

"Yeah, I *want* to," I said. "But can't we, well, get *used* to this first? You know—you and me, just *being* like this?"

"I know what I feel," said Joc.

"Yeah," I said, "I know what I feel too. And I also know that we've been friends forever, and we know each other inside out. But this is something different, something new. I just want a chance to get kind of *used* to it first, y'know?"

Joc grinned, exasperated, then said, "I hope you're not going to say you want to wait until we're married."

"No," I grinned back. "Not until we're married. But right now I just want to get used to being madly in love with your little finger. Because I am—*totally*. I am totally, madly, completely in love with this little finger here."

Lifting her left hand, I kissed her pinkie.

A definite blush swept Joc's face. "Gosh darn, Dyllie," she mumbled, her eyes flitting away. "You're a romantic."

"Well," I said, hardly able to believe that for once she was blushing more than I was. "It's like that globe Ms. Fowler has in her office. You ever seen it?"

Joc shook her head.

"She told me she bought it because it was bigger than her head," I said.

Obviously not getting it, Joc just looked at me.

"Well," I said, struggling, not quite getting it myself, "that's the way this feels to me. Y'know, sex, love—it's so *big*. Bigger than my head, my groin, my entire body. And I want...I mean... well..."

I paused, trying to figure out what *exactly* I goddamn meant. "Well," I stammered finally, "I want sex...with you..."

My eyes flicked across Joc's, and I saw we were both in power blush mode. "Well," I stammered on, "I want it to be the most incredible experience of my life. I mean, I want it to be really *us*, something we're sure of, not just something we did. Because..."

Suddenly it was all welling up inside me, the whole fucking mess—Cam, Sheila, Joc, me, even Dikker—and tears started sliding down my face.

"I don't want either of us to get hurt, okay?" I blurted. "Because I love you, Joc. And I want to feel as if whatever we do, it's love, y'know? True love, the kind that can just let itself be."

"Oh my god," mumbled Joc, and I saw she was crying too. "C'mere, Goofus," she whispered. "I promise I won't ravish you. Just c'mere."

This time I did let her pull me down beside her. And then, slowly, as if we were in some kind of incredible parallel universe, we put our arms around each other and nuzzled into each other's hair. And *then* we just lay there like that, getting used to the feel of it, the whole astonishing *impossible* sweetness.

"Y'see," I mumbled into Joc's neck, "I figure, if I work at it, it'll take me maybe one or two months to get used to being in love with your little finger. And then maybe in half a year or so, I'll be able to give you a hickey—"

"Half a year!" wailed Joc, directly into my ear.

"Okay," I said. "A couple of weeks?"

"Only if you promise to autograph it," smiled Joc, brushing the hair back from my face.

Y'know, when Joc is smiling, she has the softest, most absolutely beautiful face in the universe.

"Deal," I said, and we kissed on it.

Chapter Twenty-three

After we'd finished shoving the dresser back into its original position, Joc grinned at me over the top and said, "Tim, right?"

"Yeah," I said emphatically. "His car was gone when I got here, but…"

I shrugged.

"He went over to a friend's place," said Joc, looking thoughtful. "He might be back for lunch though."

"Crap," I said, ducking a wave of panic. "What should I do? Sneak out the back?"

Joc grimaced, considering, then said, "Why don't we pretend we're back to being just friends? He should be okay with that. The way you took off the last time you were here, he pretty much figured you agreed with him anyway."

"Agreed with him!" I said, astounded. "I was fucking *scared*. I never would've thought Tim could get so weird about something like that. And then when you weren't in school Friday, and Monday you just stopped talking to me, I wondered…"

I paused, not quite sure how to put it.

"I didn't know what to say," Joc said hastily. "Like you said, the whole thing was weird. It'd be weird with anyone, but with you…"

She faltered, her eyes flicking past mine, then added, "The best friend thing, you know."

"Yeah," I said softly, "I know."

We were silent for a moment and then Joc said, "I've always felt this way about you, y'know. Well, since grade seven. Dikker turned me on too—I'm bi-curious, I guess, like they say on the net. But it's always been stronger with you."

"Could've fooled me," I said. "What the hell did you see in Dikker, anyway?"

A huge grin split Joc's face and she giggled. "He pissed you off," she said. "Every time you saw me with him, you practically levitated off the ground. I could always count on it. Besides, Dikker was fun, at least until he got into that *Hamlet* shit. Holla bolla, moron."

Opening the door, she poked her head into the hall. "It sounds quiet," she said, listening. "Tim's probably not back yet. C'mon, let's get some lunch."

Cautiously we started down the hall, but came to an abrupt halt as laughter broke out in the kitchen.

"Tim," hissed Joc, shooting me a nervous glance. "He is back. He's with Mom."

I swallowed hard. "It'll be okay," I said. "Your mom'll help us."

"Maybe," Joc said dubiously. "I haven't told her yet—about us dancing and Tim freaking. If we go in there now and he starts freaking, she'll freak too."

"C'mon," I said, "she's a librarian. Librarians don't freak."

"She's my mom," said Joc. "Moms freak."

"My mom didn't," I said. "Neither did my dad. Even Danny didn't."

"No?" Joc said hopefully. "Well…" She took a deep breath. "Okay, let's get it over with."

With a grim look she continued down the hall, and we entered the kitchen to find Tim and Ms. Hersch sitting at the table and talking in relaxed easy voices. Until Tim saw us, that is.

"Goddamn it!" he said, jumping to his feet. "I told you, Joc— not in this house."

A flush hit Joc and her chin went up, but she held her ground. "It's my house too," she snapped back. "I'll do whatever I want here, and you can just shut up about it."

"I won't shut up!" said Tim, his voice rising. "I've got a right to say—"

"Just what is going on here?" interrupted their mom, staring at them both. "What the hell has gotten into you two?"

"It's them," said Tim, pointing a dramatic finger at us. "They're fagging around together. I caught them at it the other day and I told Joc not in this house."

"Fagging around?" repeated Ms. Hersch, shooting Joc a bewildered glance. "What's he saying, Joc?" Her eyes shifted to me. "You're not…?"

Joc shot me a helpless glance. "Uh," she said hesitantly, her flush deepening. "Mom, y'see, it's kind of like…Dylan and me, we're…"

I stood beside her, wincing as she tried to stammer out the impossible. I mean, I knew the feeling. The words, what were the goddamn words?

Grabbing her hand, I held on. Then I looked Ms. Hersch square in the eye.

"Joc is my girlfriend," I said carefully. "We're going out together, dating—her and me."

Ms. Hersch's eyes widened and she stared at me in complete silence. "Oh," she said finally, her voice flat, the expression draining from her face. The kitchen got very quiet, and for a moment we all spent time just breathing.

But then the feeling came back into Ms. Hersch's face. "Dating a girl, are you, Joc?" she said slowly. "Well that's all right, I suppose. I always thought you were a nice kid, Dylan—just the kind of friend I wanted Joc to have."

"You can't be serious," said Tim, grabbing her arm. "They're *both* girls."

"Yes, Tim—I *can* tell a girl from a boy," snapped Ms. Hersch, rounding on him. "And furthermore, it is none of your blessed business what your sister does in this house. It's my house, not yours, and if she wants to have her girlfriend Dylan in to visit, that's fine with me."

"You're kidding," said Tim, his voice skyrocketing.

Ms. Hersch crossed her arms and glared at him. "What exactly is it that has you so upset about this?" she demanded. "Is she pointing a gun at someone, or setting off a bomb, or hijacking a plane? Just what is so terrible about what she's doing?"

Tim's face screwed itself up in utter disbelief and he snorted loudly. Then he crossed his arms and sat down with a thump.

"Actually," said Ms. Hersch, sitting down too, "if I had it to do over again, I'd choose a woman as a lover. They're a lot easier to get along with, believe me."

A grin leapt onto Joc's face. "You still can, Mom," she said.

Tim's eyes bugged and he sank back in his chair. "I think I'm moving out," he said faintly.

"Well fine," said Ms. Hersch. "If you're not prepared to respect your sister and live by my rules, then you're certainly welcome to find somewhere else to live."

"I might just do that," snapped Tim. Getting to his feet, he stormed toward the door. As he passed, Joc and I took a simultaneous step back and turned to watch him stomp into the front hall. Emphatic muttering followed as he pulled on his shoes, and then the front door opened and slammed shut behind him.

Joc let out a whoop. "So much for Big Brother," she grinned. "Actually, make that Big Bother."

"Has he been giving you trouble?" asked Ms. Hersch, patting the table. "C'mon you two, come and sit down here with me."

With a glad smile Joc scooted into the chair beside her mom, and I sat down across from them. "He yelled a bit when he first found out," Joc said eagerly. "But other than that, he's mostly been grunting and glowering."

"You took him by surprise, that's all," said her mom, lighting a cigarette. "He's taking a bit of a fit, but he'll come around. Probably just scared, that's all."

"Scared of what?" demanded Joc. "Dylan is hardly Frankenstein."

"You're his sister," said her mom. "He's afraid that if you're lesbian, he might be gay."

Another flush hit Joc and her eyes darted toward the window. I knew what she was thinking—*Lesbian!* The word took some getting used to.

"It's not contagious," she shrugged finally, her eyes flicking across mine. A smile wobbled across her mouth, and I wobbled one in reply. "Anyway," she added, turning back to her mom, "he should know himself better than that."

"Should doesn't have much to do with real life," Ms. Hersch said thoughtfully. "As long as the people you spend time with are just like you, you don't have to ask questions about yourself. It's only when you meet someone different that the questions start. Anyway, Tim'll get over it. I know my son, he's straight as a pin. And as prickly. Now, you two must be hungry. How about a grilled cheese sandwich?"

"Let me make you one, Mom," said Joc, half-rising out of her chair, a huge grin on her face. I could just about see the relief coming off her in waves. *Happy*—Joc was happy.

So was I.

"No, no, no," said her mom, lifting both hands. "You'll burn the top and drip melted cheese everywhere. I don't have half the afternoon to clean up after you."

As Ms. Hersch started to get up, Joc caught her arm and held on. "Are you really okay with it, Mom?" she asked. "I mean, really?"

For a moment that nothing expression came back onto Ms. Hersch's face and she stood motionless, looking down at Joc. "Honey," she said finally, "you're my daughter. Whatever you are and whatever you do, you're mine. You've been full of surprises since day one, and I'm sure this isn't the last curve you'll throw me, but what the hell, I'm a big girl now and I can handle it. So you just concentrate on figuring things out for yourself and don't worry about me, okay?"

Blinking rapidly, Joc ducked her head. "Okay," she whispered, brushing at her eyes. "It's just...it *matters*, y'know—what you think."

Ms. Hersch stood, looking down at Joc as she dragged on her cigarette. Then she gave Joc's shoulder a quick pat.

"Well, now you know," she said gruffly, "what I think. Okay?"

Joc nodded, not looking up, and they stayed like that for a bit. Then Ms. Hersch straightened, heaved a sigh and said, "What would you like, Dylan—one grilled cheese sandwich or two?"

"Two please," I said, standing up. More than anything I wanted to go around the table and give Joc a hug, but she was still sitting with her head down, rubbing her eyes. Sometimes a person needs a private moment. So instead I asked Ms.

Hersch, "Can I help make lunch? I'm not a burny drippy kind of cook."

Ms. Hersch gave me with a broad smile, and I could feel the warmth of it reaching back through all the years I'd been coming to this house.

"Sure you can help, hon," she said. "I'd like that."

Opening the fridge, I took out a block of cheese.

The following afternoon I was outside, raking leaves from the front lawn, when the sound of a familiar engine came rumbling down the street. Open-mouthed, I turned to see a blue Firebird with leaping orange-red flames pull up in front of the house. For a long moment I stood frozen, my heart in an absolute kick-ass thud as Cam sat motionless in the driver's seat, staring straight ahead. Then slowly he opened his door and got out of the car. Coming through the gate, he walked over to me.

"Hi, Dyl," he said quietly, his eyes not quite meeting mine.

"Hi," I said hoarsely, then just stood frozen again, not knowing what to say. "I...tried to call you," I said finally. "Last night."

He nodded. "I turned the ringer off my cell," he said, studying his feet. "I didn't...feel like it, I guess."

My throat tightened. "I'm sorry, Cam," I blurted miserably. "You don't know how bad I feel about this. I'm just really *really* sorry."

"I know you are," he said quickly. His eyes flicked across mine and I saw them redden. "I've thought about this a lot," he said, glancing away again. "The whole thing between us, from the very beginning. At first I was mad. I thought how could you do this to me, waste my time for ten months leading me on like this? But after a while I could see how hard you were trying...to care about me, I mean."

"I do care about you," I said, the words bursting out of me. "I love you, Cam. I really do."

"I know," he said gruffly. Ducking his head, he rubbed a hand over his eyes. Then he took a shaky breath. "So, after that I thought maybe there was something wrong with me," he continued grimly. "I hadn't tried hard enough, or—"

"No," I burst out again, but he lifted a hand and I saw that he was working his way toward something. So I just shut my mouth and waited.

"I guess," he said heavily, "that was the way I'd felt all along—that you weren't, y'know...turning on...because I wasn't good enough. It was always there in my gut—the feeling that I wasn't doing it for you, that there was something wrong with me. But then I realized that you were probably feeling the same thing about yourself. And how could anything ever work between us if we were both feeling that way?"

He stared past me, his shoulders slumped. "I mean, it just wasn't working, even though we both cared about each other. And we were both too scared to admit it. Until *you* finally got the guts to say it. You had the guts, not me."

He looked at me then, and I could see the sheer courage in him, how hard it had been to come over and tell me this. Suddenly the impossible space between us evaporated. Dropping the rake, I grabbed hold of him and hugged tight.

"Jeeeezus," I whispered.

Cam stiffened, then let his arms slide around me. "I can't believe I let those guys talk me into that bedroom thing at Gary's," he said into my hair. "That's how wrong I was getting inside, Dyllie—I actually went along with that."

His arms loosened, and I realized that I couldn't hang on forever, I had to let him go. With a sigh I let my arms drop, and he took a step back.

"I guess the whole thing was getting me really twisted around inside," he said slowly. "When you said those things in the car afterward, you saved me from something, Dyl. I dunno what exactly—a way of thinking and being, maybe. There's more space inside me now. I can breathe better, y'know?"

"I know," I said fiercely. Oh, how I wanted to hug him again, just grab hold and never let go. Instead, I stood smiling weakly at him as he smiled weakly back. Then, as if on cue, the front door burst open behind us and Keelie came barreling out, her shoes half on and her jacket sliding off her shoulders.

"I'm ready, Cam," she hollered. "I'm ready to go driving now."

"Keelie," I said, turning quickly. "Cam's not here to—"

"Actually," interrupted Cam, putting a hand on my arm, "I am. I called ahead and asked Keelie if she'd like to come driving with me. I haven't seen her in a couple of weeks, y'know. C'mere Keelie, let me do up your jacket."

With a grin he got down on his knees, zipped up Keelie's jacket and fastened her shoes. Then he straightened, took her hand and turned toward the car. Abruptly he stopped and turned back.

"You can come too if you want, Dyl," he said. "There's lots of room."

A giant ache reared up in me, but I rode it out and let it fade, a last sad breath. "Maybe next time," I said reluctantly. "I'd really like to next time."

The same ache came and went in his face, and he turned and continued toward the car. As he opened the passenger door, Keelie glanced back at me.

"The queen of the Sirius galaxy isn't coming?" she asked doubtfully.

Suddenly then, it hit me—happiness, exuberance, *jubilation*.

The queen of the Sirius galaxy! I was finished with that bitch forever.

"No, she isn't!" I called, the words bursting out of me in a glad shout. "But you've got the once and future king to take care of you, Keelie. And you know you'll be all right with him."

A quick grin crossed Cam's face and his shoulders seemed to straighten. Helping Keelie into the car, he closed the door. "See you later, Dyl," he said, walking around the front.

"Hey—you can always come in for hot chocolate when you get back," I said.

His grin widened. "Yeah okay," he said. "Should be about an hour."

Getting in, he started the engine as Keelie waved frantically from her window. Then the Firebird pulled away from the curb with a loud rumble, its bright hand-painted flames leaping across the sides and hood.

Firebird, I thought, watching it go. *Foxfire*. All along we'd each had our own private fire—different kinds maybe, but enough sweet heat to keep us warm as we went our separate ways.

Picking up the rake, I got back to clearing leaves.

Chapter Twenty-four

Monday morning before classes, I went to the front office and asked to see Mr. Brennan. Eyebrows raised, a secretary told me that he was busy but would be free soon. Ten minutes later I was called into his office. With a questioning smile Mr. Brennan gestured to a chair and asked, "What can I help you with, Dylan? Something to do with the library display?"

Taking a very deep, very polite breath, I sat down. "I decided," I said, not quite meeting his eyes, "that I wanted to tell you why I put *Foxfire* in the girl silhouette's groin."

As soon as I said this, of course, a flush started creeping up my neck. Groin—it's such a...well...*groiny* kind of word, y'know? Not the easiest thing to say to your high school principal.

Fortunately Mr. Brennan didn't appear to notice. "I'd be interested in hearing about it," he said warmly.

"Well," I said, "okay. It was actually the same reason that I had for using *The Once and Future King*. *Foxfire* is about some girls who saw that everything around them was wrong. Society had the wrong priorities, people weren't being treated right, that sort of thing. So they decided to do something about it. Sure they made mistakes, but what they were really interested in was justice and fairness. And because they were all girls, I figured it had a lot to do with…well, with being a *girl*. I mean, we live in our whole body, right? Our whole body is our heart and mind, maybe even our soul. So I think our heart and soul and mind live in our groin, just like anywhere else. And we need to make that part of us be about truth and respect and love, just like our heart."

As I spoke Mr. Brennan leaned slowly forward in his chair, his eyes glued to my face. "I like that, Dylan," he said, as soon as I'd finished. "I think you're absolutely right. And I also think that if you wrote that up as an explanation and posted it beside your display, you could take down the censor strips and put *Foxfire* and *The Once and Future King* back into their original positions."

A huge grin split my face. I mean, I was jubilant. Mr. Brennan grinned jubilantly back.

"That's great!" I said. "Except tomorrow is the last day of October. So Ms. Fowler has to put up a new display on Wednesday."

"Oh, I think she'll be quite happy to leave this one up for another month," said Mr. Brennan. "Putting up displays isn't her favorite pastime, y'know."

"Yeah," I said. "She mentioned that." Then a new thought hit me and I blurted, "Hey."

I paused, wondering how far to push things.

"Hey what?" prompted Mr. Brennan.

"Well, *The Joy of Sex* used to be in the boy silhouette's mouth," I reminded him.

Mr. Brennan shook his head. "Sorry, but I don't think that one is appropriate for this setting. Keep it in mind for later, when you're studying graphic design at college."

"Graphic design?" I repeated, staring at him.

"Sure," said Mr. Brennan. "You've got the mind for it, Dylan. I could see you coming up with some interesting professional work some day."